Tales of the Broken Moon

the Lost Prince of Dark Leaf

Book 2

Written by Travis Hanson & Aimee Duncan
Illustrated by Travis Hanson

Bean Leaf Press

ISBN 0-9774127-1-7

Printed in the U.S.A.

First printing, May 2007

Cover illustrations by Travis Hanson

Special Thanks to Ray Bingham for the Glossary, Janae Albee for the last minute
reads, and Cathy Hanson for all the hours pushing us to finish this.

"to Janell, who continues to believe…"
-Travis Hanson

"For all the strong wonderful women in my family
but especially for my Grandma Betty who always
knew I could do it, for my Grandma Clara who was
wanting to know if Bean got his sword back and
for my mother, Alisa, who has been very patient
with me."
-Aimee Duncan

Mama Faerie

The lore singer falls silent, the fire dies and the coals grow black. Still there remains a promise of something more, a gentle admonition of "Ah, another time... another time, perhaps in the morning." Hear how the listeners beg though! A story must inevitably come to its end, but no, not just yet. Night approaches as it must but no good tale can be silenced by mere darkness. It is sometimes in the wee wakeful hours when the best of the tales begin to streak down in fierce points of glittering light, like stars falling from the sky. So the story goes on...

A door opened slowly and candlelight fell across the floor, warming the walls of the snug cottage. Outside the sounds of nature settling down for the night briefly came through the opened door before it shut again. Yet within these walls, the stifling night moved in strange and restless ways. It shamefully crept into the windows and sulked in the corners where the candlelight could not touch it. The darkness was filled with murmurs and visions, nightmares, and haunting fears.

A tiny flickering flame touched a small stone lamp hanging

from a chain on the wall, lighting the cotton wick. Threads of white smoke spiraled into the air while the perfume of burning lampsweet oil began to drift throughout the room. The candle was set carefully in a small alcove nearby. The darkness withdrew further as the room brightened with the glow of the lamp and the small candle.

"Quickly now, lay him down over here. Careful. Now bring me a basin of clean water, my darling, and whatever else you can carry," said a soft, clear voice. An uneasy silence hung heavy in the air, broken only by the rustle of crisp clean sheets, the whisper of a curtain swept aside, and the tread of retreating footsteps. Sometime later, the footsteps returned. The dull clank of a full basin set down followed the gentle clatter of terracotta pots banging against one another.

"A little yarrow and feverfew first of all for the burning in his blood. By the way he's breathing, he may have a cracked rib or two. Bindwort will do for that," said the voice again, a woman's voice. "Oh... Look at those wounds on his leg and arms... all those bruises, pity the poor child. Why just look ..."

She grew quiet and then at length, sighed. "This may take a bit more than herbs," she said. Her voice sounded hard pressed for hope. She did not speak again for a long time. Talking at this point had become completely irrelevant.

In the light of the lamp, odd and worrisome faces of stone seemed to lurk in corners, watching and waiting. The silence grew urgent and tense. Sideways glances and terse nods conveyed all the needful questions and answers. Unspoken words came in the frequent swish of the curtain as it was moved aside, the occasional soft sigh escaping from tightly pressed lips, and the rapid footsteps retreating and emerging from other distant rooms that the darkness hid. The lamp turned slowly on its chain and in its unsteady light, the shadows writhed in peculiar ways on the cottage walls. Even the hours seemed to hang on fragile chains, turning minute by agonizing minute.

Hands took up the basin with its dark filthy water and disappeared, only to bring it back a short time later, freshly filled with clean cool water. Those same hands brought clean strips of linen, whisked away pots and piles of blood stained cloth, and brought back fresh supplies. The smell of blood and worry overwhelmed the sweet scent of healing flowers and herbs for some time.

The candle guttered and died leaving a hardened waterfall of white wax trailing down the side of the alcove. Fortunately though, hope had not died with it. The flicker of light in the lamp dimmed for the fourth time as the lampsweet oil ran low again. Herb poultices soaked against numerous bruises, the last stitch had been pulled tight, and clean linen bound the cut and bleeding limbs. There was nothing more to do now, but wait out what hours were left of the night and wish for the best. Now seemed an ideal time to sit back and allow a moment to finally breathe and perhaps speak a word or two.

"That should do it," spoke the woman again. "All he needs now is a little rest and some warmth. He should recover just fine." She picked up a large clay flask from nearby, pulled up a stool, and stood on it to refill the lamp on the wall. As the light grew a little brighter, it illuminated her serene face, a face that belonged in a dim and long forgotten time, somewhere back in the morning of the world. A homely glow was reflected in the depths of her wise dark eyes and fell over her companion sitting in the corner, a stout tired-looking man.

"I hope so... he looked so pale out there in the swamp... so lost," he said quietly.

"But he is found now," she replied, looking over her shoulder at him, "and a good thing as well. Who knows what could have happened if you hadn't passed by?" She stepped off her stool and disappeared in the shadows outside the pool of lamplight.

A shrug from the man expressed his answer. "I don't wish to think how much longer he might have been there, had I not come along," he said. He paused, and the silence weighed heavy with dreadful and heart-wrenching thoughts. His deep slow voice continued with some difficulty, "It would have been a wretched way to leave this world... and his is a life barely lived, it would seem."

Her footsteps sounded across the earthen floor as she walked towards him. Her hand reached out in the dim light, clasped his larger hand, and squeezed it tightly. "Thanks to you he does live, my dear brave knight. You saved him from that fate. Think no more of it," she said and paused. He felt her studying him, her eyes following the deep lines in his old warrior's face. Under her gaze, gentle though it was, he couldn't help but feel his age.

"You should rest now," she said. "You look so tired and worn out, little wonder with you trudging around in that rainy swamp. I'll stay with the boy for now."

"Tired, hah. After all this excitement, I couldn't sleep if I tried," he said. "Really, Qwen, I should stay. It would only be right."

She patted his knee. "You are too good to me," she murmured, "but you and I both know that I do not suffer from the lack of sleep. You've already done more than enough. The boy and I will be fine, Theron, I prom..."

A soft whispering stopped her sentence. It was coming from the reading nook in the wall that had been converted hastily into a makeshift bed. Within the depths of the blankets, a small figure had begun to stir restlessly. She got up and walked over to the little sickbed and listened for a moment to the delirium-soaked ramblings filled with fragments of unintelligible words. Her cool hand gently brushed over the small pale forehead, shining with beads of sweat, only pausing when a smaller hand came up and clutched feebly at it. "M-mama," came the pitiful little murmur.

In the dim light, her quiet eyes shone with deep sorrow like diamonds. Her only answer to the plaintive statement was a soft intake of breath and a gentle pat. She turned back to the man, who had stood up with her.

"Off you go my dear," she said to him. "Back to our room and get some rest. Someone needs to stay with the pixies anyway. If one wakes up in the middle of the night with neither of us there, then

they'll all be up." A hint of a smile lingered in her tone and her eyes twinkled. "They need to have their papa about to soothe them back to sleep."

"True enough," he chuckled, "but if the great knight must be sent to his room, at least let me warm up the leftover cider and share a cup with you before I go. It won't take but a moment."

"Fair enough, dear," she answered. The tender sound of an exchanged kiss was followed by the retreat of his heavy footsteps that gradually faded as he headed for the kitchen to heat up the cider.

* * *

Sometime later that night, Theron pushed aside the curtain to their bedroom. He rubbed his face wearily, stifled a yawn, and changed his clothes before he settled with a grunt into the large and unique bed that dominated the tiny room. Three huge old ash trees made up the headboard and footboard; living trees whose roots intertwined across the earthen floor and whose trunks thrust up through skylights in the ceiling. Trailing vines of wisteria covered the walls, curled up the tree trunks, and twisted across the ceiling to form an overhead canopy of balmy fragrance. Scattered throughout the canopy of vines and clusters of flowers, hundreds of pale lights like kaleidoscopic fireflies could be seen, the glow of pixies caught up in their small and curious dreams. The slumbering pixies made a living night sky among the sweet smelling wisteria. Tiny, gentle snores and tuneless humming made gentle music above, but neither the noises nor the glow ever disturbed Theron and his wife in their own slumber. It all came together like a tranquil lullaby, lulling them into a serene peace brought by the secure knowledge that all of their unique little family members were gathered together, safe and sound under one roof.

Theron lay in the bed on his back, looking up at the little lights with their continuously shifting colors that reminded him of dozen delicate little crystals, turning and catching fragments of light.

Beside him, an empty space where his wife should have been gave him little comfort. Qwen's warm scent still lingered on her pillow. He pulled it closer and breathed in her sweet perfume. Theron sighed, closed his eyes briefly, then opened them and sighed again. His mind would not let him sleep. Thoughts of a small pale face and the shine of his wife's concerned eyes drifted behind the lids of his own eyes. Restlessly, he tossed and turned, fluffed up his pillow, and studied the empty space next to him. He ran his hand over it, rubbed it thoughtfully, and thought how cold it felt. He closed his eyes for the second time and tried in vain to relax.

Directly above him, a little light flickered suddenly. A musical drone of little wings sent a breeze of wisteria-scented air across his tired face and his eyes opened once more. The shadow of a pixie drifted down towards him and the wavering green glow she cast over the pillows and blankets indicated she was still more than half-asleep. It was his Tia-Pho-Phia. The pixie landed drowsily on his forehead, made a tiny yawning noise, and then slipped gently down the side of his face to snuggle up in the curve of his neck below his ear. Theron smiled and moved one hand so that his finger could stroke her wings delicately. He listened to her hum softly while she fell back asleep and her dreaming glow traced every line and scar on his face in muted shadows.

Theron finally sat up, carefully taking the pixie in his hand to lay her on his pillow. He slid out of the bed and sat there a minute, rubbing the back of his head, deep in thought. Then he got up, just like any other concerned father and husband, and began to pace back and forth across the room, all while the pixies dreamed their dreams in peaceful innocence.

> *"..sore afraid was she*
> *O my love waits on the shore*
> *A maid wed a bear, how could this be?*
> *He'll wait no wait-o no more*
> *Then up spake her father, with coldest glare*
> *O my love waits on the shore*
> *An' swore she'd pledge her troth to the bear*
> *He'll wait no wait-o no more*
> *Then up spake her mother, with palest fear*
> *O my love waits on the shore..."*

Theron stopped pacing and a bit of a smile crossed his face. Qwen's soft voice floated past his ears from the other room, singing a familiar old ballad. The dreamy music wound itself around his restless mind, relaxing him. He pulled up a rocking chair to sit by the fireplace and listen to Qwen's sweet voice. Strange, he thought to himself, how a simple song could make him forget all his fears and concerns so easily. He hummed the bear's part of the song to himself and thought of the times Qwen had sung this song to tease him. Other fond memories bubbled and simmered in the back of his mind, lulling him into a drowsy repose. Before he realized it he had nodded off into sleep. Long after his wife had stopped singing, he heard the song continue on in his dreams. Perhaps indeed the melody or the sound of her words had a bit of magic about them. At any rate, he slept quite soundly in deep contentment.

***

In the adjoining room, night sought every corner not under the watchful eye of the lamp. Pale moonlight spread over the windowsill and across the dark floor. Somewhere a cricket chirped. The woman sat beside the little alcove and bathed the boy's warm face with a cool cloth. She hummed softly to herself.

She studied the young boy. His lax face still bore the shadows of pain, something more perhaps than physical wounds. She listened to his anguished voice that spoke of a mind awash in nightmares and visions of the past.

"His eyes... his eyes and the... the creature... the song... I can't... ohh, please... it calls," muttered the boy before his words trailed off again into whispers. The shadows in his face deepened.

"Hush now, my little one," she spoke with a sweet voice of gentle rebuke. She placed a hand over his bandaged face and tenderly rubbed the bridge of the boy's nose. "Let calmness come, let the song drift out of your mind and back into the past..."

Back in the distant memory of the world, she had been a masterful healer and her craft she knew very well. Her hands spread over the little restless body tangled in its sheets, touching wounds and bruises with a careful deliberation that spoke of something deeper than mere gestures of comfort. The warmth of a comforting virtue spread over the room and concentrated itself in her delicate and gentle fingers. It in turn spread over the wounded child, like a flow of invisible and healing water. "Dream instead of still pools at dawn... Calm and placid waters... clear and soothing to mind and soul... unruffled and tranquil under shadows of golden-leafed trees," she said, her voice taking on the hypnotic rhythm of a

chant.

"Slumber peacefully now, dreaming of innocent days, sunbeams, and dewy grass under little bare feet. Dream undisturbed now, drifting effortlessly on clouds of healing and comfort..."

After a moment, she withdrew her hands. Her face turned thoughtful. "I wonder who you are, little one," she murmured, "and what terror or courage drove you so far into the swamp to begin with."

The boy, of course, gave her no answer, for at the moment he lay still in hypnotic slumber. Suddenly, his bandaged arm grew rigid and his hand clenched spasmodically in a tight fist. Red seeped through the linen wrappings and she pulled another clean roll from her basket and took the bandaged arm in her hands to wrap it once again.

Suddenly her own arm convulsed, reacting involuntarily to a strange electrical sensation that made her weak. The linen fell from her grasp and went rolling across the floor. A chill ran down her spine as she rubbed her affected arm, twisting and stretching her tingling fingers to settle the prickling nerves. She stood up, paying no attention to the creaking chair or her aching arm. Her demeanor turned defensive and her eyes narrowed and grew dark with anger as she felt the unmistakable warning of something evil violating her domain.

Theron slept blissfully unaware of anything going on in the next room. He didn't even stir when dozens of tiny lights abruptly illuminated the room, throwing his shadow across the vine covered wall. Every single pixie, even Tia-

Pho-Phia on the pillow, sat up in their wisteria beds, wide-awake and fluttering, while their individual lights created a dazzling brilliance in the room. Their gazes gravitated towards the curtained door, listening hard for what had wakened them all at once. Then with an unspoken sense of urgency, every single pixie darted out from the wisteria and flew out of the bedroom. The sweet breeze of their flight stirred the thin graying hair on Theron's forehead and still he slept.

A rush of air blew strands of hair across her face as the tiny pixies darted out of the bedroom as she heard dozens of tiny voices chanting, "Mama Faerie, Mama Faerie, Mama Faerie " sounding like a canticle of alarmed chimes. The pixies swept into the room and circled around their mama, fluttering fearfully. Qwen calmed the pixies and turned to gaze on the boy lying in his makeshift bed.

His restless murmurs took on an urgent tone as his wounded arm reached over the side of his sickbed, his fingers twitching in strange gestures, grasping at elusive visions. Sighing, the boy grew oddly still and a seething noise akin to the sound of water boiling dry slowly began to penetrate the listening ears of Mama Faerie and her children and reverberated through the stillness of the night. Within his hand, flickers of faint light glittered like stars across a moonless night sky and traveled down his bared arm, spreading out in spidery threads across his damp skin. The jagged streaks of bluish light grew larger and brighter and stretched out in thin, shining threads beyond his fingers, forming the spectral shape of an ancient battle sword. The shape of the sword wavered and grew brighter, throwing out sparks of energy and blue-white light.

Mama Faerie raised her hands in defense, gathering her children close around her. "Mo-i!" she said sharply.

The light flared in fierce brilliance and then without a sound, it suddenly splintered. Blue light pulsated across the floor and ceiling, flooding through Mama Faerie and her children. The lamplight vanished in a curl of smoke and the pixies quickly fled up towards the ceiling to hide in the rafters and branches. Qwen lowered her head quickly like a woman walking against a strong wind but held

17

her ground against the blue energy leaping all around her. With a tremendous mental effort, she spread her arms, made a few gestures, and managed to contain this outburst of dark power within the room. The light disappeared as suddenly as it came, dissipating in the darkness of the cottage room, leaving Mama Faire and her pixies alone with the boy once again.

The Faerie Queen remained silent and still for several long moments, breathing hard. She curled her hands, closed her eyes, and examined the weaves that held her domain safe and secure. She felt through every corner of her world, trying to restore the numerous tangles that had been unknotted in this sudden blast of energy. Carefully, she tried to reweave the tangles that kept her world hidden from the eyes of anyone passing by.

"Lammath-a-shaer..." she heard the boy say in the rich elven tongue. She opened her eyes and looked at the boy lying on the bed. The child stirred and frowned. His bruised hand groped about blindly and then finally came to rest on the pommel of a kingly sword leaning against the wall. Threads of mist still curled about the white blade and it dimly shone in the darkness. The boy's hand tightened around the grip, pulled the sword closer towards him, and then he lay quiet, breathing slowly and easily. The pixies gradually drifted down towards their mama, all of them staring at the sword.

"Well, well," Qwen finally said in a low voice. "There is more to this child than I thought." After a long silence, the pixies began chattering all at once, asking a flurry of questions.

Mama Faerie gazed at the sword, barely hearing the voices of her pixie children. What had brought it here still lingered in the air around the weapon, an unsettling force powerful enough to rend the tangles that protected her domain. She felt drained. She glanced at the window and felt storm clouds gathering uncomfortably close around her home and she shivered momentarily in the dark.

"Children," she said wearily. "Come now. We need to get you back to bed. You and your mama are all right. Shh, now. All your chatter will wake Papa. We'll figure things out in the morning."

beckoned the pixies to come close around her. Their tiny little ces slowly died into silence and she ushered them out of the room into the hallway back towards the bedroom. As she walked ards the bedroom, soothing and shushing the pixies, she kept her k and worrisome thoughts to herself. Precious time needed to der this dreadful conundrum seemed to be slipping all too rapidly ough her fingers and it would not be long before morning.

In the room behind her, the boy slept fitfully. He began to s and turn again and his feverish slumber slipped into darker imag- gs. Troubling images of the past and more recent events swirled d mingled together beneath the surface of his consciousness.

Bean dreamed and the night pressed down relentlessly upon mind.

Picking Up the Slack

"Ugh," grunted Ravna softly. "This day is never going to end..."

She tucked errant strands of stringy hair back into the scarf tied around her head and pushed her sleeve back up on her arm. She plunged her scrubber into the bucket again, churning it back and forth in a vain attempt to stir life back into the dingy suds. Filthy grease-laden water slopped over the wooden sides of the bucket and splattered across the blackened stovetop.

An despairing frown deepened the lines around her eyes, lines already set in place by another short sleepless night. On top of that she had had to deal with a tiresome morning that, like many of the Inn's customers, had overstayed its welcome. Ravna lifted the dripping scrubber out of the bucket and wearily started working again on the grimy stovetop. The back door still stood open and sunlight, as dull as the suds evaporating in her bucket, filtered feebly through the misting rain. Everything seemed to be veiled in dull gray, not just because the dismal weather outside had been going on for longer than she cared for, but it just felt like that sort of day.

Midday meal had been a disaster. It had, however, made Ravna appreciate cold cuts and cheese a little more. An attempt at a hot meal had gone miserably wrong as the blackened stovetop clearly showed. She blamed Gort and the customers entirely for putting the idea that she should cook in her head. As far as she was concerned, if anybody wanted to eat anything other than leftovers, they were more than welcome to come into the kitchen and take care of it for their own be-cursed selves. Again Ravna found herself missing Groggle's large comfortable presence in the kitchen, even if his taste in stew ingredients did leave something to be desired. She was used to serving and twittering pleasantries to the guests, not cooking in this miserable kitchen. That and well... she had to admit to herself that it was nice in a way to have Groggle around to soothe over Gort's temper and brutish ways. She wondered if Groggle was having any luck finding Bean. She wished he and the Bean would come home quickly, and not just to do the cooking and cleanup.

She wiped the back of her hand across her face, leaving a black streak. Her expression grew somber and she thought how Siv had always kept the bar, with its carefully arranged glasses and bottles and its neatly polished counter. "Odd," she mused, "how one takes for granted someone just being there every day." A wry smile twisted her mouth as the image of the neat bar was replaced with the reality of dirty glasses sitting amid puddles of various brews splattered across

the counter. Odd, realizing just how much that Siv had done on a regular basis, she added to herself silently. Gort had been running the bar in Siv's place since the day before yesterday. The benefits were that no customer had dared try to weasel a free drink out of the ogre, but still Siv wouldn't be happy to see how Gort had not taken care of his bar.

Ravna squeezed her eyes shut, blew softly between her lips in frustration, and wished fiercely for Siv to come back and to be quick about it. She could bear another quarrel about the condition of the bar for the sake of seeing Siv and the Bean back again. It wasn't even so much for relieving her of the extra workload. She wanted to see Bean washing the dishes and talking with Groggle while the old ogre cooked. She wanted to see Siv standing at his old place behind the counter, talking with the customers. She wanted things back the way they were. Most of all she wanted this day to be over and take its disquieting dampness and gray mood with it. Even Gort's bellows, which she was certain had been directed at her today more times than was necessary, didn't have the inflammatory power they ordinarily possessed. He might as well have been muttering under his breath. That in itself was worrying.

At least there hadn't been such a huge in-pouring of customers today, or yesterday, come to think of it. Actually, she mused, there hadn't been any at all at least not from the direction of the homesteads. The last one from there had been a hunter going to visit relatives and he had left the evening before Bean disappeared. He had been a friendly sort, perhaps a tad too friendly. He had flirted shamelessly with Ravna though he had been old enough to be her grandfather. His complaints at the scarcity of game in Darkleaf and the less than flattering references to his overbearing old woman back at home hadn't been enough to garner more than a forced laugh and an empty polite wish for better luck next time from Ravna. She had been glad to see him go.

The nasty weather undoubtedly was to blame for a lack of customers, turning the roads to sludge and flooding out commonly used paths. There had been a couple that had stopped in early this morning, but all from the opposite direction, returning from Heartleaf and beyond. Marathur and Maeyve had been due to show up today and there had been no sign of them either. She knew that because Marathur, bless him, always showed up a day or two behind the Pers, touting his wife's rough-made earthdweller's brandy and a few baskets of runty vegetables to sell in the local towns. He was always hopeful that Siv might purchase a crate or two of the stuff. Siv always bought the earthdweller brandy, as well as some vegetables, more out of kindness towards them than anything else. While his wife's skills with brewing (inherited from her father) were undeniably excellent, their native brandy never sold well with anyone in the Inn, except to the few earthdwellers that occasionally passed through, wanting a musty taste of home to wet their whistles. It was, no doubt, an acquired taste.

Marathur had always been first and foremost a soldier and the retired life of quiet farming never had settled well with him. He had learned long ago that vegetables didn't respond well to military orders, but still he tried his best. The sad thing was that in glancing at his produce, one couldn't tell the enormous effort that went into coaxing them from the ground.

A widgin-fly buzzed idly around her head. She swatted at it and it returned to bite her on the ear, nimbly dodging the wrath of her quick palm. Ravna scratched grumpily at the welt, turned her head, and watched the little wispy pest dance just out of reach and over the rafters. Her eyes narrowed, following her tiny tormentor. The widgin-fly skipped over the hanging pots and pans, skittered down the wall, and finally drifted back in her direction once again. It landed on the edge of the bucket, crawled down to the stove-top covered in puddles of black water, and crouched there a second, its wings pulsing. A split second before it darted off again, Ravna's hand shot out and slapped at it triumphantly, smashing it. Black ooze spattered across her face and the front of her blouse. She sputtered and rubbed her face on the somewhat clean sleeve of her other arm.

"Showed you, you little nuisance," she muttered in satisfaction as she picked her hand up and frowned in distaste. "Blech..." She wiped the bloody smudge off on her apron, picked her scrubbing brush up again, and attacked the stove with renewed vigor.

She admitted to herself that there was something to be said for the gratifying sight of the dark grey of the iron surface of the stove emerging from beneath the black sludge. It had probably not gotten a good cleaning since the day it had been delivered to the Inn. Of course, she knew at the back of her mind that it would soon be right back to its old filthiness within days. Some might even go so far to say that really giving it such a thorough scrubbing was like Gort getting a haircut; a gesture that served no real purpose and was in fact ridiculous even to consider.

However, Ravna had to admit, it did seem to serve a purpose and perhaps more than one. It kept her busy doing something so

that Gort wouldn't come storming in, demanding for her to do some other task that he was more than capable of doing himself. She felt for the moment, that she was accomplishing something, never mind if it proved to be a short-lived accomplishment. Plus the rhythmic motion of the scrubbing, demanding though it was, did have an odd soothing quality to it. When she allowed herself to be completely caught up in it, there were moments where her thought processes fell into the comfortably simple rut of "scrub, rinse, scrub, rinse..." and she didn't have time to be preoccupied with worry or irritation. She didn't have to think at all, only work.

When it became apparent that every last bit of soap in her bucket had been utterly exhausted and that she was moving the filth around on the stove instead of actually cleaning it, Ravna gave up and decided to refill her bucket. She hefted it off the stove and poured the water down the drain in the center of the floor. A trip down to

the cellar brought back the last of the lye soap. She crumbled the waxy white chunk into the bucket, reminding herself to take care of cooking up another batch once she had finished with everything else. Finally she hauled the bucket outside to get some clean water.

The day was still gray and wet with unsettled mists and the night rain had caused the rain barrel to overflow leaving puddles of mud beneath the dripping water barrel. She rinsed the wiry brush in the water, dipped the bucket into the overfull rain barrel, and turned to head back inside.

Scrub, rinse, scrub, rinse... she thought.

A gust of damp wind followed her through the door, blowing past her sweaty face, and tenderly brushing aside her stringy limp hair to kiss the back of her neck. She paused, closed her eyes, and gave a little sigh. Then she quietly set the bucket beside the stove, turned around, and stepped back across the threshold of the back door. She decided she needed a break away from the smothering warmth of the kitchen, even just a small one to refresh herself before getting back to work. She was so hot and tired.

Ravna closed the door behind her, sat down on the woodem bench beside the door, and watched the dreariness. Occasionally, a breeze stirred through the trees and she closed her eyes, listening to the leaves whispering and the branches creaking. Siv had told her once that the soulful sound of the wind rushing abruptly through the forest in the middle of a good rainstorm was the closest one could get in Darkleaf to the sound of the sea crashing against the shore. Ravna had never seen the ocean, but from Siv's descriptions, she could imagine that if the sound of the wind had such an ability to stir the sluggish blood and call up such deep buried feelings of restlessness and awe, how much more could this semi-mythical ocean do? She rested her chin in her hand, enjoying the murmur of her own personal green and leafy ocean. Damp and misty days, she grudgingly decided, could have its good points.

When the cold finally started to seep through to her bones, she got up reluctantly, stuck her hands into the clear cold water of the rainspout barrel, and splashed her face, rubbing it clean. She casually untied her scarf and ran her wet fingers through her hair until the cool dampness ran in trickles down the sides of her face. When she heard the faint bellow of Gort calling her name from within the Inn, she bit her lip, rolled her eyes, and wondered what he was wanting now. She gave her head a vigorous shake, tied her scarf back over her hair, and rested her hand on the latch of the door before turning it to go inside.

An eerie noise stopped her in her tracks. It crawled up her spine like a spider; a faint lowing drone far off in the distance that slowly grew louder. Other droning sounds slowly joined it, rising up in harmony. She cocked her head, raising her eyebrow first in puzzlement and then in genuine alarm as she looked around trying to figure out where it was coming from and what it was. She heard Gort yell for her from inside again. Clearly from the tone of his voice, he either hadn't noticed the odd noise outside or he didn't care.

Ravna grimaced and turned her attention briefly back towards the half-opened door.

Old Lore & Bad Dreams

Bean watched a moth. The pale tiny creature fluttered just within reach of his hand, shining dust trailing from its wings. It fell upon the boy's upturned face. Those he had known in his short life flickered past him like a procession of shadowy murmers. He saw Siv leap over a ditch and turn into a white raven in a fraction of a drawn breath. The bird flew away beyond his sight. Gort's angry face loomed up in his vision, shouting silently. He saw Ravna looking up in a night sky with no stars and he heard Groggle's humming while he cooked in his filthy kitchen.

Promises made for a broken blade, whispered a voice somewhere beyond his sight. Bean turned his head. Every movement he made felt painfully slow. Silent figures stood in a circle around him, people he knew, people he cared for. Their faces wore no expression and their eyes lay deep in shadow.

Secrets taken to the grave, the voice whispered again. One by one, each person stepped back into the darkness and vanished. One by one, they left him until he found himself alone again with the moth. He looked up and reached desperately for it. His fingers barely brushed the little creature's wings.

Clawed hands clapped over his hand, crushing the moth in a burst of sparkling dust. Bean felt horror turn his stomach cold. The Collector grinned down at him and flames flickered in his eyes.

"Welcome to the gates of madness, boy," the creature sneered, gripping his hand tighter. Pain shot down the boy's arm. He felt the black muck of the swamp swirl around his legs, felt himself sinking further and further into the abyss. Dreams poured into his head, spinning dank threads around him, clawing at his sanity, and dragging him down in the murky waters. Wretched claws and fangs clamped into his legs and arms.

Bean clenched his teeth, his misery escaping from his throat in a thin parched utterance of pain.

At that moment, he thought he felt the warmth of sunlight touch the back of his head. He heard a woman's sweet voice calling him. Bean turned his head instinctively towards it and he felt the light spread across his forehead and felt the pain in his arms and legs recede.

"Come out of the darkness, little one," he heard her say, "Leave the pain and fear behind."

Bean sighed once and then it all vanished as quickly as smoke in a breeze. He walked again down a winding path bathed in warm afternoon light and he saw someone standing farther ahead of him, someone who smiled and held out her arms for him. He smiled and his walk turned into a joyful run. The nightmare slipped away into distant and happier memories. The night rolled on. Eventually, as it had always done, morning came.

Dancing particles of sunlight filtered through a delicate filigreed window, framed in white wood, and shuttered on the outside by a partial curtain of willow limbs. Here and there in the window hung tiny gold-tinted crystals that winked, glittered, and refracted the sunlight into a kaleidoscope of dazzling colors that shimmered and trembled throughout the room. Flowering morning glory vines spilled over the windowsill and meandered over white-washed walls inlaid with brightly patterned fragments of colored glass and wood. The disquieting sculpted visages of the last night now could be seen as whimsical and gentle faces, surrounded by intricate designs, and peering from odd secret little corners of the large and comfortable room. Hundreds of bunches of sweet-smelling herbs and flowers hung from the crossbeams of the ceiling along with several wind chimes of rosewood and glass. Even though a brisk morning in late fall should have brought a bit of a chill through the open window, it remained surprisingly warm and cozy. The air stirred with the busy thrum of dozens of tiny wings. Someone hummed softly over the chings and hollow tocks of the wind chimes turning as they hung from the ceiling.

"Nalia, Tia..." said a voice suddenly, cutting the humming short.

"Yes, Mama Faerie?" asked two tiny voices at once.

"I need two more roots of shepherd-heart and Narva's seal, my darlings." The pixies fluttered off and Qwen began humming quietly to herself once more.

She sat by the small sickbed where she had been all night. She worked carefully on the bright patchwork quilt spread over her lap; and several dog-eared books were stacked up around her feet. In outward appearance, she looked much the same as any farmer's wife, though her skin tone held a dark gold of honey and her ears bore a hint of the elven point.

She had her black hair tied back from her shoulders with a bright fringed scarf and when she moved, small bells tied around her ankles and braided in her hair jingled merrily. Yet in her eyes, something unmistakable shone like the multi-colored reflections dancing over the walls. The air around her seemed to shimmer in the oddest way, like curtains of sunlight filtering through the branches of leafy trees.

Her eyes glanced again at the sword that the boy still held tightly in his hand. The stone in the hilt, like an unblinking eye, seemed to regard her with carefully hidden intelligence. If the sword had been a living person, it most assuredly would have worn the thin faint smile of someone who knows more than he would care to divulge. Most people would have quickly dismissed these mental perceptions and blamed them on a lack of sleep or some other trick of a creative mind. However, given the strange circumstance under which the sword had arrived here and given Qwen's sensitivity to such things, an overactive imagination proved a flimsy explanation at best.

The pixies fluttered back to the woman's side. In their tiny arms, one carried small yellow roots; the other clasped the larger white roots. She took the roots, dropped them into a stone bowl along with a few drops of oil, and proceeded to mash them up into a dark, golden paste with a worn wooden pestle. A pungent smell, reminiscent of ginger, filled the air. She rubbed her forehead with the sleeve of her arm, yawned, and looked over at the sleeping young boy still curled in his blankets. A faint weariness passed over her face, weariness coupled with a hint of unease.

"Tia, my sweetheart, watch over our young visitor for a moment would you? I think I'll see about fixing up some breakfast for papa before he wakes. Mind now, leave the sword be. It is very

dangerous and special. You mustn't touch it."

"Tia will, Mama Faerie, yup, Tia will..." Tia beamed. As Mama Faerie got up and walked out the door towards the kitchen, the pixie alighted gently upon the boy's shoulder, turned her head sideways, and proceeded to watch the sleeping boy with all the serious intensity she could muster.

"Why does Tia always get to do big things for Mama? Nalia is big too," grumbled Nalia. The other pixie landed on the back of Mama Faerie's chair, folded her wings, and pouted.

"Shh!" Tia commanded without taking her eyes off of the boy. "Nalia can watch the shiny stick that came to the liddlelad last night." She waved at the curious looking sword with its icy white blade.

"Don't touch... Mama said so," she added, peevish about being distracted from her terribly important task. Nalia stuck her lip out and placed her pointy chin in her small hand, staring intently at the sword with narrowed yellow eyes and clearly disappointed with her duty.

This morning's coziness and comfort lingered in the round kitchen, bright with various pots and pans lining the whitewashed walls. A large freestanding stone oven, shaped like an enormous vase,

was carved with a fantastic beast writhing over its terra cotta surface. It stood in the center of the kitchen beneath an open-air skylight with an intricate iron grating wrought in a sunburst pattern. The fishlike mouth of the beast formed the mouth of the oven and two spread fins supported a pair of iron-stove eyes. Small wooden containers lined the shelves in the walls and several burlap sacks slumped below, overflowing with various vegetables and fruits. Strings of dried beans and peppers hung from the ceiling. Pixies flitted in and out, filling the room with their chirruping chatter, as Mama Faerie stoked the glowing coals beneath one of the iron eyes before replacing it. She took a large pot off of the wall, walked over to the huge sink built into the wall and started filling it with water from the sink pump.

Hands rested on her shoulders and began to rub them gently. "So how is he, my dear?" A deep voice asked. Mama Faerie looked up and smiled.

"Why hello, Theron," she said. "I didn't expect you to be up yet. The boy is still sleeping... his fever's down some and I've taken care of any infection that might be lingering in his wounds. He's still a very sick little boy. He'll make it though. I feel he's a fighter."

"Sounds like I could I have used him in my old regiment all those years ago," Theron remarked with a dry smile. He looked relieved at her comments.

"That boy is probably far tougher than many of the soldiers you knew back then if your stories mean anything," Qwen replied with a grave smile.

Theron chuckled, leaned down, and kissed her on the side of her face. "I'm glad that the boy is doing well," he said. "And how are you doing? You look tired from your evening chore."

"I am fine, my sweet knight. The weariness you see is nothing more than an illusion." she said playfully and then turned serious. "I admit I'm feeling more perplexed over our unexpected visitor than tired."

37

"Perplexed?"

Mama Faerie placed the pot in the sink, dried her hands on her skirt, and closed her hand over Theron's. Her fingers intertwined with his and her eyes grew thoughtful.

"Yes. He has been through a lot. In his dreams, he mutters not only of his own life, but of old forgotten things... ancient lore that a little farmer's son should know nothing of," she answered. "He speaks the names of ancient elven lords as if they were personally known to him. He mentions red rock trolls who have been long dead all these years. Most troubling is the reek of a very old weave about him."

She waved her hand absently through the air. "All fragments drifting like sparks from a fire," she said. "Yes, there is a strange fire in the boy's blood, a fire that burns blue, and a sickness... a weaved sickness." Her expression turned distant and inward.

"A weave, eh..." mused Theron, his face thoughtful. "Then that is the oddness around him that I felt, like the tangles here at home, but different though."

Mama Faerie stirred and came out of her thoughts. "Hm? Oh..." She smiled in apology at Theron. "I am sorry, my dear. My mind was just wandering down old paths."

"Wandering. I see," Theron answered, placing his large strong hand gently on her shoulder. Mama Faerie nodded and looked solemnly at him for a minute.

"Theron, this child is dangerous," she said gently. Theron glanced sharply at his wife.

"How so?" he said. A defensive tone crept into his voice. "He's just a boy, Qwen. Is there so much danger in old lore and fever dreams?"

"More than you might realize. There's something else," she said, her face grave. "Here, perhaps we should come back to breakfast later, you need to see this." She drew Theron's hand from her shoulder and held it by her side as she and her husband walked out of the kitchen.

When they entered the sickroom, Theron stopped in surprise at the sight of the sword leaning against the boy's bed and his small hand curled around the hilt.

"By the broken moon, Qwen," muttered Theron, letting go of his wife's hand. He walked towards the boy with Mama Faerie following close beside him. He knelt down and peered at the odd sword with its green stone and white blade, studying it closely. He started to touch the hilt, when suddenly his wife's hand shot out and grabbed his. Tia, surprised by the sudden action, fluttered into the air again and gave her mother and father an inquisitive look.

"Don't," Qwen hissed, her eyes afire.

Theron looked over at her startled. "What is it, my dear?" he asked.

"Leave the blade be. Touch it and the world as you know it becomes undone in an instant," Mama Faerie said in a tone of voice that resonated through the blood in Theron's veins to the ground beneath them. Theron stared at her. He straightened himself and took his wife's hands in his. A look of mutual respect passed between them.

"As you say, then," he said in a firm voice. "But I would like to know how it got here."

"The sword appeared last night in the boy's hand," Mama Faerie said quietly as Tia settled on her shoulder. "A powerful weave brought it here."

"What else do you know of this sword, Qwen?" Theron asked. "Why does this child have it? Young as he is, is he then a weaver? Has he...?" He paused and his features darkened with sudden thoughts. "Has the madness taken him, then?" he asked in a painful voice.

Mama Faerie gave her husband a tender kiss before sitting

down again beside the boy's bedside. She stroked the boy's hair and her brows creased as she pondered things. Then she closed her eyes and her hand grew still. "His mind is still his own but how long that will last I do not know. I see the threads shining, unfolding the tapestry before my eyes, and my knowledge deepens. I hear a song and I see the threads of this child's soul inter-spinning with the soul of this sword. The nature of the weave is such that it is almost impossible to distinguish one from the other," she said in a low voice. "I know that touching the blade would have killed you, Theron. My knowledge is mostly of the forest and its lore. What surrounds this boy and this sword is outside of my domain. Thaddeus would know, for his realm is that of the scholars. Yet let us see what we can find out."

She opened her eyes and leaned closer to the child, whispering words in his ears. Theron saw the tense features on the boy's face slowly relax.

"Wake, my boy... wake," Mama Faerie finally said.

"Mm..." One blue eye opened and tried to focus on the surroundings. "H...huh?" The boy murmured.

"Easy little one. You are still sick and very warm from fever."

The other eye opened and the boy shifted his head to look up at Mama Faerie. "Where is m'sword?" he muttered.

"In your hand, child, where it belongs," answered Mama Faerie tenderly. The boy slowly pulled the sword up onto his bed, then gingerly pushed himself up still holding the sword close to him, and fingered the stone in the hilt. He stared out beyond his bed to the rest of his surroundings. A thoughtful look replaced the confusion.

"Where am I?" he asked softly.

"You are in my home. It is a quiet safe place that dwells part in twilight and part in morning. I live here with my family and no evil touches my realm," she answered.

"Who are you?" the boy asked.

"You can call me Mama Faerie, little one," she replied gently.

The boy adjusted himself and winced. "Oww..." he grunted. "Everything hurts..." He bit his dry lips painfully.

"That hardly surprises me. You've taken quite a beating and have not quite healed yet, young man. Now take a deep breath, the pain will pass. In the meantime, rest yourself. There will be plenty of time for getting up later. Are you hungry?"

The Bean nodded. "And terribly thirsty, ma'am," he added. Mama Faerie turned her head to her husband.

"Theron dear, will you fetch us a bit of cool water from the well?" she asked.

"Yes my love," Theron replied with a slight smile. His wife shooed the pixie off her shoulder and gestured to her. The pixie hovered in front of her face and tried her best to look attentive.

"Tia, darling," she said in a brisk voice. "Would you and... ah, where is Nalia? Nalia?" She looked around. "That child will be the death of me," she sighed. "Tia I need you to go find your sister and bring us a few apples."

"Nalia got bored and flew off to find Miri," Tia said dutifully. "My will find her though, yup!" The pixie darted off, calling, "Naaaaaaliaaaaaaaa!!!!"

The boy's eyes followed the broad back of Theron as it disappeared through the door and narrowed in amazement when they caught a glimpse of Tia flittering merrily off. Mama Faerie clicked her fingers sharply and he turned his attention back to Mama Faerie. His eyes searched hers for answers.

"I'd like to know who you are, young

man, before I go any further in answering the questions you are going to ask," Mama Faerie replied with a wise look on her face.

"Yes ma'am," sighed the boy. "I'm called Bean."

"Well, that is the most unique name for a little warrior that I have heard of. Do you not think so?"

"No ma'am." Bean scratched the back of his head bashfully. "It's just what I've always been called."

Mama Faerie chuckled. "No harm was meant, young sir Bean. Now what brings a little warrior such as yourself into the dark swamps near my home? It is not the safest place to be wandering, day or night."

"Warrior? Me? No ma'am. Not at all." Bean perked up his head at the thought of being referred to as a warrior. His cheeks flushed a bit.

"Judging by the elven sword you clutch so carefully in your hands, I would think 'yes indeed' rather than 'not at all.'"

Mama Faerie knelt down and picked up Bean's torn and soiled shirt from off the floor beneath the bed and studied it. She clicked her tongue in disapproval. "Filthy thing, I must say. I guess a clean linen nightshirt will have to suit you for the time being until I am able to scrounge up some new clothing. These need to be burned. No use in you getting sick again." She held it out studying it for a moment. "Hmm.... Though I do wonder why the clothes you wore tell a far different story from the sword you wield."

"I just wash dishes, ma'am. Honest," the boy

wered.

"A brave washer of many terrible dishes, you say. I cannot ⸺p but think of a knight errant in disguise." She smiled cheerfully ⸺3ean and he couldn't help but smile back and gave his nose a self-⸺scious rub.

"Well... uhm... actually..." Bean began and stopped, as Ther-⸺came back into the room carrying a drinking gourd full of clear ⸺l water in his hand. The boy's eyes brightened and he raised him-⸺ up as the man came to his bedside. "Here you are, lad," he said, ⸺ding out the gourd. Bean took it and gulped at it greedily. The ⸺er tasted sweet and cool, magical to his dry mouth. He barely ⸺pped for breath until he drank it all and wiped his mouth.

"Thank you, sir," he said. He lay back down, turned on his ⸺e, and rested his head in the curve of his arm. He watched as ⸺ and Nalia, who was grumbling under her breath again, flutter ⸺k into the room laden with several pieces of fruit and head to the ⸺le by his bed. They carefully laid a couple of apples down on it ⸺ fussed for a few minutes arranging them just so, wiping off the ⸺udges, and polishing them brightly.

Fascinated, Bean reached out and gingerly touched Tia's ⸺gs with a finger. The pixie immediately hopped up into the air ⸺ peered at Bean for a moment, as she hovered there in front of ⸺face. "Ah-ah, liddlelad," she said with the slightly exasperated air ⸺a mother dealing with a baby with busy hands. "You am keep-⸺ fingers off Tia's pretty wings, yup." Nalia giggled and several soft ⸺le giggles followed hers, fluttering through the air as more curious ⸺ies came into the room and hovered in the air above their heads. ⸺ indignant Tia buzzed her wings and zipped away holding her chin ⸺ proudly.

"Wow," Bean said in amazement.

He looked over at Mama Faerie carefully folding up his trou-⸺s and remembered what he had been about to say earlier. "Actually... I'm not really... not much of anyone, let alone a warrior," he remarked humbly.

Mama Faerie looked up at him and smiled again. "I would beg to differ, little man. In my house you may call yourself a knight as proudly as you call yourself a washer of dishes. There is no shame in being either. Even the greatest heroes must carry a washing pot now and then." She gave Theron a playful look and then looked back at Bean as her eyes grew sharp and serious.

"There is far more to you than meets the eye, I would think," she said. "I know what you battled with in the swamps. Perhaps more than a mere hungry beast..." Bean pondered these words before Mama Faerie added, "Listening to you caught in your dreams last night revealed things most strange and unsettling to me. Now that you are awake, tell us your tale young man. There is no need to measure your words. I am very curious to hear what you have to say."

Bean rubbed his nose again, thought for a minute, and then began to talk. Mama Faerie and Theron sat and listened in respectful silence as the boy spoke. Above them, the chimes gently sounded as the inquisitive little pixies fluttered about and the morning air hung heavy with soft music and the sweet heady perfume of peace and contentment.

Siv's Choice

The deep-throated rumble of thunder sounded far in the ground beneath the roots of the trees and the relentless rain fell in steadily hissing sheets. The soldiers of the Badger's army moved through the forest and white lightning flashed again, the glare glancing off a sword's sharp edge.

The goblins had chosen to pursue a deadly quarry. It was becoming more and more difficult to distinguish who was hunter and who was hunted.

Siv twisted his sword and pulled it out of the blood-smeared tree trunk with a grunt. The goblin it had seconds ago pinned to the trunk made a horrible rattling noise deep in his throat, slid down to the ground, and lay still. Siv rubbed his arm absently and stepped over the goblin's companion, sprawled facedown in the reddening mud. He knelt down, took a second to cut the spearhead loose from the dead goblin's broken shaft, and jammed it into the side of his belt. Several more spearheads and knives were attached to his belt as well, but Siv's intention was more than just idle trophy gathering. He had been putting them all to very good use, being 'thoughtful' enough to return the weapons to the goblins every once in a while; most often right between the shoulder blades or some other vital area. The forest walker was very familiar with the art of making do with what he had available.

His lacerated chest started throbbing painfully again. He glanced down at his wounds and winced. He hadn't had time to do more than plaster a hastily made poultice of moss and tree sap across it, which beside its healing qualities, had also been helpful for keeping him camouflaged. He had been on the run all night from patrols. The patrols had gone from a scattered few initially to running into a troop almost every time he turned a corner and it was slowly but surely, gnawing away at his stamina.

Siv had the sickening feeling that this Badger fellow had not hesitated in mobilizing the rest of his troops and had begun the serious task of taking down Darkleaf in one fell swoop. Siv himself was just another fly in the broth to deal with.

Well, this old fly still has a bit of a bite at least, Siv thought grimly. He touched the precious parchments he had tucked under his shirt. The edges of the paper scraped at his bare skin with his every movement. At this point that information and a few tightly knotted nerves of iron stretched to their utmost limits, were all that kept him on his feet and pushing relentlessly onwards toward Heartleaf.

Siv glanced up, hearing the sounds of goblin voices in the distance behind him. On an impulse, he grabbed the smelly tattered rag that passed for the creature's cloak and draped himself in it. He hurriedly slipped off to put the finishing touches on the welcoming party he had planned for this latest group.

A moment later, the patrol, which was now down to about five goblins, came trudging right up to the bodies of their comrades. Slitted eyes and hushed whispers filled the silent woods. There was anger in their voices, anger and frustration, and at the very center a fine needle of fear.

They scoured the area furiously for
evidence of their quarry, sniffing and glancing about.
Not more than five feet away within the trunk of a huge
old willow, split open by lightning strike, Siv's cold eyes
narrowed behind a drapery of slimy moss. His bleeding
hand finished lashing the knife tightly onto the flexible
branch. He gripped it, waiting for the goblins to find
the evidence he had deliberately left for them.

The tension of the branch held in his hands
throbbed as tightly as a drawn bowstring. This was no
ordinary farmer they searched for.

The goblins found the smeared blood on the
tree stump and the broken limbs leading off into the
underbrush. They moved past Siv eagerly pursuing
the false trail he had left them. He waited with the
patience of a spider, his eyes following the goblins
moving past until the last one had turned his back
to Siv. Siv moved the moss and let the branch whip
out. The knife lashed to its end caught the wretched creature right at the base of the skull.

The agonized gasp of their fallen fellow
immediately caught the attention of

the other goblins and they turned in time to see him drop and saw Siv dart from his hiding spot and take off in the opposite direction.

The goblins flew after him with maddened shrieks, exactly as Siv had hoped they would.

The precise expertise of Helixshire training and the rigors of his former life as Captain of White Stone Hall had sharpened him, but his brutal apprenticeship in Darkleaf had tempered him as hard and unbreakable as forged steel. Siv was a forestwalker. Darkleaf's voice spoke in time with the beat of his heart and the voice of the trees was in his bones. The goblin's ignorance of this was the most deadly mistake they could have made.

With the goblins at his heels, Siv ran. He drew out his sword while he ran and its white rose emblem shimmered in the dull light. The goblins were so close behind him he could hear their labored breath hissing between their clenched teeth. He skidded to a halt, apparently trying to find his bearings, and made sure to hesitate just long enough for them to close the distance he needed between them and himself. Then abruptly, he jumped a fallen tree, barely avoided the swipe of one of the goblin's swords at his back, and slid down a steep embankment slick with mud.

They scrambled over the tree and down the embankment after him and saw him slash wildly at a taut vine as he neared the bottom. A second later, a makeshift framework of saplings and vines sprang up out of the loose-packed earth like the gaping jaws of some hideous skeletal creature rising from a grave. Spear points and knife blades glinted along its edge. The slick mud and the steep incline, coupled with the goblins' mad eagerness to catch their prey sealed their fates.

A sickening noise like punctured melons filled the air. Siv slid gracefully to a halt at the foot of the embankment and crouched there a moment, breathing hard, and staring up at the motionless bodies of the impaled goblins. He closed his eyes, shook his head a little, and heard again the distant sounds of soldiers moving through the woods.

Siv gave a little sigh. He rose, draped in his tattered goblin cloak, soaked with filth from head to toe. He trudged off down the narrow ravine, ankle deep in mud and rotten leaves.

Some time later, he found exactly what he had been looking for; an old earthdweller's entrance beneath the shadow of a rock, all but invisible to those who weren't looking for it. "Illusions and ghosts," Siv mused softly to himself before he knelt down. Opening the grille took some effort. It had been many years since it had last been used and the effects of time and the elements were working against Siv's overtaxed muscles at the moment. Somehow the forest-walker managed to get it open and quietly slipped into the darkness below.

The air in the cavern was chilly, damp, and ancient smelling as Siv moved stealthily down the dark winding corridors. He stopped momentarily when his footsteps disturbed a cluster of small creatures in the darkness that scuttled off down another tunnel in a flurry of whistles; skylocs, he thought and managed a faint smile.

He could feel several pairs of eyes on him as he walked; studious and careful eyes of other small creatures seeking shelter from the rain. They watched him, trying to determine whether he was an immediate threat or not, scurrying away or scratching down further into the earthen walls when he passed by them. Somewhere in the distance, the kwok-kwok-kwok! of a chorus of little frogs, happy for the rain and the damp and happily oblivious to Siv's difficulties, echoed down a tunnel off to his right.

He stepped carefully over huge twisted roots, the collected roots, both living and long dead of generation upon generation of Darkleaf trees that reached far, far down into the living heart of the world. He could almost hear through the roots, the beat of Darkleaf's heart if the old folktales of the earthdwellers were to be believed. He kept his hand on his sword while he walked. Illusions had their ability to conceal, but he dared not trust their dependability over the wretched talent of the goblins to pry into and discover the hidden places of Darkleaf. He trusted the keenness of his blade first, a trust that had been proven true in times long since gone. His services to the Hall had been unique as had been his training. His abilities to think and react on the spin of a coin in terse situations had made the less tutored swear he could rival the skills of an elf in one-on-one combat. Siv had never discouraged nor encouraged these speculations though he had always been secretly amused at the thought of comparing himself to the Helixshires who had trained him and his household in the art of both statesmanship and warfare. His own sword strokes and moves would have been as clumsy as a toad's alongside the ethereal glance-and-fade swordsmanship that even a novice warrior of Helixshire blood had an innate knowledge of.

Those elves moved with a deadly artistry that was like water pouring over polished stone or light glinting off a

diamond. His instructors had once commented to Siv that it was a pity for the shortness of human years since the only thing indeed that kept him from mastering the full understanding of the dance of blades was about a hundred or so more years of training. Helixshire elves tended to give back-handed compliments that both praised and patronized, but due to the rarity of any sort of compliment, Siv had learned to take them in stride. It had all been part of the training.

His sword had been a constant companion from his days of wearing costly silk, when Darkleaf was no more than a spot on a map. Those days the forests he walked were forests of pikes and broad-swords held aloft in salutes by eager boys who knew nothing of the savagery of true warfare, who had never tasted blood in their mouth or felt the shamefully triumphant rush that accompanied the slaughter of one's enemies. Siv wore plain coarse wool now and his leather boots hadn't seen a good polishing for decades. His sword was all the status he had left and for reasons even he wasn't sure of, he still found himself sheathing his sword deep in those memories, deep within that tattered pride.

The dim light of dawn began filtering in here and there above his head through places where parts of the tunnel's ceiling had fallen into disrepair. He stopped in one faint column of light and turned his head up towards it while mist drifted down on his face. His face grew thoughtful and he gave a wearied sigh.

The information he held, those few fragile parchments delicately rubbing against his side, had the potential to work a miracle. It was, in a way, the oldest kind of weaving, an everyday power that re-spun frayed threads of shame back into a tapestry of respectability; the kind of weaving that wove and healed the delicate strings of a heart broken in unrequited love. He had willingly turned his back long ago on those who had esteemed him, who had loved him, and to some degree had utterly loathed him. He knew what was done was done and he was no longer welcome within the Hall. But for this moment he only felt the deepest and most poignant pain of longing to spin the threads backward in time, to undo the mistakes, to return to his post and protect his king.

His thoughts cleared. He lowered his head and looked ahead.

A few steps ahead of him a rusted old ladder led upwards. He rubbed his face, wiping away the moisture, and hurried towards it. Ascending the ladder brought him to a trap door. He edged it open, took a quick glance around, and then climbed out.

The woods by now were deep in a thick mist of light rain as early morning light spread through Darkleaf. He stood now at an old stone marker in the middle of a road. He took a moment to study it. The marker placed him directly midway between the Silver Dagger and Heartleaf. If he could get to Heartleaf in time then he could find a mount there to take him directly to the Hall.

He looked down that road and touched his side unconsciously, feeling the parchments beneath his shirt. The rain slackened up a bit and the forestwalker stood there in the road with an aching heart, muddy, worn, and drenched and pondered his situation.

In the distance he could hear the calls of the goblins behind him and he turned to see if he could see them. Through the early morning fog and the surreal landscape of the silent forest, Siv could see the torches being carried aloft by the misty shadows of the goblin patrols. Those goblins were no longer hunting for him; they were mobilizing. His visit to their camp had sent them pouring into the forest. They had other tasks to tend to now and the Silver Dagger stood in their direct path.

The seconds ticked by like years. Siv couldn't afford the delay. He couldn't risk being cut off from Heartleaf. He dared not throw his hopes and this information out on a gamble. Siv knew the goblins and he knew they would raze the Inn to the ground. He knew they would leave no survivors.

Feeling too exposed, Siv stepped back off the road, walked a few feet back into the woods and found himself at the edge of another ravine. Something light-colored in the weeds caught his eye. He crouched down and gazed at what lay at his feet. He absently plucked up a soft bright blossom.

In his ears he heard a low droning sound begin, droning that

echoed all over Darkleaf. Siv turned the delicate flower over in his hands. Its silvery petals felt like silk between his fingers and their tender fragrance lingered over his mud and bloodstained hands, as in sympathy for his woes. His brow creased and his face softened in concern. The forestwalker in Siv knew the flower to be soul's-tears, a common little wildflower found all over Darkleaf. The man in Siv thought of Ravna, how she loved this flower, and of his deep feelings for her, feelings that had no words to describe them.

How much keener that loss would be... he thought to himself. It would be something he could never forgive of himself. Everything else; his old life, his dreams of regained honor, his desires for what once was, that was all dreams and illusions. Ghosts. This he held in his hand was all he was. This was all that remained, all that he could call real. Redemption and the favors of White Stone Hall would just have to wait.

He gently opened the pouch at his side and tucked the little flower away. Turning his back from the direction of Heartleaf, he pushed his way back into the woods, becoming another shapeless wraith in the mist lying close and thick to the ground. The eerie drones and cries of the goblins rose into a dawn that held its breath and waited for blood.

Fireflies

Aside from an occasional stop-over by the road to catch a few winks, Father Per, his son, and their wagon had traveled uninterrupted through most of the night. They had passed a canteen of pepperbark tea back and forth between them to ward off most of their drowsiness and over swallows of the spicy-sweet tea, they had talked. The elder Per had more or less led the conversations while Fencer had listened and offered his own thoughts when it seemed appropriate. Both men, however, had gingerly skirted past any mention of the politics of White Bird Cove or Darkleaf.

They had spoken of local gossip, small personal tragedies and joys that friends and relatives had experienced in the years Fencer had been gone from Darkleaf. Any of Fencer's acquaintances back in White Bird Cove would have been yawning by the second word of how Lon's prize boar had torn a hole in the pig-sty and gotten itself wedged under the steps of his house and even Fencer had found his mind wandering now and then. Nevertheless he had tried to give his father's words the proper attention they deserved. Sometimes he hadn't had to try so hard. He'd laughed at the old jokes and sang a verse or two of the songs he'd heard a thousand times before. At times, he found himself settling into the same comfortable old rut he had enjoyed with his father before leaving Darkleaf. But then again, there had been times where he'd sipped quietly at the tea, thought about White Bird Cove and felt a dull emptiness settle over him. The jokes seemed silly, the songs off-key, and Fencer would retreat into his thoughts until he felt like talking again.

Both men sat in their seats now, waiting to hear the first signs of the forest waking up. Neither had spoken for about two hours and Fencer, despite gulping down a bit of pepperbark tea only a few minutes ago, still found himself rubbing his eyes and struggling to stay awake.

He paused and looked down at the poplar branch twig in his hand, the one he had started working on with his knife about an hour before at the first sign of proper light. It had started out as a heron and somewhere within the last thirty minutes it had decided to turn into the head and shoulders of a young woman. He couldn't call himself a master woodcarver by any stretch of the imagination but to his faint surprise, Fencer realized it rather looked like Ravna. He smiled and a hint of mischief came into his eyes. "Or maybe not," he thought to himself, "She's not scowling enough." He brushed the shavings off himself, slid the knife back in its sheath, and tucked away the little carving in a pocket inside his coat. He lifted his head up and then tilted it curiously.

"What's caught your attention, boy?" Crimson Per asked, finally breaking the long silence. He stifled a yawn and stretched his arms skyward as the old cart rocked slowly forward.

The young man sat up straight and alert in his seat. "I don't know," he muttered. He gazed into a dream-like landscape, deep in shadowed trees and thick misty rain. It was that uneasy quiet time of the early aurora that was sister to the twilight. The birds hadn't stirred, the last stars were dying in the sky, and silence hung heavy over Darkleaf. The morning was just defining itself from the night and it promised to be a rainy morning at that.

There were fireflies, hundreds of them. Points of yellow light danced in the distance, fading and brightening in the thick damp fog. "Look at that, now..." Fencer said as his brows lowered. "Fireflies, I guess? But they don't move right." He blinked and narrowed his eyes, wondering if they were playing tricks on him. As he watched, the lights abruptly winked out like they had never been there.

"Eh? Fireflies? Not this time of the year, lad," said Crimson, squinting to look where the little points of light had been. "You HAVE been out of the woods too long. They take off at the first sniff of cold weather."

Fencer shook his head and rubbed his face. "Yes. Odd, really. They seem to be gone now. Maybe a trick of the fog and the light," he said. He turned to his father with a faint smile while the rain started pattering down in earnest around them. "Or maybe I just need a better sleep than a wagon seat can afford."

His father shrugged and turned his eyes back to the road. "Wonder where the birds are? They oughta be singing by now," he remarked and almost the minute the words left his mouth, a strange high-pitched whistle sounded in the silence of the woods. However, it had not burst from the throat of any bird.

Something hit poor Mab's flank with a sharp "thunk!" and the startled mult-ox bellowed and thrashed and leaped off the path into the woods, taking both elder and younger Per on a horribly surprising detour. Two more dull "thunks" sounded from the back of the cart, and a keg broke open, spurting wine across the cart floor while the cart itself bounced and jolted wildly over the rough terrain.

Fencer heard his father curse while his hands floundered for one of the reins flapping loose. Fencer stood up in the seat slightly and glanced back at the cart. His eyes widened as he saw two arrows

buried in the floor of the cart among the broken remains of the keg.

Fencer's head jerked up when he heard deep savage calls issuing from the throats of many horns. In the dim light of dawn, the young man saw scuttling shadows leaping over bush and log, pursuing them, blades glinting in their hands. The cart slowed a bit while the elder Per tried to regain control of the mult-ox to see what had startled her. Fencer whirled around.

"PA! NO!" he shouted. He suddenly reached over, pushed his father behind him, and grabbed the reins from Crimson's hands. He snapped them savagely and urged the mult-ox on faster.

"What the blazes are you do-ing, Fencer!?!" Crimson bellowed. An arrow hissed by his head sud-denly, nicking his ear. Crimson touched the side of his face and looked in bewildered horror as his hand came away flecked with red. Fencer pushed his father down in the foot of the seat and tried to keep his own head low. He jabbed a finger at Mab's bleeding flank. "That's an arrow, Pa! It's got two brothers in the back of the cart. Someone's after us!!" Fencer shouted. "Gee-up Mab! C'mon!" The wounded beast needed no further urging.

Tree after tree shot up in front of them and Fencer jerked the reins this way and that, narrowly avoiding them while raindrops stung his face. The Pers bounced violently in their seats. The cart rounded a curve and started up a hill and Mab's panicked gallop quickly slowed to a painful canter against the upward slant and the dragging weight of the cart and its occupants. Crimson raised his head again and stole a glance behind them. His brows lowered.

"We gotta lighten the load, boy," he grunted and before Fencer could reply, his father pulled out a knife from his belt, climbed over the side of the seat and slashed at the holding ropes secured on the side of the cart. The back of the cart banged open and the remaining casks and kegs slid off and rolled down the hill bursting open against the trunks of trees and knocking a couple of their pursuers off their feet further down the hill.

The cart crested the top of the hill and skidded wildly down the other side where it abruptly jack-knifed and smashed into a tree at the bottom. Crimson grabbed his son by the back of his belt and yanked him over the side of the cart seat moments before the impact. Father and son smashed through a canopy of thick undergrowth spread over a deep ditch and hit the shallow line of murky water at its bottom with a dull splat! Mab staggered out of the wreckage and continued on, vanishing into the misty forest.

Fencer groaned and picked his face up out of the water while droplets of rain puckered the shallow water around him and pattered on his head. His father's hand tapped his shoulder in warning and he looked over at the old man whose eyes showed white in his bruised and muddy face. Crimson pointed up at the foliage over their heads.

Beyond it, the noise of running footsteps and cries filtered down to them and they heard the sound of their pursuers growing closer. Both men grew still and held their breaths as they bent low in the water. Minutes became centuries. The damp crunch of inquiring footsteps sounded very close to them and stopped. They heard the clatter of boards falling against each other and being pulled aside while the wreckage of the cart was investigated. A muffled conversation in a foul-sounding language carried on for a few minutes above their heads. There appeared to be a disagreement about where Fencer and his father had gone, made more difficult no doubt by the rain and the thickness of the undergrowth in this area of Darkleaf. Suddenly a lowing noise sounded through the air, a noise that seemed to thrum through Fencer and Crimson's bodies and filled them with cold dread.

The voices bickered for a minute more, fell into a surly silence, and then footsteps crunched rapidly off in the opposite direc-

tion. For a long time Crimson and Fencer listened to the sound of the rain pattering on the leaves and dripping gently into the water around them. Finally they each dared a soft sigh and raised their heads.

Crimson looked around. "Come on, son," he muttered and pulled at his sleeve. "We'll keep our heads low and follow this for a bit."

"Pa..." Fencer started slowly, not sure what he was wanting to say or how he wanted to say it. His game leg hadn't liked the recent abuse it had taken and was letting him know in no uncertain terms now. "I don't know that... " he said and fell silent.

His father turned and raised his eyebrow. "You know what you're in son?" he asked.

Fencer's mouth twisted in a faint smile. "Either a mucked-up mess or the finest sort or a ditch," he answered. "Do I get to choose?" Crimson snorted. "Look at what's under the vines. Know what's under this line of water, under our hands and knees, Fencer? Feel it? That's fitted stone. Earthdweller made too. We're in one of the old ruined aqueducts. We keep following it, it'll take us underground before too long." His father grinned wearily. "Trust your old man on this one, all right?" he said. Fencer nodded and on hands and knees, they continued on through the dripping rain under the canopy of the concealing vegetation.

The duct had fallen into general disrepair. Along with chuckholes and the spots where the stone sides had collapsed and been overrun by vines and roots, the hard stone itself wasn't easy to bear, as they crawled along like any other four-legged forest creature. Eventually, however, with bruises on their knees and the heels of their hands, the Pers reached the underside of what had once been a bridge. Here the duct ended in a cul-de-sac and the trickle of water dripped through a corroded iron grill. With a little effort, Fencer and his father managed to pry it open. Once a runoff pipe had collected the

er and deposited it into a stone cistern below. The runoff pipe
disappeared a long time ago, though the cistern with its rust-
ned sides and pipes running haphazardly into the walls and the
r still remained. Fencer and Crimson dropped down into water
o their waists, waded to the edge of the cistern, and climbed over
stumble off into the safety of the underground caves.

"This is bad, my boy," Crimson muttered, his voice echoing
ly around the walls of the tunnel. "Bad indeed. Those weren't
highwaymen after us up there. Y'heard the filthy language?"

Fencer nodded mutely. "Too many of them to be bandits,"
aid in a grim voice. "Goblins, you think?"

Crimson nodded and his eyes grew dark. "Goblins back in
kleaf," he grunted. "There's a smell of ill weather in the air and it
t got nothing to do with the rain." They fell silent and neither of
m spoke while they continued walking.

The earthdweller blood made for an effortless adjustment of
r eyes to the darkness of the caverns and Fencer watched his father
king ahead of him. Crimson held his head high and his eyes were
ght and alert while he confidently followed the dizzying twists and
is of the tunnels. Unquestionably, the old man put a tremendous
ount of confidence in his internal underground compass, another
t of the earthdweller heritage he and Fencer shared.

"Dirty little beasts," sniffed a melodic voice in his mind
denly, and he saw the aristocratic sneer curl around a fork full of
-gras. "We were foolish enough to welcome them into the city all
se centuries ago and they never stopped coming. Pray, what have
to show for it now? White Bird Cove being devoured by two-
ged vermin from the ground up, that is what."

Amid the pretty laughter and ill-mannered jokes, Fencer had
od there in silence, listening with a pasted on smile when proper
duct had called for it. While Fencer had moved in the social
les of White Bird Cove, none of his employers had ever known

what he shared with those who dwelt below the city.

By the Darkleaf law of survival, he had kept his secret since the genteel class of the southern cities and the predators of Darkleaf had more in common then they realized. Mixed blood was a weakness to both of them and the weak didn't survive long. Yet now he walked with his father through tunnels built when most of the southern cities had been the passing dream of a ship's captain far out at sea. Again, Fencer wondered as he often had during those times lying in his bed, listening to the sounds of the city below the window or the music of a social gala beneath his floorboards, if silence came at too great a price.

Crimson came to a stop at a crossroads. He turned thoughtfully and studied the paths laid out before them. Fencer stopped behind him. A deep silence fell upon them, broken only by the distant drip of water.

"Son," said his father suddenly in a low voice. "If I asked you to do something now, would'ya do it?"

"You don't even have to ask me that, Pa," said Fencer. He spoke quietly but his voice seemed unnaturally loud in the heavy silence that surrounded them both.

Crimson motioned down one of the tunnels. "I don't know goblin language that well," the old man said. "I know though I heard them say "Heartleaf" and "army." You need to go to Heartleaf, Fencer. Warn them even if they don't want to listen. Bring any that'll come with you down below to the old cities. They'll be safe there." Fencer closed his eyes. "What about Ma? And the rest of the family?" he asked.

"I'll get to them," said Crimson firmly. "We'll meet you there. Now get going. You may have to go topside at some point. Don't get yourself caught. I know that gimp leg'll give you trouble but you have to go quick and go careful, nevertheless."

Fencer opened his eyes and they glinted hard in the darkness.

"It's not going to slow me down, Pa. I'll get there," he answered. "I'll take care of myself. I always have."

He turned towards the tunnel that would lead him towards Heartleaf. "Fence..." came his father's voice suddenly. Fencer glanced back at the old man standing and watching him.

"Yes sir," he replied.

"You've always made me proud, son," Crimson rubbed his jaw. "Don't you forget that." His voice grew quieter. "Don't you forget... your old man loves you better'n his own life and the finest brew in Darkleaf."

Fencer smiled. "I know." He reached over and embraced his father briefly.

"I feel the same, Pa," he said, his voice muffled. "I love you as well." He stood back and looked at his father for a moment, his expression lost in thought.

"Tell Ma I honored our name," he said finally and turned and hurried off in the darkness, his hand on the sword slung at his side. The elder Per turned without another glance and set off down the opposite way.

"I know, son," he muttered under his breath. His stout form quickly vanished into the uneasy darkness. "I will tell her. Don't you worry about that."

69

the Emerging Storm

In a slumber brought by the extremes of exhaustion, dreaming must sometimes be pushed aside and so it was with Bean when he woke in his little bed. He remembered nothing of the previous hours except the sensation of drifting along within a peaceful dark silence, punctuated by bits and pieces of odd memories and sounds.

He rolled over and his drowsy eyes roamed over the room while his mind went about the hazy task of gathering his senses back from their deep period of stillness. What had woken him was a gentle rhythmic humming filling his ears, a humming that seemed very hard to explain. If someone had asked Bean later if it had been a voice humming or a sound of nature he would have quickly answered "Yes" to both. If he had been asked where the humming had come from, he probably would have thought about it for a moment and then answered, "Everywhere... the walls, the ceiling, the carvings, and the flowers. Maybe somewhere far off but still close by." At that point the questioner most likely would have sighed heavily and given up asking anything else, figuring that the boy's confusing replies could be explained by his recent fever and bewilderment upon waking up. However, that wouldn't have changed the fact that Bean's first impressions had been more or less correct.

He lay there and listened to the humming for a while, humming that was not quite a voice or a sound of nature, but came from everywhere and nowhere. Such was the peculiar quality of it that he wondered for a while if he might not still be asleep and possibly dreaming after all. If so, it really wasn't a dream he was in any hurry to wake from, for it soothed him to the soul.

Gradually the source of the humming grew less all encompassing to the point that Bean finally could pin it down as coming from somewhere outside the window. He sat up, slowly wrapped the blankets and sheets around him, and slid to the edge of the bed. He pulled the stool near to him and used it to support himself, tentatively stepping onto the floor. The injured leg caused some discomfort but nothing that Bean felt he couldn't bear. Through a bit of maneuvering and using what was handy to support his weight, he limped towards the window and finally settled himself gratefully into the seat beneath it. Pulling the blankets beneath him, he got up on his knees, moved aside the vines spilling through the window, and rested his elbows on the sill, looking outside. A breeze stirred the delicate drapery of willow branches beyond his window, which gave Bean a glimpse of a garden, and such a wonderful garden it was. By the standards of a rich lord, it lacked somewhat the formal topiary beasts, the regal layouts of flowerbeds, and fine marble statues. Yet it was just the kind of garden that a little fellow like Bean could wander into by chance and still be utterly awed, yet without a self-conscious desire to hastily wipe his face clean on the edge of his shirt.

The garden stretched out a considerable way beyond the house and at the edge lay a fringe of dark trees that signaled the beginning of the swamp. Instead of a fencing of stonework or posts, Bean saw markers made of round flat white stones stacked on each other at regular intervals where the garden met the swamp. Vegetables and herbs grew, not in rows, but in the midst of a large circular maze of rich black earth against pale green grass. The grass looked as soft as feathers and just right for kicking off shoes and running barefoot. Every once in a while he saw a pixie dart by in a flash of iridescent wings. The humming came from somewhere just beyond his sight and Bean realized it was the voice of Mama Faerie. He smiled.

"H'lo ma'am," he called from the window and the humming stopped. He heard the soft thump of footsteps crossing the ground and he saw Mama Faerie duck under the willow branches and smile back at him.

Her hands were in a pair of rough canvas gloves covered in rich black earth, her hair was tied back with another of her bright scarves, and a dark green apron covered her simple clothes. Dirt was across her face and the front of her apron. She rubbed the dirt off of her gloves, pulled them off, and reached through a gap in the intricately made window shutter. The back of her hand rested briefly against the side of his temple and then moved down to the hollow between his neck and collarbone for comparison while a thoughtful expression crossed her face. She withdrew her hand and said cheerfully, "How are you feeling, my little man? I think you might be getting a bit warm again."

Bean shrugged, held up his hand at chin level, and waggled it gently. "Not so bad, not so good ma'am," he answered. "Down the middle I guess." His eyes glanced mournfully past her shoulder. "Wish I was outside," he added, "It looks so much better than in here. Could I please... maybe just sit in your beautiful garden? For a little while?"

"Ah... thank you. But one thing at a time," Mama Faerie answered gently. "I have another row of sage to transplant to the other side of the house and then I'll be inside to give you a dose more of sallow bark and yellow gentian root tea for the fever. For now a little fresh air and sunshine from the window will be fine."

She unlatched the shutters and then stepped back from the window. Cupping the willow branches gently in her hands, she closed her eyes and whispered something. To Bean's amazement, the branches curled themselves gracefully away to afford him a clearer view of the garden. She opened her eyes and met his astonishment with an expression of tender reproach.

"One can command that which lives and grows and make it do wondrous things, but I prefer to ask permission. Compassion is preferable to dominance," she said and smiled again. "After all... they were here first." Mama Faerie ruffled Bean's hair affectionately while he pondered this bit of information and slipped off again to tend to her gardening. Bean sat back down on his bottom, found a comfortable hollow spot where the seat flowed into the wall, wrapped a blanket around his shoulders, and felt very content.

He must have dozed off at some point because he suddenly blinked and found himself wide-awake. His injured leg had started tingling and going numb where he had folded it under himself. He made a face, shifted himself, and stretched out his leg, all the while rubbing it. He shrugged off his blanket and rubbed his shoulders when an odd draft of chilly air made his skin prickle. The warmth seemed to have gone right out of the room. He could no longer hear

Mama Faerie's humming and the silence was more than a bit unsettling.

Outside on the other side of the house, Mama Faerie's hands curled tightly and the tiny sage plants lay in their boxes, untouched. Her face was pale but grim; her eyes gleamed with fierce energy. Almost the moment she had left Bean at the window she had felt it; a breach in her tangle. Normally this did not cause her alarm. Small forest animals and birds often blundered into the tangle on occasion and were turned away in the same instant, leaving them bewildered but otherwise unharmed and the tear would heal itself immediately. This, however, did not feel like a mere innocent of the woods stumbling upon her territory. Though it was small, a deliberate maliciousness lingered about it like salt in a cut, a poison she felt in her blood. It was worrying enough that Mama Faerie had spent the last thirty minutes going through her intricate threads, trying to pinpoint the source of the intrusion. She felt she was getting closer but as she did, her concern grew and so did a disquieting sense of familiarity. She had dealt with something like this before.

Theron had gone gathering wood and hopefully would be back soon. Mama Faerie would have been grateful for the presence of her dear knight at this moment though, as much for reassurance as for anything else. Led to the edge of the garden, Mama Faerie discovered the source quickly enough. By one of the stone markers, the white stone was spattered with flecks of blood. Mama Faerie stopped, her eyes gone cold. An oriole lay there, its bright feathers and the soft green grass beneath it stained with red. A dagger pinned it to the ground, a brutish looking thing with a red-wrapped handle. What was worse... the bird was still clinging to life and fluttering weakly. Its own small eye looked up at her in terror and agony, its beak opened as it gasped for breath and then while she watched, it died right before her eyes and she felt its passing on a level of understanding few had in this world.

Almost in the same instant, she herself grew paler and pain crossed her face. She held up her hand to her face and closed her eyes. Then she clenched her teeth, opened her eyes, and swung her head around in sudden alarm, looking back towards the house. A diversion... she realized. Invaders were in her domain, reeking of the innocent blood of the recently slain. They had ripped through the tangle... The boy... they were after the boy. She took off running for the house.

Bean's hands closed around the sword hilt and he relaxed. It didn't seem right when the sword was out of his hands for too long. Doing so caused an unnatural yearning in him, a hunger beyond what food could satisfy. He got up on his knees again to look out of the window and to call for Mama Faerie and ask her if she was alright. What he saw instead were several pairs of narrowed yellow eyes glaring back at him. The ludicrousness of the peaceful garden contrasting with the murderous gleam in those eyes didn't register in the boy's shocked mind for a split second.

The goblins took advantage of the boy's momentary confusion and eagerly set upon Bean, sinking their sharp little nails into his arms and pulling him right through the window. Bean's yell of horror was cut short to a "HNGH!" when he was slammed into the ground and the breath burst from his lungs. Hands pinned him to the ground and a goblin leered in his face. Something made a metallic scraping noise and the blade of a dagger pressed lightly against his throat. "Don't move boy... or I slit your throat and gut you like we did the woman out there," the creature croaked and gave him a nasty grin.

Bean struggled for air. Throat slit? Gutted? Mama Faerie... no! She had just spoken to him... not true, not dead... NOT DEAD! His thoughts screamed. Cold blossoms of horror and fear spread through his heart. In the corners of Bean's vision, a searing blue light began to flicker. "Liar," the boy finally gasped. "You lie..."

In a burst of adrenaline, Bean writhed away, tore his hand free and grabbed at the goblin's wrist with a strength that caught the creature off guard. The boy savagely drove the hilt of the dagger straight into that ugly leer. The goblin howled in pain, a couple of yellow fangs bounced off the boy's chest and blood flecked across Bean's forehead. Bean drove his foot into the creature's chest and sent him flying against the wall of the house. He twisted and kicked and then pulled his sword arm free and squirmed out of the goblin's grasp. He scrambled to his feet and began slashing viciously at the goblins clustered around him, driving them back and clearing a space for himself. His young face wore an expression of deadly calm and a smear of blood showed red against his throat where the goblin blade had nicked him.

He breathed hard, stepped back, and brandished his sword. Those goblins that still possessed their wits charged at him with shrieks and weapons drawn. Suddenly thorny vines burst from the ground at the goblins' feet, twisting around them and catching them fast. While the vines snaked relentlessly up their bodies, a voice, that seemed to reverberate from the very ground and air around the boy, rang out, "Bean RUN!!!!!"

The boy's head swiveled around, his eyes clearing for a moment, and he saw Mama Faerie standing a few feet away. She did not look like the sweet farmer's wife anymore but a being of incredible power as she manipulated the vines all around Bean's attackers. She grew angry, her face far from serene, cold as a deep forest pool. Arrows hissed out of nowhere. One struck her in the leg, another in the ribs and she reeled back a moment, her face contorted with pain, while the vines wavered. She straightened herself up again. Her dark hair had come undone and floated wildly about her face and she stood, straight and terrible, while the garden seemed to come alive with goblins from every corner. Her gaze fell briefly on Bean who shouted and began to limp quickly towards her, brandishing his sword. Her eyes shimmered with ancient power, a power barely contained, for she declared again, "Go to the STONES... and BEYOND... RUN AND DONT LOOK BACK!!!!"

An out-thrust hand in the boy's direction sent a wave of invisible force that literally lifted Bean off his feet and threw him backwards across the ground. He lifted his head, shaken but otherwise unharmed, and realized then that it was not a suggestion but a command that was not to be disobeyed. He jumped up, his heel gouging a scar of black earth into the soft grass. Without another second's hesitation, he stumbled as fast as he could towards the stones standing at the garden's edge. He felt the ground rumbling under his feet. Within a stride or two of the wood's edge, the ground began to shake more violently beneath him and thorny vines, huge snaking things as large as the vines he remembered seeing in the underground, burst out of the earth, lifting him off his feet and sent him tumbling through the air towards the stones. He hit the ground hard by one of the marking stones, staggered upright and without meaning to, his gaze turned back toward where he had been. He saw the beautiful tidy garden being rapidly overrun by the huge vines and within the vines the bodies of goblins struggled while others tried to clamber through, hacking at them vainly. In a gap, Bean briefly saw the face of Mama Faerie, calm and shining like the reflection of firelight upon pearls, red blood staining the corners of her mouth. Beneath her lightly closed eyelids, a golden light, brighter than the sun, flowed out across her face in amber trails and down her neck. He heard the thrumming of tiny wings and saw a flood of pixies burst from the windows and the door of the house, to encircle her in a maelstrom of tiny points of fierce gold light. The gap in the vines abruptly drew shut and Bean heard the sound of swords hacking at the vines and the sound of goblin voices growing closer. His eyes flashed a fierce blue; he closed them and turned away and painfully walked off into the woods, clutching his sword close.

The sound of carnage grew faint behind him. Dappled shadows crossed Bean's face, which oddly enough was devoid of any emotion save for the unnatural blue shine in the depths of his eyes. He held up his sword and glanced back and forth at the trees, alert for any sounds of pursuit. The further he walked, the less he seemed to limp. His previous injuries had been forgotten, swallowed up in an unusual surge of stamina and adrenaline. In his mind, the landscape around him shimmered and continually changed in subtle ways. The wheel of time began to creak backwards, gently taking the boy's perception of his present reality with it.

He paused a moment at the snap of a twig and whirled on his heel. Beneath his feet the ground had grown rocky and sloped upwards and the trees grew sparser. He stood a moment, looking up toward the sprawl of trees. Nothing seemed amiss between their lichen-encrusted trunks, but everything was silent. Neither the chirp of a bird or the chatter of a squirrel could be heard. His eyes narrowed and he turned casually as if to resume walking back into the thicker part of the woods. Then he suddenly took off towards the higher ground, kicking up a flurry of loose gravel. Behind him several goblins had suddenly burst out from the undergrowth and ran after him. Bean's bruised and cut feet pounded against the hard earth and his breathing came in quick gasps. A cold smile played faintly about the boy's lips. Some warrior sense inside him, older than he could fathom, told him that the higher the ground, the better the fighting advantage. The power of the sword surging through his blood drove him on, masking all pain, even as traces of blood began showing in the footprints he left behind.

He jumped off the side of the path and slid with elegant grace down a slope of loose rubble. Near the bottom, he swept his foot out, brought himself to a stop and took off again like he had never paused to take his brief detour. Before long, Bean found himself erratically running through a shallow pass full of twisty curves and turns. A minute later he skidded to a halt, brought at bay by the sheer red stone wall of a low cliff that stretched several feet above his head. All around him walls of red stone relentlessly hemmed him in. He glanced back, hearing the sounds

of his pursuers growing closer. Bean bit his lip. He used the sword blade to quickly strip off the bottom edge of his nightshirt. He twisted and looped the strip of cloth around the hilt of the sword, swung it over his back, and tied it snugly around his chest before he found a good handhold and began to climb carefully up the stone wall.

Halfway up, the goblins came into view and spied him easily. They headed towards the wall and began to climb up after him. Bean lost his footing once and rock bounced down towards his pursuers, nicking one in the side of the forehead and causing him to curse loudly. Bean looked down and viciously kicked at another jutting bit of rock, knocking it loose to hit another rock, causing a large slab of the wall to come loose and fall towards the goblins. The falling rock took three goblins with it. The others pressed themselves flat against the wall, escaping injury, and kept climbing. At the foot of the cliff, one goblin lay still, bleeding from his mouth and head. The others who had fallen staggered to their feet and peered up at Bean. They swore in their foul language and stepped back a few spaces, reaching for the bows and arrows at their backs.

Bean made it to the top of the cliff, got to his feet, and loosed his sword from off his back. Some of the quicker climbers scrambled to the top right after him only to be met with the deadly blade of the sword that sent them back over the edge of the cliff. While the boy engaged in desperate combat, still more inched their way up the rock face. When Bean had done away with yet another goblin and caught a moment's breathing space, one of the goblins still climbing glanced down at his comrades on the ground taking aim at the small figure on the top of the cliff. He urgently signaled to them to hold their fire and looked back up at Bean.

"You, boy!" he called in a harsh voice. "Throw down your sword, then you live! Else we throw down your arrow-riddled carcass for the buzzards!"

Bean glanced at the creature and that cold smile crossed his face again. "Loose your arrows then! I will die with a blade in my hand!" he called back boldly, brandishing the point of the blood-stained sword in their direction. The sword and his eyes glowed with that eerie blue light. "You think I fear you, rat-face?"

The goblin bared his teeth. "Foolish boy," he hissed. He shouted down to his fellow fiends and swept his free hand towards the boy. The other goblins screeched in fury, lifted up their arrows and took aim.

Suddenly, a huge shadow darkened the entire face of the cliff and a hollow THROOM, like the noise of an enormous drum-skin reverberating from a blow, rolled across the rocks. A blast of wind scoured the walls of the cliff, battering the climbers with stinging bits of loosened rock and threw the boy back from the edge. Something winged and colossal beyond comprehension dropped from the sky and gave an unworldly call as deep as the voice of a hunting horn. A huge claw raked across the cliff wall where the goblins clung, gouging the stone and knocking several from their precarious perches. Those goblins not flung from the cliff and those at the bottom scrambling away for cover swiftly faced a horror of another kind. A boiling jet of acidic steam blasted the survivors, scalding them even while they screamed and ran. Bean staggered to his feet, half-dazed. Another call from this unknown beast shook the ground under him and part of the cliff came loose, taking Bean with it. The boy clung tight to his sword, tumbled down, and then found himself snatched up in mid-fall. Gigantic talons closed around his body and a fleeting thought crossed his mind that here now he would meet his death, crushed by the claws of this terrible beast.

Instead, he found himself borne into the sky with a speed that drew the breath from his lungs. Sunlight hit his eyes and blinded him for a moment. He gasped for air and the light faded; the force that had driven him thus far drained from him without warning. Pain beyond belief took its place; pain from his injured body, fresh wounds and old wounds reopened. White light eclipsed his vision, the roar of the air rushing past him fell into silence, and the boy lost consciousness.

a Debt Repaid

Without warning, something slammed into Ravna's side. The breath burst from her lungs and she went tumbling head over heels through the back door and into the far wall. A sharp rapping noise like " thock-thock-thock!" hammered against the door behind her and her attacker moved off of her with the swiftness of a flicker of lightning.

Ravna gasped and coughed, trying to catch her stolen breath, and picked herself up off the floor. She got to her feet and shock flashed into a sudden hot surge of fear-fueled anger. She whirled on her heels and screamed, "You wretched, filthy villain, GET OUT OF MY..." She cut herself off when she saw Siv throwing down the crossbar across the door.

"Siv?" she muttered. She saw three nasty looking bolt heads protruding through the door and her face whitened when she realized that she had been standing there moments ago.

"Ravna, arm yourself, dear, and be ready to fight," Siv said in a terse breathless voice. He moved behind the huge old table, braced himself against the wall, and heaved and pushed it towards the door. The legs of the table groaned and scraped across the stone floor and Siv stopped a moment and his head dropped down between his shoulders. He breathed hard while he gathered his strength again.

Ravna automatically grabbed one of Gort's knives, which was as good as a short sword for her and hurried over to him. Bracing herself behind the table she helped him push it along, somehow up-turning it to jam it against the door. Glancing at Siv, Ravna spotted the wounds raked across his chest. Siv wiped his brow and saw her staring at his wounds with an expression of concern and horror.

The door shuddered violently. Siv looked over in that direc-tion, shook his head in disgust, and carelessly flipped open the nearest cabinet door. He reached in and closed his hand around the neck of a bottle, one of Gort's stash of special 'medicinal' wines and popped the cork with his thumb. Gesturing to the wounds, Siv remarked, "Just a scratch and a good story to tell once I get a moment." He gave her a faint smile and took a hasty swig from the bottle.

A sudden harsh thud sent a pin flying out of one of the door-hinges. Siv swallowed and flung the wine-bottle at the door. It smashed and pale wine ran down the wood while fragments of glass scattered across the kitchen floor. "That'll feel nice on their feet," he said and grabbed Ravna's arm, "We'd better go, young lady. It is about to get nasty." They flew through the curtains across the door into the common room.

They stopped short when glass burst through the main windows and the ugly grinning faces of a swarm of goblins appeared, surrounded by spears and swords. The goblins thrust themselves through the empty frames, clawing and scrabbling to get inside. The front door of the tavern banged violently and burst open. In the space of a moment, Siv and Ravna found themselves in the midst of bloodthirsty goblins and screaming chaos.

Both of their faces grew cold and emotionless. Without sparing a second for thoughts and without a word or a glance exchanged between them, Siv and Ravna took up defensive positions beside each other. The wave of enemies burst upon them and they met them on the upsweep with their weapons; Siv's sword flashed and screeched against the palestone of a goblin spear and Ravna's knife drove itself through leather armor. Dark blood slopped onto the floor, blood that ran between the cracks of the stone like eldenberry wine.

At the center of the brutal conflict, the two spun and stepped across the slick floor; Siv and Ravna waltzed with deadly and cold perfection to the grim music of clashing weapons and goblins cries. Where Siv swept out with his sword, Ravna whirled back to deflect a blow aimed at him. When Ravna caught a goblin in the ribs, Siv swept him aside like so much chaff. To watch them together bore witness to the smooth and intricate convolutions of the machinery of pure battle. They fought with precision; they fought with grace and they fought with the fierceness and the tenacity of those trained to barter their life's blood at the end of a blade.

Still the goblins came on and on. Their foes recognized in the moves and strokes of the two humans, the ancient training of elven warriors and it drove the goblins even further into rage and battle-madness. They trampled the dying and slain beneath their feet, practically cutting their own soldiers to ribbons to reach Siv and Ravna and satisfy their desires to be the first to see them both cut down.

What the goblins lacked in swordsmanship, however, they made up for in sheer numbers and brutish strength. With nicks and bruises beginning to show on them, Siv and Ravna found themselves falling back and being forced up the stairwell. Goblins had apparently moved past them at some point in the battle and fallen upon the inn's guests as well, for further up the stairs in the hallways of the higher floors came the gruesome sounds of fighting, shouting, and screams. Travelers and farmers who had thought themselves in for a quiet evening, a nice drink, and perhaps a game of cards struggled for their lives only to be stabbed and cut down without mercy.

At Siv's heels, Ravna deflected the onslaught coming up the stairs while Siv battled those coming down. The narrow and confined space of the stairwell couldn't have been a worse spot to inconvenience the two. At one point, a wild-eyed man with blood on his face appeared at the top of the stairwell. In a desperate attempt to escape, he plunged headlong into the fray. An out-thrust goblin spear killed the man right in front of Ravna's eyes and just narrowly missed stabbing her through the side. She ended up roughly pushing the man's lifeless body into the midst of the snarling goblins, using him to buffer the wave of pressing enemies and to buy herself a fraction of a second to breathe. Some small part of her, not preoccupied with fighting to save her life, cringed at the inhumanity of her actions.

Without warning, a distant bellow shook the stairs beneath them and feet pounded so hard on the floor above Siv and Ravna for a moment it seemed like the wooden slats would crack under the abuse. A bristling hedge of enemies at the top of the stairwell dissolved with a crackle of snapping bones and flying blood when the looming figure of Gort smashed his way through them. Beneath his bloodshot eyes, his teeth bared in a yellow-stained snarl and he clenched a

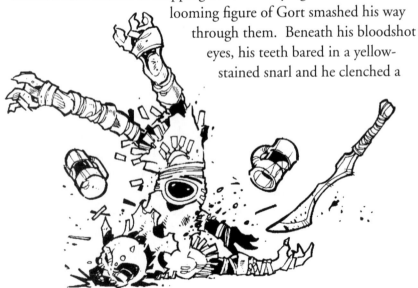

wedge-bar in his hand.

"WRETCHED RATS... SPOILIN' MY INN... FILTHY
LITTLE RATS!" the enraged old ogre bellowed down the stairs.
He started down like a veritable juggernaut, smashing foes in the
face with the wedge-bar, snatching up goblins and throwing their
broken bodies aside. Siv and Ravna barely jumped off the stairs in
time. Gort literally swept them and their enemies behind them back
towards the kitchen once more.

Pushed backwards through the curtain, Siv and Ravna caught
their balances and spun on their heels to see the kitchen door shuddering and splintering under the merciless attack of goblin hatch-
ets. Beyond the curtain they could hear Gort fighting off goblins
and then a cry in the goblin tongue started up from the wretched
creature's throats, a shrill cry amplified and passed down through the
ranks.

"They're... they're calling for the crossbows..." Siv panted.
"We've got to..." Another roar from Gort drowned him out and three
or four bolts shot through the curtain and drove them down on the
floor. A second later the ogre himself came through the curtain with
goblins pressing behind him. Gort cleared out a few goblins at the
front with another sweep of his wedge-bar. Siv and Ravna leaped
to their feet when the ogre came bursting in. The kitchen table and
the door shuddered against the brutal blows of goblins still trying to
break in. A fragment of wood flew out of the door and the glinting
curve of a hatchet blade framed an evil narrowed eye. The hatchet
hacked its way through the door and started splintering the crossbar.

"Goin' to just stand there lookin' pretty for th' goblins, barkeep?" Gort bellowed while Siv and Ravna fought off several of the
other soldiers who had nimbly circumvented the deadly reach of the
ogre's burly arm and surged past him. The ogre pushed the goblins
back, grabbed a wooden keg of dirty dishes and pots and swung it
into the creatures' faces with an ear-splitting crash. Soapy gray water

washed across the floor and Gort crammed broken dishes, pots, the keg, and a few dead goblins into the doorway, making a temporary barrier. He splashed towards Siv and Ravna, smashed a goblin in the face, and sent him skidding into the sink. He waved the wedge-bar at them and sent another goblin flying with his other fist. "Get down them cellar stairs, both of ya!" he shouted, while Siv and Ravna dispatched the last of their foes and staggered back, gasping for breath. The kitchen table shuddered violently and moved inward. Meanwhile, several dishes in Gort's makeshift barrier slid down and smashed on the floor while the goblins digging through on the other side filled the room with their cries of rage.

Exhausted as he was, Siv looked ready to swear at the ogre. Ravna elbowed past him and beat him to it. "Are you MAD?!" she screamed at the ogre at the end of a string of obscenities . "There'll be no way you..."

"SHUT UP AN' MOVE, WOMAN!!!" Gort roared in a voice that made the rafters tremble. At that moment, they all heard the groan and scrape of the kitchen table being violently pushed aside. Goblins began to pour through the narrow opening of the forced door, while to their right, more goblins clawed their way towards them over the rubble of broken dishes and pots. Gort was through with arguing. He pushed Ravna and Siv through the cellar door, almost causing them to fall over each other down the stairs. Their enemies pressed into the narrow space, clambering over each other; sure they had their prey now right where they wanted them. The goblins forced Gort, Siv, and Ravna down the stairs inch by inch and the trio fought for their lives the whole way. The shelves shook under the onslaught and pots and sacks came tumbling down, smash-ing across the cool earthen floor, while goblin feet clambered eagerly over the mess.

Gort swept a whole shelf of clay pots into the goblins' faces and while it threw a good bit of them off guard long enough for Gort

to clear out the ranks with his wedge-bar, it did little to hold them back.

The battle raged its way clear across the cellar and into Gort's room, which was really more or less the back half of the cellar, partitioned off by flimsy mud-and-daub walls and two main support beams. Old chests and sacks of hoarded 'gifts' unwillingly or unknowingly donated by many a poor traveler lay upon the floor. With Siv and Ravna semi-protected behind him, Gort held his ground at the door. His huge hand closed around an old battered helmet hanging within his reach and he lashed out with it, the metal edge cutting a swath of red in the cluster of goblins before him. They retreated for a split second and Gort whirled around and flung the helmet into the room towards the stone wall directly behind them.

It almost caught Siv across the forehead before it ricocheted off the stone and clattered into the corner. Something hissed amid the noise of grinding stone against stone and a black hole gaped open in the wall. In a rage the ogre press-ganged the rest of the attackers back out through the door and slammed the door in their gibbering faces. He grunted and braced his shoulder against the door while it shook with violent thuds and cracks appeared in the plaster around the frame. The whole front half of his body looked like it had been dragged across a massive grater.

"Now Mistress Dragon... an' you, forestwalker..." the ogre panted and waved at the hole with his bloodied wedge-bar. "There's your way out..." Ravna looked desperately over at Siv while she tried to catch her breath. The man held a hand over his bleeding chest and breathed heavily, clearly worn down, yet he still held his blade upright in his other hand. He shook his head at Ravna, unable to speak for a moment. She glared back at Gort.

"Stupid... and repulsive as you are, ogre... we're not... we're not leaving you," Ravna said breathlessly. Another violent blow made the door jump ajar for a second.

"GO!" the ogre bellowed. "GO NOW!" Neither one of them budged. Gort scowled and his huge frame buckled again from another blow on the other side of the door. He clenched his teeth and glared at the door, knowing it wouldn't last another assault by the little wretches. The ogre jammed his weapon in his belt, turned himself around, grabbed the doorframe with both hands and slammed his massive body against it, over and over again. With a guttural roar, the ogre wrenched door and frame out of the wall and holding it like a shield in front of him; he heaved it at the goblins crushing a good portion of them. The door shattered under the abuse. Standing in the gaping hole left by the door, the ogre pulled out his wedge-bar and went to work. His blows lifted several more goblins off their feet and into the air. Siv caught his second-wind and leaped next to the ogre in an instant, slashing whatever creatures came within range of his sword. In the heat of the battle, Gort's eyes caught the forest walker for a moment. He gave Siv little more than a furious sneer and kept fighting. While the goblins pressed into the room, Ravna hit one soldier in the face, whipped her knife around, and drove it into the shoulder of another enemy. She sent him backwards with a vicious kick in the chest as she pulled her knife out. A brief curl of disgust lingered around her lips. Siv drove his sword into the gut of a goblin, swung back and slashed another's throat. His pale face appeared the epitome of calmness and self-control. Again the foe fell a bit back to regroup. Most of the front wall had fallen in by this time, leaving a mere patchwork of mud bricks and splintered wooden beams that offered no protection at all

At the top of the cellar stairs, shadowy figures slunk down towards the fight and stopped halfway. Their eyes glinted over the barrels of a dozen taut crossbows. The goblin archers sighted on the three figures through the gaping holes and waited patiently for an opening in the seething conflict that would afford them a fatal shot.

Gort suddenly loomed up beside Ravna and Siv, clenching

his bloodied weapon tightly in his fist. His other hand rested briefly on one of the two support beams. He glanced over at the Mistress of the Inn, the barkeep, and his treasures for a brief moment and then lowered his eyes, knowing full well none of them would last this final battle. If the ogre could ever allow himself to feel anything akin to sadness, that would have been the moment to do so. However, rage proved a stronger emotion than sorrow in the old ogre when he heard the gibbering of the savage little beasts gathering themselves for one more assault. Before any of them could draw another breath, the goblin forces swarmed into the room and the three of them found themselves hard-pressed and fighting for their lives, quite literally with their backs to the wall. Ravna found herself slowly being cut off from Siv and Gort and driven back towards Gort's secret door. The barkeep slashed and struck at the jabbing weapons in an increasing frenzy to keep her from being separated from himself and the ogre.

Gort continued to lay about with the bloodied wedge-bar and his bare fist. A command rang out from the direction of the stairs. In that instant, Gort paused in his assault and glared at Siv, battling and oblivious to the ogre's hard eyes.

"No more debt... barkeep. Gort's paid it..." the ogre spat out between his teeth.

The ranks parted and a dozen crossbow catches released with a metallic hiss. Gort swung out and his arm slammed into Siv knocking him backwards towards Ravna and towards the black opening in the wall. Ravna glanced up and caught a brief glance of Siv diving towards her, his teeth gritted in determination, his eyes mad, his free arm outstretched and reaching towards her. Then his eyes closed and she felt Siv's breath burst violently across her forehead. Blood speckled her face.

A split second later Siv slammed into her and they both tumbled backwards through the opening in the wall and into the complete darkness beyond. Gort flung his wedge-bar at the wall. It rang

against the stone, triggering a mechanism hidden in the framework of the wall. Hundreds of pounds of crushed rock tumbled down and sealed the opening of the secret doorway within seconds.

Gort grunted and turned back towards the goblins. Crossbow bolts stuck out from his chest and lay shattered at his feet, broken against the unyielding stone. A slow smile crept across the ogre's face and a shine of blood lingered in the corners of his mouth. He remembered the smell of fire and the bellows of warriors in the night. This was what it was to really live, he thought.

With all the strength left in his old body, Gort roared and bulldozed his way through the goblins, sending them flying in all directions. He drove his shoulder into the nearest support beam and snapped it like a twig. An avalanche of rock and wood came crashing down as the Silver Dagger Inn collapsed, burying scores of goblins and the secret door with it.

When the last rumbling echoes had died away, Ravna finally raised her head, winced in pain, and propped herself up on her elbow. Siv lay on his face beside her.

"Siv," she whispered painfully, unable to see much of anything in the darkness. She sat up, took his shoulder and with some effort rolled him on his side.

"Siv," she whispered again.
Her fingers felt a shudder run through the barkeep's body. A long sigh escaped his throat and he lay still. She felt blindly across his chest and her finger found the iron point of a crossbow bolt. It was wet and the air smelled of blood.

"Siv..." she said, fear constricting her throat, "Siv... oh... answer me please... answer me... answer me..." She clenched her teeth and her trembling hands closed around his shoulder, her fingers dug tightly into the fabric of his shirt.

"Don't leave me alone in the dark, Siv," she whispered, "Don't..."

Her face dropped into the hollow between his neck and his shoulder. Her body tensed. She drew in her breath and then a hoarse scream from the depths of Ravna's soul filled the narrow space with grief and anguish. She screamed until the sound thinned to a razor's edge of pure pain, screamed until there was no breath left in her lungs.

When she finally gasped for air, wild sobs began to rack her body and the tears flowed down her face. She sat up and rocked back and forth like a woman gone mad, pressing her hands to her mouth. Then she leaned her forehead into Siv's shoulder and clung to him, clung to his lifeless body and sobbed.

Far above her head, Darkleaf died.

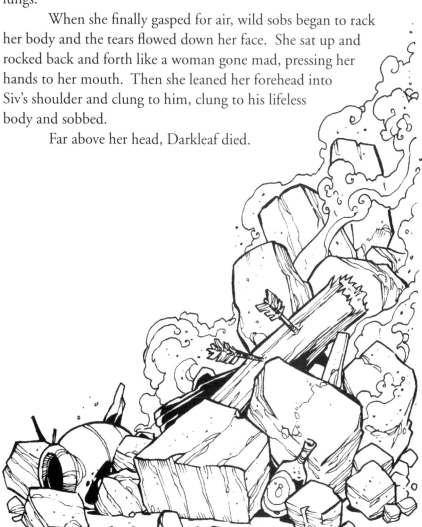

Brutus

A high-pitched whistling in his ears roused Bean from his stupor at last. He opened his eyes to see only thick mist and felt himself lying on his back at an angle, his feet elevated a bit above his head. His hair flapped fitfully against his forehead from a constant gust of cold wind that blew against his face and made his eyes water.

The mist parted. Bean blinked, lifted his head a little, and saw a distant landscape of upside down clouds and a thin uneven line of green where the sky should have been. He seemed to be enclosed in the middle of a gently swinging tangle of huge gnarled tree roots. He could move his arms and his legs and he still clutched his sword but his body appeared to be caught fast and he had the most dizzying sensation of moving. Disoriented, he closed his eyes and let his head fall back again. He wondered if he was in the middle of some fever dream again.

Moments later his eyes shot open in sudden terror when he felt the tree roots shift and tighten around him. He felt himself swiveled upwards and instinctively clutched at the roots, fearful of slid-

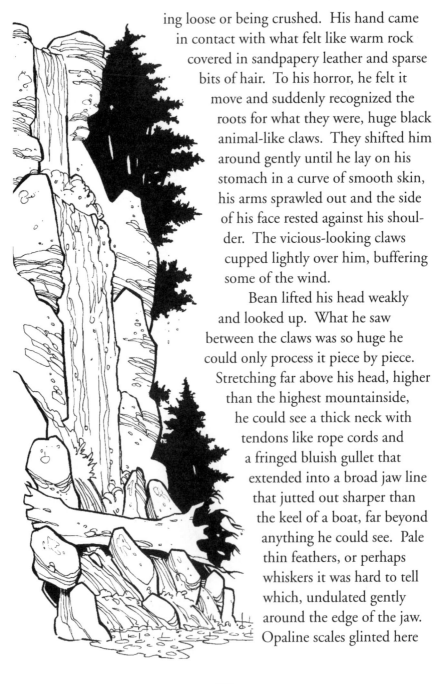

ing loose or being crushed. His hand came in contact with what felt like warm rock covered in sandpapery leather and sparse bits of hair. To his horror, he felt it move and suddenly recognized the roots for what they were, huge black animal-like claws. They shifted him around gently until he lay on his stomach in a curve of smooth skin, his arms sprawled out and the side of his face rested against his shoulder. The vicious-looking claws cupped lightly over him, buffering some of the wind.

Bean lifted his head weakly and looked up. What he saw between the claws was so huge he could only process it piece by piece. Stretching far above his head, higher than the highest mountainside, he could see a thick neck with tendons like rope cords and a fringed bluish gullet that extended into a broad jaw line that jutted out sharper than the keel of a boat, far beyond anything he could see. Pale thin feathers, or perhaps whiskers it was hard to tell which, undulated gently around the edge of the jaw. Opaline scales glinted here and there where the sunlight reflected and danced off them and he marveled at the grandeur of the huge dragon cradling him so gently.

Dazed, Bean stared at it all for a moment, then shifted his head and tried to look down. Far below him he saw wispy clouds drifting by and the scrubby dark fringes of what he realized were tree-tops, thousands of miles down from where he was.

The world he looked at started to spin clockwise. Bean closed his eyes and his weary head sagged against his shoulder again. Too drained to wonder what it was that had him, too emotionally exhausted to feel anything more than a dull calm, Bean struggled to hold his drifting consciousness together while he floated through a world of feathery clouds and endless blue sky.

At times he must have dozed off and dreamed, for between periods of white silence a mingled and confused stream of images passed through his head, images that occasionally blurred the borders between fantasy and reality. It seemed that he saw at one point the tops of the trees, not as a collective mass of shapeless greenery far below him, but so close that he could pick out the details of each trembling leaf and could hear them whispering collectively while the breeze blew through them. Another time he watched a monstrous sword of pure silver, with a blade that curved like the edge of a new moon, unsheathe itself ever so slowly from the forest. It transformed into a huge silver snake and writhed across a mirror of gold and jewels, its scales glittering fiercely.

Bean raised his head slightly at the bewildering vision, shook his head a little, and his eyes and mind cleared. Only then did he realize he gazed down at the curving body of a magnificent river, its waters caught by sunlight, and bordered on either side by lush fields of golden wheat and a scattering of towns. Mesmerized by the winding sweep of the river, Bean's eyes followed it as it wound its way across the landscape far below him. He clutched at the claws that held him when he sensed the creature adjust itself in midair and veer sharply to the left. He saw the riverside villages culminate into two magnificent cities in the midst of the rich golden fields. Then for a brief instant, he caught sight of a large lake and the turrets of a large intricate tower, that Bean was sure was too beautiful and unearthly-looking to be real. He glimpsed walls glittering with stained glass where the sun caught them and columns of silvery grey and white before it was all swept away in a white mist. He sighed and his chin sunk down to rest again on the smooth warm skin.

He woke later; unable to remember when he had last dozed off and saw they were passing over the fringes of another forest. Civilization seemed to be fading once more, or at least that is what it seemed from Bean's particular vantage point. At least, there didn't appear to be any more indication of farmlands or settlements, though it was possible the thick green foliage of this forest covered any hint of that. Bean thought briefly of Darkleaf and then saw rolling hills capped with snow emerging from the heart of the forest below him. While he watched the hills gradually grow taller and more angular, the forest melted away from his sight and vanished. The hill grew into a vast terrain of dark-colored mountain ranges.

Bean sensed then that they were climbing higher in the sky. The mountains below grew smaller and smaller and the clouds thickened around his range of vision. The air had become sparser and every breath he took felt labored. He gulped like a fish out of water and pressed his forehead in his hand, taking deep breaths and feeling sick while black specks swam in front of his eyes. They burst out of a damp cloudbank and Bean's eyes flickered up to behold a magnificent sight. He and his captor (or rescuer, Bean couldn't be sure either way) now drifted silently on a light air current through a strange other world.

Beneath him lay a dazzling white plain of clouds, run through with spidery veins of glittering silver and mottled with slate blue shadows. They looked so solid Bean half-fancied he could step down and walk across them. Over his head curved a perfectly clear blue sky, so blue it was like the heart of a dazzling sapphire.

The dragon dropped lower and Bean found he could breathe a little easier again. The tips of mountains broke up the flawless plain of clouds. Bean found his mind straying to quiet times when he and Siv walked in the forest on errands and he listened to the older man's voice describing in great detail ships and sailors and a mysterious body of water called an ocean. Larger than the largest pond or lake, Bean remembered, large enough to have sitting on its restless waters, whole pieces of land large enough for people to live on, an idea Bean still found impossible to wrap his mind around. While he gazed down at this scene below him and watched this vast white sea with its mountain peak islands, it suddenly occurred to the boy that it could look something like this.

However, the thought of the magnificent sea of clouds was quickly followed by the last terrible memories of Mama Faerie and Theron. Even the beautiful sight below him couldn't shake Bean out of the black misery that had settled on his head and his heart. He curled his arms tightly around his shoulders and buried his face in his arms, trying not to think about what had happened, but not succeeding very well. He made a small noise of discomfort.

It seemed it was his luck to never have somewhere he could call his own for too long and it also seemed his luck to be constantly separated from people he had grown to like or in the case of Theron and Mama Faerie, had just been introduced to. It was cruel luck, Bean thought, feeling overwhelmed, cruel and unjust. It seemed he had no more power over what happened to him than he had over the creature that now bore him aloft to an unknown destination.

He startled when he felt a rumbling vibrate along the creature's claws and he looked up to see the creature's bluish beard on the underside of its jaw shrink and then expand as the creature inflated its throat slightly. Bean felt a tiny stab of cold fear in his stomach at the thought that the creature might be growling, but then as he listened, this noise the creature made changed. Bean had never had the chance to hear a grand organ or a set of shepherd's pipes as they swelled into majestic life and began playing their music, otherwise he would have made the connection between that and this sound immediately. As it stood, the closest comparison he could make was a cat's deep throaty purr that suddenly turned wonderfully musical.

Subtle tones and inflections wove themselves within the underlying steady rhythmic beat. It was a deep and ancient music the creature made, music that drummed in Bean's blood in time with the beating of his heart and caused strange chills to run over his skin and the nape of his neck. Little sensations and images came into Bean's mind, of diving into a river warm from the lazy heat of a summer's afternoon or of a crisp breeze fresh from the budding of spring whirling itself joyfully around and through him. The music grew in intensity and awe while Bean listened and his thoughts and feelings became more and more complex until his mind could no longer make any comparisons to such humble little pleasures he had experienced in his short life. This was more then just pleasant music. Bean realized that it was music filled with a fierce joy, music that burned him clean and hollow and then brought him back from the ashes feeling more alive than he'd ever been before. Bean rested his head on his arms and felt the waves of the strange song wash over him. Whether the creature had somehow sensed Bean's sorrows and sang in response to that or whether it simply sang to amuse itself while it flew along, the boy couldn't tell, but the song, despite its unworldly power, had a mercifully quieting effect on him and he was somewhat comforted.

After a while, it seemed the creature's focus became intent on a certain hazy mountain range surrounded by clouds off in the distant horizon. It lowered its neck and its rumbling hum took on an eager tone while the mountain range grew larger and closer. They reached it in another few minutes and the creature scaled over the jagged peaks with ease. It suddenly dipped, so quickly that Bean felt like his stomach had been left behind in the sky. Nestled in the misty curve of a cliff's embrace, Bean saw a magnificent castle of slate-colored stone appear before his eyes, rising up out of the lighter hued raw stone surrounding it. Surmounted by a tall lonely tower, the main building was an odd-looking keep made up of sharp corners and strangely angled roofs. Several bridges branched off from it. A couple led to a trio of small towers and the largest one led to a huge watchtower with small slots for windows. On the cliff, just below it, a huge dark hole yawned. The dragon fell silent finally, circled the building lazily and flew lower, affording Bean a closer view. The whole castle had the look of a military severity in its overall design, nothing very elaborate or decorative. It didn't look very inviting at all.

Before Bean had time to react or be alarmed, the claws unclosed around him gently and the huge head loomed up in his vision. He saw his reflection in a dark eye bigger than himself and then the creature with astonishing delicacy caught Bean up in a mouth edged like a hawk's beak, holding him in jaws that very easily could have snipped him in half if it so chose. It beat its wings furiously, raising a cloud of dust beneath itself as it settled heavily on the ground. Its head lowered and promptly deposited Bean on a courtyard, extending out like a shelf from the main building. It rested its head beside him, studied him for a moment

108

with intelligent eyes, and then closed its eyes and snorted a great gale of warm breath at him.

Bean staggered to his feet and stood there for a moment, trembling unsteadily. He gazed up at the side of the enormous building, took a few staggering steps towards it, and then everything turned sideways and the corners of his vision dimmed. The metal blade rang clear as he drove the sword into the stones of the courtyard and he sank to his knees and sagged helplessly against it for support. His eyes closed by themselves and he found himself unable to keep them open any longer.

He heard the patter of peculiar sounding footsteps coming towards him. The blade wobbled and tipped and then rang against the stones of the courtyard when Bean collapsed completely on his side. His hand tightened involuntarily around the hilt of the sword, and he could do little else but clutch it tightly.

"Brutus!" said an exasperated voice somewhere above his head. "Tish, lad... great numskull you are, Brutus! You've only gone and dropped the poor little chap at the doorstep! Dragons... fft. Here now, young fellow, off these nasty and freezing old stones with you and we'll get you someplace warm to rest and recuperate... help me get him up now... there we go."

Bean felt hands curl under his arms and his legs and cradle his head gently while he was lifted up, hands that felt strangely cold and dry. He heard the edge of his blade scraping against the courtyard stones while the mysterious hands carried him off. The speaker chattered amiably to him, most of which Bean couldn't understand at all, but soon even that noise finally faded into a welcome silence, taking Bean's awareness of his surroundings with it and he slept.

the Storm Worsens

Deep in the secret heart of Darkleaf, a dismal and foul fire burned, its greasy black smoke drifting up into the evening twilight. Theron stood at the doorway of their home, his eyes dark-rimmed and tired, watching the fire on the far boundary of the garden while it consumed the last of the immense vines he had cleared away and the twisted bodies of the dead goblin soldiers twisted within them.

He held a bloodstained rag to the side of his painfully throbbing face, where down the side of his jaw and alongside his temple ran the ugly black marks of foul claws. He counted himself extremely lucky it hadn't cost him an eye or his whole head for that matter.

The air was bitingly cold and quiet. A while ago it had started snowing; great fat white flakes drifting idly down from the sky, covering the few patches of grass left among the fragmented sections of raw earth. The grass, which had been green and tender this morning, now had turned brown and died, even as he had watched. Creeping frost etched the tips of the dead grass blades and devoured the vegetables still on the vine and the young fruits that had escaped the earlier destruction. Flakes dusted the stones white on the edge of the garden and delicate flowers that had blossomed and thrived this morning had closed their petals against the chill. They hung their drooping heads low as they vanished under an increasing blanket of whiteness. The garden, once at the height of an eternal spring, had slipped quietly into somber winter's dream while he stood and watched, powerless to keep it from happening.

There were a lot of things he had been unable to stop today, he reflected ruefully while the fire burned and flakes of snow fell in tiny hisses on the hot coals. He had not, for instance, been able to keep the goblins from finding their home and trampling upon the peaceful life he and his sweet wife had built for themselves. That in and of itself made his blood boil with wrath and also deeply disturbed him.

Mama Faerie's tangle had been powerful even by weaver standards. To break through it, the goblins would have had to have had an uncommonly strong talent for unraveling, however they shouldn't have been able to find their home to begin with. He suspected that the horrific beast he had struggled with, the one who had slashed at his face, might have had something to do with it all, both in discovering Mama Faerie's home and in breaking through her tangle. He had been on the thing in an instant when he had emerged from the woods and saw it creeping stealthily towards his wife while she was deep in the throes of her power, placing her full concentration on entrapping the goblins. Theron thought back on the feelings that had been dredged up from deep inside of him when he had seen the murderous glint in the creature's eye and had known its intentions. It chilled his blood in a way that the frost, now clinging to the ground, never could.

Flakes had started blowing in the front door by this time, dusting the doorstep and Theron's feet, sending a cold draft of air through their home. The fire had almost burned itself out by now but Theron turned his back on it and shut the door.

He walked through their house, heading to their bedroom to check on his dear wife. He stopped in various rooms, closing shutters and drawing curtains that had never needed to be closed or drawn before, in preparation for a long cold winter. The warm comfortable atmosphere that had always occupied the house had been replaced by the cold and withdrawn silence that settled now in the corners of Mama Faerie's home.

Theron stopped briefly in the kitchen. A cap of metal blocked the pleasant open-air vent above his head, leaving just a bare minimum of space for the cooking smoke to drift through. A dusting of snow drifted down through the small hole, lightly covering the big freestanding oven and the floor below it. A chill lingered in the air. Theron stopped and absently brushed the snow off and peered inside the oven's mouth. The snow had melted and gone down inside while he had been dealing with cleaning up outside, leaving nothing but damp and black coals. He sighed, reminding himself to stoke the oven again with live coals from the fireplace and hopefully get some warmth in the kitchen after he had visited with his sorely ailing wife and tended to her needs. He placed a stone cap over the oven's top to keep out more snow until he could get back to it and closed the kitchen door behind him.

A rustling noise in the hallway made him spin around,

heart drumming with anger, ready to fight and defend his home in a instant from more secret intruders. The intruder, however, that emerged and stared back at him with shining black eyes happened to be a small field mouse seeking shelter from the cold. Its little whiskers twitched at the sight of the large man standing in front of it; a man, the mouse would flee from had it found itself under any other roof than this one.

Theron smiled faintly at his small refugee.

"You're welcome here for the winter, little one, you and your family," he said in a deep gentle voice. "Provided you don't go being a rude houseguest and gnawing where you shouldn't, but you know that already, don't you?" He turned and continued down the hall. The mouse watched him go and then scurried off at its leisure, knowing there'd be no fear of traps or poison within this home.

Theron drew the curtain aside to their bedroom. A fire popped and crackled in the fireplace and the shutters were drawn and draped with thick heavy curtains to keep out the frigid air. The skylight overhead had been shut and Theron had seen that every nook and cranny that might let in the cold had been securely blocked. The canopy of wisteria had lost its tender greenness and delicate flowers and was now just a tangle of hardened grey vines above their heads, vines that now hung empty and dark. On the bed, blanketed in sheets and hundreds of mournful little pixies, Mama Faerie lay with a pale face and closed eyes, her dark loose hair spread over the pillows and her arms curled and limp across the mattress. The light of the pixies gleamed a dull and sickly yellow while they clung close to their mama with solemn little faces. Theron had never seen the little pixies stay so silent and still while they were awake. That broke his heart almost as much as seeing his dear injured wife lying in their bed. He paused over the bed and his bruised hand rested gently on his wife's forehead. He leaned down and kissed her and pulled up a chair to sit beside her.

"You needn't worry about me, my dear Theron," came Mama

Faerie's low, tired voice. "I'll be fine. I will take some time to heal, but I will be my old self again before long." Theron heard her sigh and she opened her eyes to look up at him. A few pixies stirred their little wings in response but they all remained silent and sad.

"Did you find the boy?" she asked.

Theron shook his head. "It looks as though he cleared the garden," he said sadly. His wife turned her head and gazed at the shuttered window while he continued, "Beyond there, I haven't taken the time yet to track him properly. It happened so fast, Qwen, and you…"

"Within him, dreams and memories seek a life they lost in ages gone," she said lifelessly, causing him to fall silent. "A beast even now shadows his heels."

Theron furrowed his brow at her words and her detached tone of voice. Then he nodded. He touched the scars on his face gingerly. "A beast, yes," he muttered. "We fought but a moment and then distant horns sounded, calling it, I would guess. It bared its teeth at me, struck me one final time and then vanished beyond the garden. I do not know what it was."

He shuddered. "It was shaped like a beast… yet its eyes were not those of an animal, more of a madman. I have never seen such madness," he added. "Even now where its claws marked me, it feels cold, a weaver's icy touch that no fire or medicine can seem to banish. If it had not been called away…"

A disturbed frown touched Theron's deeply lined face and he stopped talking. A long pause stretched between them as the words sunk in and then Mama Faerie turned and looked up at him.

"I know what it was," she said gravely. Theron saw tears of relief shining in her eyes. "I know what it was and you met it in battle and are yet spared. Be thankful for the horns, Theron. I cannot tell you how grateful I am for them," she said and her voice trembled a bit. "Very few have been able to fight a gren-el and tell of it afterwards."

"A gren-el? I thought those were legends to scare children..."

"No legends, I fear," Mama Faerie answered and her face turned solemn again. "Look in the sky on a clear winter's night. You see the full moon in her shattered glory, the points of light that are the stars and her children and the darkness they are framed against. So when you look into the soul of man or ogre, troll or goblin, elf or dragon, those that think and make choices for good or ill, there is light and there is darkness."

Theron smiled sadly. "It is such a grim thing to consider, my dear Qwen. Surely the darkness is far greater than the light?" Mama Faerie gave him a wise look. "Only if you look at the darkness as evil. In and of itself, it is neither good nor evil but simply exists. Darkness is a beginning and an end of all things, the frame of our inner thoughts. Our own world and on a lesser level, our life began in darkness. Whatever fear or evil we may think it hides is only what we call forth from it, nothing more. Could we truly love the light if not for comparing it against the darkness? Would we truly understand the darkness if we never saw the light? A word makes us love silence and silence makes us long for a word. That is what makes balance in the world."

"It is still dark, though. You still cannot see through the darkness and you fall and lose your way," Theron answered.

"We don't always see with our eyes, my love. Think of your heart, your feelings, and your senses. When you realize that light comes from many sources, then perhaps all paths are not so shrouded and obscured after all."

Theron sat quietly, pondering her words. "I think however there was no light left in that beast. Indeed I am doubtful there was any to begin with," he finally said. "Nor would I believe there could be such within the goblins or any other of the fouler creatures in Darkleaf."

"There is perhaps the memory of light," said Mama Faerie solemnly, to herself as if reminiscing of some tale long forgotten.

"Even the goblin race before the darkness had been created with honorable intentions, to defend and battle skillfully in war, before hatred and deceit twisted their ancestors' paths. Once the beast you fought held the fair form of the elven child, but he raised his prideful eyes and looked too long into the night that surrounded his soul, searching for eternity, peering until he was blind and could see nothing but the ending of all things and his own mortality. He looked until his soul shrunk with rage and fear and he sought to create immortality with the weave. The weave devoured him and his hopes from within and in his madness he took on the form of the gren-el. He lost himself and who he was in the weave and he became the gren-el, a slave to lust, destruction, and blood. It is an old story that sadly has been repeated many, many times before."

She reached out her hand and Theron took it and kissed it absently, holding it and rubbing it with his calloused hands. He felt very depressed then to know such heavy truths and he didn't doubt they were the truth, coming from the lips of his beloved wife. The world itself at the moment seemed dim and horribly distorted with shadows of madness and sorrow and he closed his eyes, feeling his heart sink.

"Theron…" said his wife gently and he opened his eyes and looked into the warm darkness of her eyes. She did not smile but her face was clear, calm, and untroubled. She gestured him to move closer and tenderly kissed him, first on his lips and then on the side of his wounded face, brushing the ugly wounds lightly with the tips of her fingers. Almost immediately he felt the virtue of her love and the healing touch she held within her hands move over the wounds, bringing warmth to the unnatural chill that lay in them and bringing his heart out of the shadows and despair. He closed his hand around hers holding the side of his face and felt that although the wounds were there, they seemed to have healed as if he had received them some days ago, instead of hours. They were, however, no less troublesome than any other injury would be mid-way through the normal process of healing. He felt stronger and the room felt warmer.

"I apologize, Theron. It is not any kind of a strong weave, but it is worth a day or two more of my own healing," said Mama Faerie in a fainter voice.

"You need not have done that," spoke Theron in concern.

"You would not have let me if I had asked anyway. You never were one to accept gifts, but only accept this small one and don't protest further about it," she answered and finally smiled again. "It will see you through the next few days of your traveling, I think."

Theron raised an eyebrow, but before he could ask the question, she shook her head. "Nothing remarkable my sweet knight, no weaver's mystic ability to read minds. A wife knows her husband's thoughts as well as he knows hers and your thoughts and your troubles were plain on your face." Her face grew concerned again. "Yes, you do need to go and find him. Protect him, Theron. You fear as much for the boy as I do."

"What makes it a difficult decision is leaving you here alone... hurt," admitted Theron. "Between the lad and you, it's a wretched choice for one man to make."

Mama Faerie closed her eyes in deep thought and then opened them and turned her head. "Nalia? Tia?" she said. One pixie drifted up into the air and hovered in front of her.

"Yes, Mama?" she asked in a pitiful little voice.

"Why, where is Tia, little one?" asked Mama Faerie and the pixie shrugged half-heartedly.

"My haven't seen her all the day after Papa Theron brought you in," she replied and Mama Faerie looked up at the rest of her children.

"No one has?" she asked and coughed a bit. A chime of sad little "no's" filled the air. Qwen cleared her throat and looked over at Papa Theron who also shook his head sadly.

"Nor have I. She was here when I laid you in the bed because she kissed your forehead," he answered. "She was very upset and trying not to cry. I wouldn't be surprised if she's gone off somewhere to hide. She never liked us to see her cry."

Mama Faerie looked troubled. "Poor little Tia," she murmured. "Nalia, you and Vespa go fetch my bag for me then, my darlings. It's the little blue velvet one in the storehouse, on the shelf behind all the empty bottles."

The two pixies flew out of the room. Before long they came back, holding between them a velvet sack tied with a simple white ribbon, which they gently laid in Mama Faerie's hands. They dropped down beside her, folding their wings and nestling themselves on either side of her face. Mama Faerie opened the little sack and turned it over. Two wristlets, beautifully carved of some nearly translucent stone and fastened with tarnished silver clasps, dropped in her hand. An oval crystal, dark and smooth was set in the center of each wristlet.

She took Theron's hand and laid it over the two wristlets, cupping her hands over his hand. She closed her eyes and whispered something unintelligible under her breath and Theron felt the cold stones grow warm under his palm while she whispered. When he lifted his hand, the dark crystals glowed, one a brilliant gold and the other a more subdued but steady soft blue like moonlight. She placed the dimmer one in Theron's hand and took the gold one, fastening it around her wrist and laid back against the pillows looking very pale

now. When she spoke, her voice had become still weaker.

"These are lifestones, Theron. The gold tells me you live and are strong and healthy," she said.

"What of the blue?" asked Theron, gazing down at the wristlet on his arm. He was almost afraid to ask what it meant, but not knowing would have been worse.

A faint smile touched Mama Faerie's lips. "It means that I live, but that I am as you see me now. Sick, weak, and wounded," she said. "You will have me with you while you are gone and I will have you here. Distance will not matter. The only thing either of us should fear is if the stone goes black."

A fit of coughing caught her again and Theron leaned forward in concern, but she only waved her hand at him and shook her head. After the fit had passed, she cleared her throat and rubbed the side of her face. "I need to rest now. I am so tired," she murmured. "I have not been this worn down for many an age."

"Yes, sweetheart. Rest then," said Theron quietly and when she had closed her eyes, he got up and walked out of the room. This close to nightfall and in this weather he knew he could not start until early the next morning, so he spent the rest of the evening in preparations. He left packing his gear until the very last. He felt he had to leave their home in some semblance of order, so he went about taking care of that first. He found himself approaching his tasks with a sweet tenderness.

Little everyday routines he ordinarily did suddenly became significant and worth dedicating a little more thought and energy to than he usually took with them. He handled each one with patience and a delicacy that didn't seem to fit such coarse work; stoking the coals and stacking wood for fuel, plugging up any cracks or crevices that might let in the cold, going over the food supplies, seeing that the sink pump was in good working order, and wrapping the pipes against the cold so they would not freeze and burst. The doors and windows he checked last. In between, there were many little things he did that no one else would notice much. Theron took care of them all regardless. He also took the time to look for Tia who he missed terribly and worried about, but no matter how hard he looked, he could find no little pixie in any of her usual moping spots.

Far into the night, he went back to their room and with a long face carefully packed all the supplies he would need to see him through a possibly long, wearisome, and harsh journey in a hostile world. He checked over the things he had packed twice, making sure he had only what was absolutely necessary for him to survive and what the boy might need once Theron had found him. He laid his axe across it all and crossed back over to Mama Faerie. She was sound asleep, the stone glowing bright and golden on her wrist. He stood a moment, looking down at her with immeasurable tenderness and love; then leaned over and kissed her. He settled in the chair by the fireplace, folded his arms and attempted to sleep away the few remaining hours left to him. The night passed uneasily but without incident. Theron thankfully suffered no nightmares in his sleep, but neither did he dream.

The next morning he rose in the grey light of early dawn. After one last tender conversation with his weary wife and a kiss for the journey, he whistled a merry little tune to the pixies, calling them down to wish them good bye.

"Little ones," he whispered to them, as they raised their little heads and looked up at him expectantly. "Know your papa and your mama loves every one of you. Protect your mama and our home. Hide her away from the world and away from prying eyes while your papa is gone and I'll be back before you know it."

He glanced over the little pixies and his heart sank, still not seeing Tia-Pho-Phia's bright little face among them. "Please tell Tia too when she comes back that her papa loves her," he added. The musical hum of little beating wings filled the air and the pixies flitted off of the bed and surrounded Papa Theron like a shimmering cloud of stars. He felt hundreds of tiny little kisses on his face and head and hands. He touched his fingers to his lips and blew a gentle draught of air over them all, his way of returning the kisses. He picked up pack and lantern, hefting the axe on his shoulder and walked down the hall. The pixies followed him in attentive silence.

He opened up the door and the cold winter air blew over his face. He felt the chill down to his very bones and in the wounds on his face. He stepped outside, his heavy oiled boots crunching across the frozen ground, and the pixies flittered out of the door after him. They followed him as far as the white marker stones, then fell back and surrounded their home. When Theron turned back to watch, he saw a shimmering curtain fall over his entire home, over the dead garden and over his dear little pixies and heard the delicate sounds of what seemed like a thousand small wind-chimes ringing in a breeze.

Moments later the shimmering and the chimes ceased. He turned and walked away from what was now merely an old tree stump sitting in a silent grove of yew trees, unremarkable except for an odd glimmer of the air here and there, clinging to the dark green branches. Beyond that the snow drifted over the mound of dead ashes and bones lying at the edge of the swamp. Snowflakes lightly brushed over his face and hands and the wind picked up. Theron thought of small warm kisses as he trod steadily on in the direction that he had last seen Bean. The brewing darkness of the bitter winter storm embraced him.

Somewhere in the silence, in the long stretches of emptiness and darkness, Ravna dreamed of ice. It crept up her arms and legs, casting a fine sheen of silver over her hair and skin. She felt her heart-beat slow and finally fell into silence. She felt her breath cease. With it came a small sense of relief, that everything was over and done with and there would be no more pain.

124

Roc~Noc

When she awoke, she breathed in a great shuddering gasp and clutched herself. She felt her heart beating steadily under her hand and reached up to touch her eyes. She felt her lashes brush against her fingers, telling her that she wasn't dreaming and that her eyes were indeed open. Her hands reached out blindly in the darkness and touched Siv's face. She recoiled for he was so very cold.

The tightness built up in her chest and stomach again and she felt the grief in her throat choking her. She breathed in and her body trembled, while thin keening noises escaped her lips in dark dispair. She had no more tears. She had wept them all a long time ago, but even so, her body still went through the motions in a cruel parody of grief. She squeezed her eyes so tightly shut that sparkles of light gathered in the darkness behind her eyelids. She clutched at her face, shook her head and felt numb.

Afterwards, she remembered very little of this time she spent in the blackness and the silence. Nor would she have wanted to re-member it any more clearly than she would have wanted to remember any hideous nightmare. Between the periods of numbness, there had been tears and after the tears there had been irrational horrors, wild hopes, and crushing guilt. At one point she found herself whispering to the lifeless body of Siv while her hands fumbled over his chest in the darkness. She remembered thinking quite calmly, and it made so much sense at the time, that if she merely pulled the bolts from his chest then he would start breathing again. He would sit up, talk to her in his soothing quiet voice, and guide her out of this hellish black hole back into the light and her old life. She had managed to extract one before she had collapsed again in horrible grief-filled rage, beating his chest with her hands over and over again and screaming profanities at the walls and the ceiling of the cavern until she had no more breath left to scream. After that she had spent a few hours crying silently while she smoothed the hair from his forehead over and over again, a ritual as useless as trying to wrench the horrible feathered bolts from his body.

Grief had reduced her mind to that of a child or an animal. Sometimes she thought the darkness itself had come to life. Horrors lurked in this place. They, those unspeakable things she couldn't even conjure up in her imagination, would come while she slept. They would take Siv's body from her and ravage it like beasts. They would come for her. They were there now in the darkness, watching her, waiting for her guard to slip. She would sit with her back to the wall, staring in the darkness and then awaken hours or minutes later, her heart pounding with fear, not even realizing she had fallen asleep. Black guilt often placed terrible thoughts in her head while she sat there. Perhaps a few hours ago Siv had still been clinging to life and she had let him lay there unknowingly, caught up in her own selfish grief and let him bleed to death. Perhaps if she hadn't turned him over, perhaps if she had moved quicker, struck faster in the inn. Perhaps it would have been different if she had pulled Siv behind her; perhaps, perhaps, perhaps.

Siv's sword still lay clenched in his hand. At some point or another she remembered she still held Groggle's knife in her hands and pressed it close to her face, trying to tell herself nothing was there in the blind dark, fighting against the fears. She had felt the cracked leather wrapping against her skin and the coldness of the knife's edge against her forehead and a chill had run through her soul. She then placed it carefully away from her, still within hand's reach if she needed it, but far enough away that she could breathe easier. For at that moment, another fear had risen to join that of the dark and the unknown; fear of herself, of what she might do if she kept holding the knife for much longer.

Fear dominated her for a long time, holding her within its spidery black claws; fear of never being found, fear of the cold still body that lay just an arm length's away from her, fear of ghosts and the unknown things that crept where she couldn't see, and fear of dying here alone and no one ever being the wiser. Thinking became an almost unbearable torture. She stared into the darkness until she almost imagined she could see it moving, taking on a more solid shape. Then she blinked and thought surely that she was either dreaming or that her sorrow had finally driven her mad because at that moment, her ears caught the sound of a delicate sound-fall of chimes in the darkness and a golden light began to grow in front of her eyes. Ravna blinked at the brightness and shrank back, unsure of what she was supposed to be feeling at the sight of the apparition looming out of the darkness.

It was man-shaped, but much larger, almost ogre-tall and dressed peculiarly in threadbare but richly ornate robes. A long silvery-gray waterfall of a beard cascaded from the jaw down the front of the chest. The strange steady light, that Ravna had now come to realize was a lantern held by the creature, rose higher, illuminating a grave face framed by large ears that flickered occasionally like an intent cat. A deep silence dominated the moment. He held a long

walking stick, but the arm and hand that held it appeared relaxed and unthreatening. The wary dark eyes studied her and then a flicker of recognition passed through them.

Ravna's hand reached out and closed around the knife lying on the ground and moved back slowly, positioning herself in front of Siv. An image of a bristling and terrified rat backed in a corner came to her mind. She felt that way now, trapped like a rat with Groggle closing in. She'd be stew for sure. The corners of her lips twitched and she swallowed down a sudden crazed urge to start laughing hysterically.

The creature lifted his fingers in a placating gesture and carefully knelt to lay the walking stick at his feet. "By the beards of the Great Honorable Judges," he said in a deep rolling voice and stood up again. "What have we here? You must be the young lady he so often spoke of, Ravna, is it?"

Ravna did not move or answer. Neither did she lower her knife.

"I am unarmed, little mistress," the creature said. "I mean you no harm. Now why would you be down here in this dark damp cavern? Pray speak."

"Go..." Ravna said in a raw voice that echoed off of the ceiling. She sounded like a stranger to her own ears. "I don't know how you know my name or what you are. I don't care... leave us..." She swallowed hard. "Get out of here," she managed finally. She clutched the knife to herself and felt herself crumbling again, wracked by an agony of dry sobs that shuddered through every inch of her body.

The creature moved the lantern further to the side and saw for the first time, Siv's lifeless body behind Ravna. The most profound expression of horror and sorrow cut deep creases of pain in his gentle face. Now he understood what had brought her to this state of misery. He set the lantern down, closed his dark eyes and touched them lightly, letting his fingers trail down his face. He touched his palms together, brushed them down across his forehead and sighed heavily. Finally, he pressed his hands to his own chest. It was a ritualistic and graceful set of gestures that expressed both grief and deep empathy with quiet eloquence.

"Let me offer assistance," he said in a quiet soothing voice, lifting up his hand towards her. "Surely you..."

"We... don't need... h-help..." Ravna stammered. "No help... at all... NOTHING!" she screamed suddenly in the creature's face. Rage at herself, at her angry words, at the entire cold cruelty of her situation welled up in her and fairly shook her. "We... need... NOTHING! NOTHING! NOTHING!" she shrieked, raising the knife with sudden savagery.

For appearing to be old, the creature moved very fast. He made a sudden gesture with his hand and the handle of the knife splintered in Ravna's grasp while the metal twisted like something alive. Ravna gasped and flung it away, more shocked, however, than hurt. She heard it ring against the stone somewhere in the darkness and stared up at the creature with wide white-rimmed eyes.

"That will be enough, little mistress," he said in a firm tone of voice. "There is no more need to shed blood. Is that clear?"

"What are you?" she said hoarsely, nearly paralyzed with fear.

The creature closed its eyes and murmured something under

his breath. He lifted his hands again, noting that she flinched and then held them out to her with the palms up.

"I apologize. I do hate violence. What I am, hm..." He pondered this a moment and closed his eyes. "Last of the ancients, mayhaps; a holder of secret knowledge, teacher and scholar, father and son. Ah, no. I am none of those anymore, just an old and sad red rock troll, Mistress Ravna," he said and opened his eyes again.

"Better methinks to ask who I am. I am known as Roc Noc." Ravna peered at him, wondering if he jested with her in some way but he spoke in such a grave tone of voice, it was hard to tell.

She saw his face soften as he looked down at Siv for a moment. "My dear friend..." he said addressing the still body. "You entered the journey that few desire to seek but all must follow. How fitting you chose to go on ahead of me... always so eager, yet I held great hopes for you. Pity." He looked back up at her with an expression of mutual sorrow. "I only ask for your trust, mistress, and nothing more," he said solemnly. "Will you give me that?"

Ravna hesitated a moment. Then she lowered her head and closed her eyes. She lifted her hands and placed them gingerly in the troll's broad palms. They felt warm and rough. His fingers curled gently around her hands and a brief memory went through her mind of the smell of rain in the air, honeysuckle, and her hands ever so much smaller than they were now, being held tenderly by weathered old hands. She felt a mingling of peace and loneliness. The red rock troll stood up pulling her to her feet. He picked up his staff from off the floor, slid it through the ring of the lantern and rested it on the floor. He then knelt down and gathered Siv up in his arms as though the grown man weighed no more than a child. The sword slid loose from Siv's hand and rang on the floor.

"Take his sword, Mistress Ravna. Such a blade as his is no trinket. It should not be left here for the creatures of the dark to crawl over and desecrate," came the red rock troll's deep voice. Ravna bent down and picked up his sword. The red rock troll adjusted Siv's body enough to take hold of the staff with the lantern on it. He balanced it on his shoulder, tucking the end in the crook of his arm.

"Now we need make haste. It has been many ages since these halls and roads have been infested with enemies and the tunnels are still safe for now, but that does not mean that trouble will stay above ground," Roc Noc remarked and set off. Ravna followed after the red rock troll, leaving behind in the darkness Groggle's ruined knife and a single bloodied crossbow bolt.

For a long time she walked after this strange but gentle creature. His lantern that burned with no flame guided her steps. She kept her eyes downcast and her head slumped while she held Siv's sword close to her. Gradually the darkness began to open up from the narrow tunnel into a larger cavern. The air was not so close and stifling here, but still just as damp and cold.

Ravna slowly started to take notice of her surroundings while they walked, mostly because such odd and mystical things occurred as they went by. She had fully expected to be trailing along behind this creature with only his lantern for light but as the tunnel opened up, she became aware of lights gently coming on all around her with a soft melancholy ringing of chimes, illuminating what in fact was no rough cavern, but one that bore signs of a great civilization. The lights here shone in shades of blue and pale yellow, not as brightly as the lantern but enough for her to see they traveled down a paved avenue through what might have once been an underground hanging garden. Vegetation with pale coin-shaped leaves and star-shaped blossoms spilled over high walls. They passed under delicately carved and hollowed-out arches that looked like lace, purist white and all cunningly worked out of stone. Scraggly skeletons of dead vines twined through the arches and some of the vines trailed all the way down to the cracked and ruined pavement to create cobweb-like curtains.

Ravna caught glimpses through the rampaging vegetation of

freestanding statues, seats, busts, and mounted crystals set in alcoves, lining the walls. Whether it was her sorrowful mood or just the mood that the atmosphere itself projected or even a little of both, everything spoke to her of being lost in a sad and subdued dream, caught up in the ghosts and ruins of a past still aching with troubles. Had she been in higher spirits, she may very well have allowed herself to be swept away in the wonder of this place, but her heart hung as low as her head. The ruins that surrounded her seemed an all-too fitting backdrop for her mood.

Sometimes she became vaguely aware of the red rock troll addressing her on occasion or just talking in general, speaking in his low rolling voice that seemed like an extension of the half-lit darkness that surrounded her. He spoke of events of the past and names which she didn't recognize. Curiously enough though, he also spoke of familiar things above the ground. Apparently he was as well acquainted with the goings-on of the above world as he was with the vastness of the underground world. He also talked in quieter tones of the training of a young man he had come across in the forest of Darkleaf years and years ago, a displaced and ragged man, a prince it would seem with a sad troubled past and an uncertain future. He spoke of his character with the keen and well-placed observance of a master teacher assessing a favorite pupil and his words frequently took on a tone of lament over the fall of such a great man.

Ravna, half-listening, began developing a picture of this young nobleman in her mind; quiet and intense, quick to learn and if possessing any faults, it was only those of being impulsive and a touch prideful. Yet he had been a man who talked carefully and with deliberation and listened well, a student who took in knowledge like dry ground in a rain, a young man who came to know the forests of Darkleaf as intimately as if he had been born in the shadows of the great towering trees rather than the swaying silk curtains and golden tapestries of the privileged class. The kind of person, Ravna thought numbly to herself, that she could have grown to be very fond of, to even love. Prince and forestwalker...

Ravna raised her head, her eyes widening. "It was all Siv?" she whispered suddenly to the red rock troll's back. "He was that man?"

"He was, little mistress," said Roc Noc.

Ravna's eyes dropped again. "He never told me. Why?" she asked, her voice thin and filled with quiet hurt. Roc Noc shook his head. "I do not know. He came to me at a crux in his life where all his pathways that both stretched out in front of him and behind him seemed shadowed and grim. He saw no need perhaps. Siv was ever that sort of person. He never looked back."

Dark and chaotic confusion churned in Ravna's mind while she processed this. She wanted to ask more, pry into why Roc Noc addressed Siv as a prince when she knew he was no such thing but tears started in her eyes, tears she had thought long dried up. She pressed her free hand across her eyes and wept again, but in silence, her shoulders shaking. Roc Noc fell silent then on his recollections of Siv, thinking perhaps to save them for another time. He turned his words to other matters, but Ravna could not bring herself to speak any more for the rest of the journey. It hurt too much.

The ruined gardens fell away behind them and they now walked down a road which went through what appeared to have once been a central square, with homes built on varying levels of stone, sometimes directly in the walls themselves. They traveled through alleys and up stone stairs caked with mud and grime and plant growth until Roc Noc stopped at a great round portal, with a latched stone door, carved with the same elaborate patterns that shone in faded silver and red across the old red rock troll's attire. On either side, stone cisterns stood, covered with delicate patterns of shining crystals and bubbling with fresh clear water. Ravna glanced up at Roc Noc and remembered her thirst. At a reassuring nod and a spoken "Drink, little mistress," from Roc Noc, she crossed carefully to the cisterns, drank her fill and rubbed the cold clear water across her face and eyes, still swollen and puffy from weeping.

The heavy door itself was cleverly weighted, hinged, and positioned so that it swung lightly aside at a touch, as if it weighed no more than a feather. It opened to a beautiful courtyard. Beautiful fountains stood here, fountains trailing into reflecting pools and tiny waterfalls scattered in an orderly manner among the carefully placed tiles of the courtyard floor. Along the high walls of the enclosed courtyard, more crystals winked and glittered, casting a soft almost spring-like artificial light on their surroundings. Lanterns hung here and there from the walls, from the hands of statues and from carved stone trees dotting the peaceful scene.

Roc Noc led her to a bower of stone and metal, carved and wrought to resemble a grove of flowering vines with blossoms of tiny crystals that winked and glowed in a dazzling array of multi-colored lights. A hammock hung in it, draped in blankets and cushions.

"Sleep here for a while, little mistress. You are weary and need to rest," Roc Noc told her. "I will take Siv and prepare a place for him." He perhaps then sensed the anxiety that flickered inside her at the comment, the fear that even though she knew him dead, she dreaded having him go out of her sight for even a moment. "He will be well taken care of," Roc Noc assured her. "We will send him on his journey a day and night hence. The living must be attended to first."

"I wish to take part in his final rites," she said in a dull voice.

"I will see that you are a part of that, young mistress from beginning to end," Roc Noc replied. "For now though you will need to sleep. We are not pressed for time, my lady."

Ravna stared at Siv's pale relaxed face feeling no more emotion at seeing him then she would a stranger. It occurred to her that she should do something at that moment before the red rock troll took him away; touch his face, smooth back his hair, kiss his cold forehead, or hands. She couldn't make herself move towards him to do any of those things. Instead she sank in the hammock and lay back, drawing up her legs and holding the sword close to her while she stared dully up at the shining lights.

Roc Noc left her there, taking Siv with him. At some point she drifted off into sleep. Her last thought when she closed her eyes was that she never wanted to dream again. This time at least, that mercy was granted to her.

Thaddeous

Bean didn't recall how long exactly he had been awake, he only figured he had been staring up at the vaulted ceiling for quite sometime now, watching it define itself while the darkness had paled to the grey light of early morning. One hand rested on his chest and he idly rubbed the edge of a blanket between his fingers. The other hand lay curled around the hilt of his sword. He could hear a fire crackling somewhere and every once in a while, the rattle of shuttered windows and the bluster and howl of the bitter wind outside.

Bean lay deep in an empty and dazed calm, not really thinking about anything in particular, but not really wanting to make the effort of moving just yet to see where he had ended up this time. He didn't want to risk breaking this moment of peace. It seemed he had been getting so few of such moments lately.

Eventually though, thoughts began intruding on the cocoon of peace surrounding him, mostly unpleasant thoughts involving goblins, fighting, and the uncertainty of his current situation. Bean felt a mental kind of wince.

"Pfiff..." The noisy burst of air that escaped from his grimacing mouth stirred his hair. That sound summed up the various churning emotions he felt inside him at the moment. He didn't even know if he ever could sort them all out. Bean's restless spirit began to goad at him. He had been sleeping off and on... how long had it been? He recalled vague memories of brief awareness between long periods of unnerving and troublesome dreams and could twice remember seeing darkness and daylight passing him by. So, two days, maybe? Perhaps more, it was hard to tell.

Bean rubbed his face and a resigned frown crossed it. Two days at least, lying here asleep. Wherever here was, he figured there was no sense in just lying around and wondering idly about it. He might as well sit up and see where he was this time.

A little nightstand stood within arm's reach of the bed he found himself in, a bed comfortable, ornate, and small. Reasonably soft and well piled with blankets, so thick and richly woven that Bean almost felt he shouldn't be touching them, much less sleeping on them. Ornate carvings covered the headboard and posts, fascinating, perhaps a bit excessive to the point he wondered how anyone could get a good night's sleep in a bed with such distracting decorations and small in comparison with the rest of the room that he found himself in. The bed indeed seemed almost an afterthought here.

Walls of bluish slate stretched far up over the boy's head. The tapestries softened the starkness a little but not much. Even Bean could see that in the growing morning light the woven colors of the tapestries that once had been bright and vibrant were faded and threadbare and the ragged edges gathered fringes of dust. The tapestries themselves seemed rather like the bed... just after thoughts. Bean glanced around at the rest of his surroundings. He saw the fire burning in the fireplace and a cozy-looking old chair beside it with its back facing him. Near the arm of the chair, a small table stood with a glass sphere and an arrangement of tiny strange items upon it that he couldn't quite make out from where he sat. Shelves lined the lower half of the walls, shelves full of old dusty books and the occasional odd trinket.

Bean pulled the blankets aside and still holding his sword, slid cautiously onto the floor. Outside of the warmth of the blankets, he quickly found that the room, even with the fire burning in the corner, felt bitter cold and the floor even more so for a pair of bare feet. On consideration, he grabbed one of the blankets and wrapped it around himself and walked towards the center of the room.

The boy still felt weak and tired. He walked as slow as an old man and had to use the sword as a support. Taking a mental assessment of his overall condition while he walked, he could tell that whoever had tended to him had done a remarkably good job of it. He patted his side absently, glanced down at his arms, and paused to give the leg that had been wounded the worst, a gingerly swing. He thought to himself that he'd probably always have a bit of a limp regardless, but in pulling up his nightshirt to get a better look at his leg, he saw merely a few patches of clean linen running across pinkish scars and a laceration or two that was almost healed, a far cry from being completely covered in winding bandages and every step a misery and a struggle.

His small hands, cut and scarred, brushed thoughtfully against the books on the shelf and he turned his head upwards to look them over. For a moment he found himself reminded of the dreadful Collector's home with its haphazard collections and rotting books. This place undoubtedly was far neater and more organized, but seeing that difference still didn't keep Bean from feeling a cold sick lurch in the pit of his stomach. He shivered and made his way to the fireplace.

He stopped once to examine the table beside the chair and what lay upon it. The glass sphere had what looked like a delicate white rose perfectly preserved in the middle of it. Otherwise it didn't seem anything more than a mere trinket. He puzzled briefly over the significance of what looked like a game of war, with carved pieces of armored men and dragons placed across a round board decorated with a complicated map made up of circles and grids. Age had split and weathered the board itself and the gold leaf and paint had worn thin on the wood. Bean slid a playing piece half-heartedly across the board. His eyes roamed around the chamber and he then turned his attention to the fireplace.

He pondered on things, reflecting that he didn't feel any foreboding or fear in this atmosphere so much as feeling misplaced in it. That in itself was a feeling that Bean was more than familiar with. The Inn had been a comfortable, noisy, and accepting family of sorts, but he quite literally had worked to fit into his particular niche there. In doing that, Bean had always been left with a sense of missing out on something vitally important. Granted, he hadn't quite figured out yet what that something should be, only he knew quite firmly it was something he wanted to have. There had also been Mama Faerie's home; the closest he had ever come to feeling like he could really belong somewhere without having to make so much of an effort, but even there had been a mere pause before being violently pushed out into the cold again, shuffled off to this new place . Who knew how long he'd stay here?

Bean sighed again, a deep, heavy sigh worthy of one of Groggle's wordless exhalations of woe. He glumly took a step backwards from the fireplace and plopped down in the overstuffed chair.

"Here now, I SAY, young man!" came a sudden muffled and indignant exclamation from somewhere at his back. A badly startled Bean whirled to his feet faster than he had sat down. His blanket slid to the floor in a heap, his sword flashed up at the ready in an instant and baffled, he he lowered it slightly.

A small lizard-like creature, a little bigger than a skyloc, looking slightly crumpled and more than a little miffed at being sat upon, raised itself up on its hind-legs and appeared to take a moment to gather back its dignity. It adjusted a pair of glasses that were a tad too big for its pointed little face, shook itself, and groomed its scales for a quick second.

"Humph... and a pleasant good morning to you, I suppose," the little creature sniffed. "It is a great day to be alive... and un-squashed, thank you very much. More so for you, I would imagine. Do try and be more careful about where you go sitting from now on. There's a smart chap."

Bean blinked and did the only thing he really could, given the circumstances. He sat down heavily on his bottom in front of the fireplace. He pulled the blanket up around his shoulders again and stared at the little creature while it slinked off the chair and scuttled over towards him. The boy found himself completely at a loss to say anything.

His silence didn't keep the little lizard-like thing from talking though, which it did so in a brisk and cheerful tone of voice, while it twitched its head about this way and that to get a

better look at him.

"Well, well, well," it said, apparently well satisfied with itself. "You look a bit much better than you looked when Brutus first brought you in. Hold fast, now." The little creature stretched itself as tall as he could and pressed a stubby claw to the center of Bean's forehead and looked him dead in the eye while his voice took on a ring of command. Bean suddenly felt himself go completely still, mesmerized by the peculiar stare. A faint sense of disquiet pricked at the back of the boy's brain. "Did a bang-up job of patching you back together," the little thing chattered on while it circled him, giving him a thoughtful prod now and then and studying his wounds.

Bean felt one of the little thing's claws poke him in the side. "Still smarts a bit there, chap?" The boy winced. His head felt strangely heavy when he nodded in the affirmative.

"Brilliant!" came the cheerful reply. "That means you're healing well. Good sign, good sign. Now the lovely Queen Mum of the Faeries knew what she was doing when she patched you up. I just helped it along a trifle. Now, release," the little creature added and Bean suddenly felt himself relax. His small caretaker must have sensed the question in the boy's head for he went on to say, "What I just did to you was a bit of weaver knowledge and a snippet of old dragon wisdom, that's all. Sorry about that, my boy. It is just that these days not many people trust a dragon anymore. They think of us as repulsive disgusting beasts, running about devouring people and ravaging villages and other such nonsense. I just take a tiny smidgeon of precaution, that's all." He smiled and his pointed little teeth glinted. Bean raised his brow, not quite understanding just what was happening. He rubbed his side and sorted through a multitude of thoughts all crowding into his mind at once.

"The strong, silent type, are we? Quite all right, quite all right. I don't think that I would be up for talking much after having gone through all that you've been through. Oh, you needn't raise those brows again. I know all about it. You'll find Thaddeus knows quite a lot, in spite of being a short scaly chap. That's what they call me, Thaddeus, and if I might be so bold, what is your name, young fellow? You needn't feel shy now. Speak up. I haven't had much company up this way for a long time, not that it's such a bad thing, but I do enjoy a good repartee now and then... a chat, if you like," said Thaddeus.

Bean felt a faint stab of annoyance. "Am I a prisoner here, sir?" he asked and surprised even himself with his rather cold tone of voice. He rethought it almost the moment he said it when Thaddeus carefully pressed his little claws together and gave Bean an uncomfortably knowing look.

"Far from it, my boy," Thaddeus replied coolly. "We don't believe in prisoners here." Bean remembered the massive dragon that had brought him in and the sensation of being held ever so carefully between his huge jaws. The boy rubbed his face and rested his forehead in his hands. It seemed everything he had been through in the last... what? Days? Weeks? However long it had been, it had worn him thin for certain but still that wasn't much of an excuse for being ill-mannered to this little creature that had taken great pains to bind up his wounds and that, by all appearances, seemed friendly enough.

"Bean. I'm called Bean, sir," he said at last, keeping his eyes carefully fixed on the stones of the hearth. Thaddeus held him in that stare for a moment longer and then raised his scaly brow.

"As in the vegetable, then?" Thaddeus asked finally in a lighter tone of voice.

"I suppose, sir," said Bean humbly, looking up at the little creature. "That's what they call me."

Thaddeus nodded and scratched the ridge of his snout thoughtfully. "And they call you nothing else, then? No other name?"

Bean shook his head, feeling rather ashamed, "No sir, just

Bean."

"Come now, you don't need to feel bad about it. It's, well, it's a good name, as far as names go," Thaddeus said carefully. "Not one I'd suspect for noble blood, that's all."

Bean smiled in half-hearted apology. "I think you must be mistaken, sir," he said in a quiet voice. The Guardian had mentioned something along these lines as well, Bean recalled, and this would be the second person to make that assumption. The boy didn't feel that he could believe either of these claims.

"Well, just thinking here, the blade of that sword you carry is sharply edged with a notable and ancient lineage. Authority and anguish went into its forging," Thaddeus remarked. "It's not just any young chap who would be swinging it about. Besides," he added and his sharp little face grew deeply thoughtful while he gave the Bean another one of his keen gazes. "When you first spoke, there a moment ago, in your voice I heard the ringing of gold through stately halls and over your eyes fell a silken mantle of azure blue, as the poets would say."

Bean's mouth twitched a moment in embarrassment. He wasn't sure how to take such elaborate compliments. He lifted up his sword, crossed his legs and laid it in his lap.

"I'm no more or less than Bean, sir," he said, running his hand across the white blade. "And it's just a sword."

Thaddeus thought about this for a moment and then nodded gently. "I have been imaginatively wrong before. I read a good deal in my spare moments, you see. It's the most a dragon can do in such a draughty old place as this," he said. He closed his eyes, took off his glasses and his tongue darted out and began to busily lick the lenses clean.

Bean looked up at him. "So, you're not a talking skyloc or lizard then. You're a dragon?" he asked.

Thaddeus stopped in mid-slurp and glanced down at his

glasses as he realized what he had been doing without even thinking. He then looked up at the boy with a bit of indignation, huffed, and hastily picked up the edge of the blanket and polished the glasses in all properness.

"Of course I'm a dragon, my dear young fellow. Why in the world would you think that I could be one of those disgusting miniscule bottom-feeders scuttling about after bugs and vermin? Ugh. Makes me ill to even think about it," he answered primly.

"Where are your wings?" asked the boy curiously. "And do you breathe fire and all?" Thaddeus drew himself up to his full haughty height at the questions.

"I would suggest in your spare time, my little man, that you pull down one of those books and read up on dragons," he sniffed. "There are several of them that go into the finer points of all the variations of the species. Many that I've taken the liberty to write myself actually and I would think I would be an expert on the subject."

Bean smiled. "I meant no rudeness, sir," he said politely and sought to change the subject to something else that had been gnawing on his mind. "You said... you know Mama Faerie?"

"I know the dear lady well, yes."

Bean had a difficult time keeping the concern and desperate hope from rising in his voice when he asked, "Then, you'd have heard something? That they're all right? Anything? There were goblins that came and... things were happening all at once..."

Thaddeus's face softened. "I haven't heard anything, Bean," he remarked and the way the boy shrank down and looked so destitute was heartbreaking. "Take comfort though, boy," he added quickly. "She's a more powerful lady than her demeanor would let on and Theron is a protective hardened warrior. I'm not worried. You, yourself, would know that appearances aren't everything."

Bean sighed and didn't reply. Sometimes, he reflected, it just plain hurt to get one's hopes up about anything.

Thaddeus patted him gently on the arm. "It's a lot you've had to take in at once, young fellow. Put your mind on resting and healing now," he said reassuringly. "You're safe here."

"I've been told that before," Bean commented in a wry tone of voice. Thaddeus gave him a very pointed look.

"You've not been in the company of dragons yet. I assure your safety shall not be an issue," he remarked dryly and as Bean opened his mouth to ask another question, the little dragon tut-tutted and said, "All in good time young fellow, all in good time. You're not at your best just yet and there's quite a lot you'll have to be doing before much longer, so you'll need to be fit as a butcher's dog, eh? There's a bit of breakfast by your bed there, tea and scones and jam. Rest, relax, and eat. Give yourself some time now. Then we'll get you some decent gear and fix you up right smart. I must be going away for a short time but I'll be in now and then over the next few days to see you. Fair enough?"

"All right," said Bean. Considering things, he had to admit that the little creature was right. He wasn't himself just yet and he knew it, but thankfully he seemed to be well on his way there. He stood up, pulling the blanket around his shoulders. Thaddeus chirruped a polite farewell and while Bean shuffled off back towards his bed, the dragon scuttled off beneath a high doorway to the right and down a set of stairs spiraling off beyond. Bean stood a moment in the center of the room watching Thaddeus vanish. He thought with a bit of amusement that despite Thaddeus's obvious pride in being a dragon, he so did make the boy think of a slightly bigger skyloc. He then heard the little creature's pattering steps echoing up the stairwell and then they paused and Bean caught snatches of the dragon talking.

"...that the boy gets everything he needs..." came Thaddues's faint voice apparently talking to someone. The way the echoes bounced around and as far down the stairs as he must be by now, it made it hard to determine everything he was saying. Oddly enough, Bean couldn't catch a reply though it was apparent that Thaddeus was addressing someone else. Finally the dragon fell silent and his pattering footfalls started up again. Bean listened to them fade into silence. He then blinked and peered hard at the stairs. For a second he thought he saw a shadow flicker across the wall further down the stairwell and he waited a moment, anticipating someone coming up to his room, a servant of some sort perhaps. However, he heard no approaching steps and no voice and after thinking about it, decided maybe it had been his imagination.

He walked back to his bed and sat down again. On the little table beside him there was indeed a plate, neatly stacked with what the dragon said were scones, but looked more like plain, old, buttered flour biscuits to Bean. A dainty little dish held three kinds of jelly; apple, strawberry, and blackberry. Another little dish held marmalade and both had tiny silver spreaders lying beside them on a neatly folded little napkin. There was also a little pot of tea and a cup on a platter. Bean gave it all a suspicious look. He picked up the paper-thin porcelain cup and examined the delicate gold leafing around the rim. It even had a trellis of pink roses delicately painted around the handle.

He made a face and set it very, very carefully back down on its saucer. It was, truth be told, a little too fussy and fancy for his taste. He'd not have to worry so much about breaking something if it had been just a plain mug and a bowl, or worry about having to refill it after one good gulp, he thought to himself while he gave the very tiny and delicate cup another critical look.

Still tea was tea and food was food and he couldn't argue with his empty stomach or with the generosity of his odd little host. The boy started gingerly on his breakfast. While he ate, a mystifying thought suddenly came to him; he was sure all of this hadn't been there on the table when he had first woken up. He would have remembered those little pink roses, that was for certain.

A Surprise in the Dark

The forces ravaging Darkleaf town by town and settlement by settlement had finally found themselves at odds with something just as savage and merciless and just as intent on reclaiming Darkleaf for its own. Little concerned with the affairs of goblin or human, winter had begun launching its own counterattack and a fierce and uncanny blizzard had claimed more of the forest than the goblins forces and the Badger could ever hope to claim. Then again, the weather had had many more years of experience with the besieging of Darkleaf after all.

Morning crept through mottled grey skies that promised more snow within hours, if not sooner. The feeble sun stretched over a still white landscape and the small birds and beasts of the forest that kept it so noisy and alive during the warmer months, dared not raise their voices now. The desperate times had begun. Silence meant either several months' commitment to deep sleep or focusing on survival from day to day and hour to hour. Either way it didn't do to attract unwanted attention. The snow could be morbidly equalizing about things. Under drifts of white, a pine tree could pass for a bush and a careless rabbit could be frozen to death quite as easily as a careless goblin or human being.

Snow slid down from a nearby embankment and with many a grunt and mumble, a burly figure pushed its way out of a shallow cave, which was more a scrape in an embankment than a true cave. The figure shook off a thick blanket of dead leaves, pine needles, and accumulated snow while it pulled itself up to its full height. Someone passing by would have surely thought it to be a drowsy bear suffering a bit of insomnia. It was, however, no more or less than a very weary Theron. Again, such was the illusion of winter and men could be mistaken for beasts.

Theron gathered up his things and set off again through the drifts in the direction he had been walking for the past few days. His knowledge of Darkleaf perhaps did not meet the same level as his wife's or Siv's, but a sailor and a fish had different understandings of the ocean as well. Theron firmly chose to understand Darkleaf as a barely civilized and hostile wilderness. He treated it much the way he had treated most things in his life... guardedly. Even now it would seem the forest and the relentless storm conspired against him to hide what traces might have been left of the boy's flight. He only hoped now that he still headed in the right direction.

Before the snow had covered everything, he'd tracked him as far as the cliffs. The evidence that had been left behind there of the distorted goblin bodies, the hissing puddles of acidic liquid, and the damage done to the rock face had done little to comfort him. He hadn't found any trace of the boy and that had been even more disheartening. Then he had come upon the goblin at the base of the cliff. Its body had been shattered, blood spattered its face, and the thing yet lived. It had opened its yellow eyes, gazed over at the distraught human and laughed weakly in his face, while deep red blood oozed from the corners of its mouth.

"Shan't find the boy... that big scaly beastie snatched him up... flown off... et him I won't doubt..." the goblin had gasped, taking one last malicious pleasure in seeing the reaction in Theron's face at his words. Theron, who hadn't a harsh bone in his body, who had no more desire to hurt another living creature than he would his own little pixies or his wife, reached the vile creature in two strides, pulled him up, and slammed him against the rock face. A horrible twisted desire had welled up in him to hit the thing's head against the rock over and over again until it was pulp.

Goblins, if they had anything even remotely resembling a virtue, had boldness. Whether through that or because the dying creature knew its time was up, either way it had merely grinned at the man holding it by the front of its ruined cloak collar.

"It gets in yer blood, human... them hates and that mad fire what eats ya up... an' once it gets in, it becomes sweet as wine... don't it?" the goblin had whispered. "I seen it... in the boy with his little sword... an' I see it in you. Go ahead... y'know yer... thinkin' it..."

It had been then that Theron found his eyes fixing themselves on the wristlet on his hand, exposed when his sleeve slid up his arm. The stone set in it glimmered a weak blue. He had abruptly released the creature, letting it slide back down to the ground. He had turned away and walked off; ignoring the derisive "...coward..." the creature had spat out between its red teeth before it expired behind him.

Thinking about that now, Theron rubbed his thumb over the stone again. "There's a difference between thinking and doing," he said to himself while he worked his way across snow, that here and there, drifted nearly chest deep. He pushed the words of the goblin and that moment of weakness out of his mind. He had more impor- tant things to focus on.

He knew about Thaddeus, of course, and the big fellow, the only 'big scaly beastie' in these parts that he could think of. He guessed, hoped really, the boy had not suffered any harm. He tried to put his mind at ease about it, but he found himself unable to do so. He couldn't relax until he had found the boy again. Qwen trusted the dragons and Theron trusted Qwen and her good judgment, but try as he might, he could not be completely comfortable with the idea of the boy being with unpredictable dragons. Some things were just too much to ask of one man.

In addition to that, the sinister marks of another on the boy's trail did not set well with him at all. He only hoped that his determination to find Bean first could beat the murderous determination of the gren-el. Time and the weather conditions continued working against him though.

Later in the afternoon, it started snowing again; great fat flakes that layered themselves on Theron while he trudged onward, melting and refreezing, until his outer oilcloth cloak and clothing became as rigid as iron. The wind picked up and the skies darkened until seeing more than two feet in front of him became almost impossible. Frost built up around the muff across his face and turned his eyebrows white. He kept walking onwards, pacing himself, so as to

conserve as much energy as he could and humming all the songs he could remember, matching the tempos with each step he took. At length, the ground sloped down into a secluded grove, where close-set trees had warded off the deeper accumulations of snow. Theron headed there to throw together a lean-to to wait out the worst of the storm. It would do the boy no good if Theron expended all of his energy fighting Darkleaf nor did he dare face a gren-el exhausted.

He cleared out a spot and gathered pine branches and scrapwood while bits of ice in the wind stung his grease-smeared face. Within a few hours he had a decent lean-to and a small fire carefully positioned and burning at the foot of it. He settled himself inside, wrapping himself up warmly to watch the snow fall. He sighed, feeling tired and discouraged, and fished around in his haversack to pull out strips of rendered sloth-fat to chew on.

As he settled down to eat and then rest, deep in the cold silence, his tinderbox sneezed.

"Mm?" Theron murmured in sudden surprise, lifting his eyebrows. He turned himself around a bit and shifted the tinderbox to where he could open it. A furtive scuttling among the dry tinder made him wonder for a minute if one of Darkleaf's tinier inhabitants had somehow made its way into the box seeking food or warmth from the harsh cold. Then he heard an unhappy little whimper and he slid off his mitten and brushed aside the dried moss and bits of twigs only to discover a very ashamed looking little pixie rubbing her nose.

"Hullo Papa Theron," the pixie whispered.

"Oh Tia," sighed Theron, while the little pixie fluttered out of the tinderbox and lightly landed on his arm. Her little wings drooped a bit and her face bore a mixture of delight at being with her papa again and apprehension at being chided for stowing away. She looked closely up at him, watching him, and waiting to see what he would say. Theron cleared his throat and kept his expression quite grave.

"What? No chatter, my little Tia?" he asked. "I would think you would at least be telling your papa how you came to be in my tinderbox when I was sure all my little pixies were safe at home with their mama. I couldn't find you anywhere to say good-bye to you. You had your papa very worried."

Tia wrapped her arms around herself and her eyes roamed around the lean-to before she glanced back at Papa Theron, tried her best to look endearing, and said, "My didn't want you to go without your Tia, Papa Theron. My goes everywhere with you." She gave him a bright smile and then her face fell seeing that the grave expression on Theron's face remained unchanged. "My would have missed you terribly if you had gone away looking for the liddle lad without Tia," she said, with the beginnings of a frown touching the corners of her mouth.

"I missed you terribly too, Tia-Pho-Phia," Theron replied and his face softened. Having the contrite little Tia in front of him, Theron suddenly realized how keenly he did miss his sweet wife and the pixies. The distance between his home and this rough little lean-to seemed even further away. "Now you shouldn't have come, Tia," he went on, "but I wouldn't dare send you home now. Even pixie magic can only do so much against this winter storm and we're much too far away. So I suppose you will have to come along. The going will be very hard, though, and dangerous. That's why your papa wanted you to stay at home where it would be safe and where you could look after your mama. Now I will have to worry about looking after you and finding young Bean."

Tia's lower lip shook a little bit and her head dropped. "My am sorry," she said. "The gobberlins brought the sad winter to Mama's home, nasty mean gobberlins. Tia w-was very sad to see Mama sick... b-but all the pixies are with her and Papa was sad too and he had no Mama and no pixies at all to be with him and make him happy... no pixies at all! That's terrible, yup!" The little pixie looked ready to cry. "My likes the liddle lad Bean and Mama had said a nasty mean beast was after him... and Papa was going after Bean... oh oh too many things for Tia to worry about..." she sniffled and wiped her eyes with her tiny fists.

"Oh little Tia," said Theron and took her tenderly in his hands. It broke his heart to see the cheerful little pixie so distraught.

"Now Tia look at your Papa and listen a minute. Since we're here we'll take care of each other so you needn't make yourself sick with all the worrying. You'll take care of me and I will take care of you. That means one way or another we will be all right and we will find Bean. Do you believe your Papa?"

Tia gave a woeful little sigh and said, "My always believes you, Papa."

"That's good." Theron stifled a yawn and settled back underneath the edge of the little lean-to, watching stinging white streaks of ice whistle by and the drifts of snow piling up outside. The pixie spread her wings and hovered over his face.

"Are you tired, Papa?" she asked. "You're blinking a lot. Tia blinks a lot when she is tired and needs her nap. My thinks you should nap, yup."

"I don't know that I should, Tia," Theron replied, folding his hands over his stomach and struggling to keep his eyes open. "I am tired, but I need to be watching to see when the storm lets up a little so I can keep moving. I don't want to really stop until nighttime comes and I can't see to travel."

Tia pondered this and then settled herself down on his shoulder to watch the snow fly by.

"How far away is liddle lad Bean? Is it a short time walking or a long time walking?" she asked, placing her chin in her hand. Theron smiled faintly. "A long time walking I would think, Tia. But we will catch up to him," he reassured her. He thought to himself how long and hard a day it had been and reflected that he hadn't yet put a dent in the miles to go. It couldn't be called completely cozy or comfortable in the tiny lean-to but at least the small fire had started warming things up a bit. Maybe closing his eyes for just a moment wouldn't hurt.

Tia nodded her head and regained some of her cheerful good nature at the thought. "Yup, my thinks we will. My will be so so double so happy to see the bean liddle lad again..." She chattered idly on for a while longer going from Bean to other things of interest to a small pixie. When she finally turned to Theron and asked, "Papa Theron, what do you think makes the snow white?" she instead received a gentle snore as an answer. Theron wrapped in his blanket had fallen fast asleep.

Tia smiled, fluttered her wings, and rose up in the air to give her papa an affectionate kiss on the bridge of his nose. "Papa has nothing to worry about. Tia will watch for him and wake him up when it is time to walk again. My takes care of Papa, just like I said," she said softly. She then settled herself in the brim of his faded hat and carefully watched the snowflake swirling by, while the wind rattled the branches of the lean-to and ice packed into the chinks.

***

Deeper in the woods some miles past from where the lean-to stood, the pitiful remains of a frozen and mutilated deer lay beneath a bare-branched elm. Moment by moment the pristine whiteness of the snow gently obliterated all memory of it and the sight of the huge dark red tracks leading away from it. A shadow drove itself relentlessly onward through the trees and against the blinding snow. Bloodstained frost gathered at the corners of a hideously grinning mouth and the slitted eyes saw things no normal inhabitant of the woods would see or, for that matter, wanted to see.

The grim world before that relentless gaze manifested itself in the twisted mind of the hunting gren-el in stark shades of black on red... red on black... black on white... and white on red... like blood on the snow.

Its master, the Beast King, had been perfectly clear in his commands. Find a boy with a sword. A youth wielded the weapon now and the gren-el would know him by the smell of the weave and the gren-el's kindred that lingered in his blood. Kill him and return the sword. Honor would be heaped upon the first gren-el to do so. Its brothers, the thing thought smugly to itself, would bear the disgrace of failure and the torture that would follow.

It would find the boy first, yes. The boy would die...

Vision of the King

"...Come now, my young elven friend. Tell me of your lord, the great weakling that sits upon the throne of White Stone Hall ... tell me how many more men that craven boy who calls himself a king is sending my way...."

The words hung in the cold gray air, spoken by a calm almost fatherly voice. Bean stood looking down at a wounded young elven soldier maybe four or five years older than himself. He bore numerous ugly bruises and wounds and crouched on his knees with his hands tied behind his back. Around him lay broken weapons and the bodies of elves, men, and goblins, most of them face down on the bloodied snow. Many of the dead elves and a few men had likewise been bound. The remains of a fort, black and despoiled, stood in the distance. A company of grim-looking humans stood around the burning ruins, idly watching the constant drift of oily smoke rise up into the overcast sky.

A thin, sharp, keening rather like the sound of a wet finger sliding along the rim of a wine glass rang at the edge of Bean's hearing. He couldn't move.

Someone stood at Bean's side and a bit in front of him, a slight, thin man dressed in old-fashioned armor. "No, not a man," Bean realized, "He was an elf; the one that had spoken in the calm, reassuring voice." Bean could see the delicately pointed ears, the white hair intricately knotted and tied with silver ornaments that rang against each other when the wind stirred them. He had his face turned away from Bean and was looking down at the young elven boy. He seemed to take no notice of Bean standing there nor did the humans. They all stood at ease, glancing around their surroundings in disinterest or watching the elven man interrogate the boy.

Bean's eyes fell upon the sword in the armored elf's scabbard, a sword of which the hilt bore an eerie resemblance to Bean's own sword, minus the green stone. The thin ringing grew more piercing, making Bean's head throb.

The armored elf knelt down and Bean did the same. It seemed the boy had no control over the movements of his body. Bean could only puppet the one he stood beside, as if he had become the elf's mindless shadow. Bean saw the elven man's hand curl around the young soldier's chin and lift his face up. He felt his hand mimic the same motion.

"I need the numbers of the soldiers and who leads them. Tell me and you might yet reach the stars by your choice," came the gentle command again. The elven man's voice carried the tone of someone who had no time for any idle nonsense or useless

164

bravery, someone accustomed to getting answers. Bean's lips moved, echoing the words silently. The younger elf, however, didn't let this order deter him. His mouth tightened and his bruised face, though damp with tears, showed a battered defiance.

The armored elf moved his hand away and closed his slender finger around a dagger in his belt. Without warning, he drew his weapon and the blade flashed through the air. Bean to his horror, found himself imitating the strike. The boy saw the body of the young soldier crumple to the snow-crusted ground. Bean's head throbbed fiercely now. He wanted to clench his ears and shut out the screaming cutting through his hearing like a thin blade. The corners of his vision began to blur mercifully into a blue haze.

The elf in armor wiped the dagger on the back of the dead elf's cloak. "Standing your ground to the end," Bean heard him murmur, "and yet courage could not save you." He sheathed his dagger again and then looked to the human soldiers standing and awaiting their orders.

"Hang them on the walls of the fort as a warning. Let the crows dance over their bones and feast while we blind the Eyes of the Hall. We march on Dark Arrow tonight," Bean heard him instruct his warriors. He stood up and the boy did the same.

The elven man turned and said something to the company of goblins directly to his left. Bean couldn't hear what he said for by this time the intensely high-pitched noise in his ears had all but deafened him.

The elf turned his face towards him. Bean saw only soulless black eyes lost in a haze of blinding blue. They pierced right through his head, sharp and cold as a shaft of black ice or the edge of a sword with a blinding white blade.

"...the cuff, of course, but that shouldn't be a problem. Now I say, young man, look here, are you even listening to me? Bean? BEAN!"

Bean shook his head and inhaled sharply as he returned to the present. He stared at his reflection in the full-length mirror and saw himself standing there, dressed in princely clothes finer than anything he would have ever dreamed of wearing. He clutched his sword, sheathed now in a fine scabbard of wood and mahogany leather. The scabbard was detailed in rich greens and gold and echoed the deep green and dark red of his fine clothing. On his feet he wore boots made of some peculiar leather, soft and comfortable, if not a little over sized.

"Away in a dream, eh boy? Well you look right noble, dressed to match the heritage of the sword you bear," Thaddeus chatted while he darted to the other side of the boy and pulled at the boots a moment. "Hum, not bad, great clumsy clodhoppers they are right now, but boys grow so fast, they'll fit you soon, I should know. Here now!"

The dragon jumped back and glanced up in alarm when the sword in its scabbard slid from Bean's grasp and dropped, caught in midair by the leather baldric that the boy had wrapped around his arm. Bean had pressed his forehead and other hand against the shining surface of the mirror and closed his eyes, while the sword swung gently back and forth, bumping against his legs. He looked deathly ill.

"Look here boy! You look far through, are you feeling ill again?" asked Thaddeus in concern.

"I saw... something horrible," the boy muttered, curling his hand into a white-knuckled fist. "Just now. I don't know what it was... I think I need to sit down." He opened his eyes and stared again at himself in the mirror.

Thaddeus's face grew grave. He stood up on his hind legs and tugged at the boy's sleeve, holding his arm, and guiding him towards the chair nearby. Bean sank down in it. He slung the baldric over his shoulder, folded his arms tightly, and bowed his head, not saying anything. Thaddeus scurried off and returned a moment later with a steaming cup of fresh tea and offered it to the boy. He took it but didn't drink it, only cupped it in his hands and looked down at it.

"I was somewhere else. It was snowing hard and I saw an elven man. He was pale, with white hair, dressed in armor. He killed someone, an elven boy, who wasn't much older than me. He cut his throat," Bean said in a low voice.

Thaddeus didn't say anything for a moment. He only gave the boy an absent-minded pat on the back of his hand and pulled up the footstool to sit down beside him.

"I thought at first it was Ganadon but..." Bean began and stopped. He gave Thaddeus a guarded look.

Thaddeus's eyes hooded over wisely. "Ah... the elven youth who lost his life at Dunsidne and who lost his soul in that very sword you carry now?" he said in an innocent tone of voice. "He was a stern young man but not given to cruelty against his own kindred."

He hopped off of the stool. "I'll give you a bit of time to drink your tea. Rest yourself in the meantime," the little dragon remarked. Bean nodded and sipped morosely at his drink. The intensity of the disturbing vision in his head faded soon with the warmth of the tea, but it had shaken him deep to the bone.

At length he set the teacup down on the table beside the chair, stood up, and made his way back to the mirror to study himself again and take his mind off of the things he had seen. He picked up the edge of the shirt and rubbed the fine material between his fingers. He sighed hopelessly and dropped his arms at his side.

"I look like some lord's son," he said.

"Indeed you do, boy. A young lord yourself no less," Thaddeus said.

"This isn't me though. I'm not any kind of prince," Bean mumbled. "These clothes are probably worth ten times what Gort paid for me back at the Inn."

"Tish! Stand up straight and hold your head up like a soldier, boy. Many young men born with blood as royal blue as the depths of

the ocean would not wear those colors half as well as you do."
Bean felt strange in these new clothes and the more he looked at himself, the more unsure he became. He wasn't sure if he should feel pride or awkwardness, standing in these nobleman's trappings.

"Do these belong to the lord of this house?" Bean asked. Thaddeus gave him another of his cool stares.

"The lord and master of this dwelling left the mortal realm long years hence, young fellow. I am the lord here now and I assure you, the young prince who once wore this apparel would be honored to know that a young chap, such as yourself, wears them now," said the dragon. As was typical of him, he switched the subject deftly to something else. "Are you feeling well enough to walk about and see the rest of the castle? You've been shut up in this room for about four days now. I daresay, a busy young fellow such as yourself would be bored to tears."

Bean raised an eyebrow at the dragon's odd words but brightened considerably at the prospect of seeing the rest of this castle. "Yes sir," he said eagerly. "Lead the way!"

Sometime later, Bean found himself walking down a long, narrow hall with the dragon skittering ahead of him. The boy's head turned this way and that trying to take in the sights of the dozens of ancient tapestries hanging on the walls and the various free-standing statues and busts in the alcoves along the way. He began to pick out the recurring themes of hunts, dark-haired heroes, the insignias of two crossed black arrows, and of course, dragons. The fierce beasts whirled and danced with deadly grace through the tapestries amid spiraling threads of embroidered flames and smoke. Most of the time, the ancient artisans portrayed them meeting their deaths in as cruel a manner as the dragons themselves and had sewn them with dazzling splashes of bright colors no less. Bean felt a little uncomfortable thinking about it. Having seen his fair share of fighting with goblins and huge beasts lately, battles in such cheerful colors seemed

almost an insult. The boy wondered why Thaddeus would have such things in his home at all.

It then occurred to Bean how little he knew about this place and in fact, how little he knew about Thaddeus. During the days while he had been recovering, he had stayed within his room, seeing Thaddeus now and then when he came in to chat and check on him. While the little dragon seemed prone to go on about all sorts of subjects, such as ancient history or swordsmanship, he grew strangely reluctant to elaborate when asked about himself or this grand castle. When Bean tried to coax more out of him, usually Thaddeus would change the subject or suddenly remember something else that he needed to attend to.

There had also been little... odd things. Regular meals appeared on the nightstand at the proper times. Every morning, Bean had found the basin and pitcher of the washstand over by the window filled with warm water with a washcloth and towel folded neatly beside them. Occasionally, when Bean sat down in the chair by the fire, he found some interesting book or game or wind-up mechanical whimsy sitting on the little end table by the chair, to keep him entertained during the long hours of his confinement. They appeared to be occurrences no stranger than the tasks of any discreet servant providing for an honored guest of his lord. But the bewildering thing was that Bean never saw the servants that so neatly arranged these little luxuries for him and not just because they were so discreet about

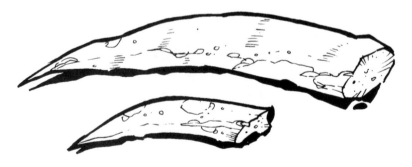

it. He would be standing at the window trying to figure out the latch on the shutters and turn and find that the empty cup and platter on the stand left over from the lunch he had just finished had completely vanished without so much as a rattle of porcelain; or else he might be deeply absorbed in a book late in the evening and the flicker of movement in the corner of his eye would catch his attention and he would look up and see fresh bedclothes spread out over the bed, a mug of warm cocoa on the nightstand, and the covers turned back neatly, waiting for him to come to bed. Given the overall strangeness of his surrounding, it didn't exactly frighten Bean, but it did leave him a little unsettled. Bean hoped with this little outing, things might be made clearer to him. Of course there was just as good a chance that it would become even more puzzling, but Bean was ready to take that chance.

They turned down another corridor, and the walls looked bleaker. Here it finally appeared that the ancient weavers of these tapestries had started getting the hint. The colors had become more muted and the scenes, while still very stylized, depicted the grittiness and despair of true warfare more accurately. They focused more on the deeds of one young dark-haired man taking out personal vendettas against scores of dragons. Below each tapestry evidence of the kill had been mounted or hung; fangs and convoluted claws, most of them about as long as Bean's hand, but a few nearly as big as the boy himself. It made the boy ill at ease walking among these relics and he wasn't sure why. It didn't seem to be because of the trophies themselves, though they were a bit intimidating. After a bit of pondering, Bean came to the conclusion that it was more along the line of not understanding why Thaddeus, a dragon, would care to have such tapestries and trophies hanging in his own home to begin with.

Movement flickered in the corner of Bean's vision. He turned his head and got the distinct impression of a shadowy figure disappearing down a smaller corridor branching off from the one he was

standing in. He stole a quick glance at Thaddeus trotting along some distance ahead of him and decided that he couldn't pass up the temptation to finally be able to see one of the mysterious servants. He carefully stepped back and slipped down the side corridor. "I can at least tell them thank you or something," the boy reasoned silently to himself. The whole idea of someone waiting on him the way he had waited on others all of his life didn't sit well with him.

No tapestries hung on the somber bare walls of this smaller corridor. A chill lingered in the air and his cloak billowed out behind him from a slight breeze coming from somewhere. Ahead, Bean could see daylight and heard a soft humming sound. He quickened his pace. At the end of the corridor he paused, crept silently forward, and stuck his head quickly into the shafts of sunlight crossing through the archway of the simple doorframe. The humming instantly stopped and Bean found himself staring into a small open-air rotunda. He glanced both ways for signs of life and his face fell. Snowflakes spiraled down through the skylight overhead but other than that, nothing moved.

He allowed himself a suspicious frown, sure that in some quiet secretive passageway someone was having a grin at his expense, and then walked out in the middle of this room. His footsteps crunched over the snow already coating the cobblestone floor and he stopped, pulled his cloak closer around him, and stared up into the polished stone face of a proud-looking young man. The blank eyes gazed up into the sky. He had one of his feet planted firmly on the stone head of a dragon. Below half-closed eyes the dragon's mouth was creased in a faint snarl. Bean found himself idly wondering about what kind of person had lived behind those blank stone eyes.

"Pompous-looking young dandy, eh?" commented a voice behind him and Bean turned to see Thaddeus standing there at his side looking up at the statue with a droll expression on his face. "Between all the tapestries and the statuary, you would expect that he would have at least given a nod or two towards the ones who accompanied him on the hunts. Many a brave lad met his end on those hunts, and later as well, when the hunts turned to territory disputes and finally to blood vendettas against the dragons. You will never see them or read their names on the records. It was all about his young Lordship here and after a time, there was no one left of his house to remember or write it down. They had all been killed or left for parts unknown and the young prince was left to his own devices. The dragons remembered though, at least those that remained after the wars. They have very long memories."

Bean rubbed at his cloak-covered shoulders and didn't know what to say. Standing beside a dragon and talking about a dragon hunter certainly made things awkward.

Thaddeus appeared to sense the awkwardness. He tapped at Bean's elbow and when Bean glanced down at the little dragon, he had an understanding look in his eyes.

"This is history, young fellow," he said in a calm voice. "We often times have to face up to it, and good or bad, it is still ours. We change it, we apologize about it, and we pretend it doesn't exist and still it exists, unchanged and unapologetic. The important thing is that we remember it for what was, learn from it, and try not to make the same mistakes twice."

Bean looked back up at the statue again. "Who was he? What happened to him?" he asked.

Thaddeus stood a long while in deep thought. After a moment he said in a hard voice, "Who was he? He was a fool. What happened to him, sorry to say, was rightly what he deserved." He dropped on his forelegs again, nodded his head towards the archway and added, "Now come along, young chap, we must be off to the study."

Bean followed Thaddeus back down the corridor. Behind him, he heard the humming start up again. It echoed down the hallway after him, but this time he couldn't take the time to turn and look back. He had to keep up with the little dragon that seemed quite insistent on having him follow closely this time. The mysterious servants regrettably would have to wait for another time. Bean tagged doggedly behind Thaddeus, preoccupied with thoughts of the young man with the blank eyes and the smell of snow and blood in the air.

Flowers in the Dark

Time had stopped.

Both logic and the animal instincts in the back of Ravna's mind dismissed this notion, of course. Days had passed. Deep in this underground world lit by flickering crystals, the distinction of morning and evening had blurred. She knew there had been days and nights, though she had lost track of exactly how many had gone by. In grief, however, time stops. Life for Ravna, in a way, had stopped also.

She woke, she picked at food that had been brought to her, she slept again, and so the cycle went on. The whole time Siv's sword always lay within reach. She could not bear to have it out of her sight. Sometimes she cried. Sometimes she just lay in the hammock underneath the wrought metal bower, looking up at the artificial flowers, just not thinking of anything at all. This was where she found herself now; only the burial of Siv preoccupied her thoughts instead of the usual quiet and empty void. Had they laid him to rest an hour ago? A week ago? She didn't know or care anymore.

After the days of waiting had passed, Roc, true to his word, had summoned her to an inner stone chamber within his home where Siv's body had been laid on a simple white cloth. He had explained to her what he would do for Siv and gathered sweet-smelling oils, water in basins, white linen rags, and other necessary items. With the old rock troll murmuring something half song and half liturgy under his breath, they had solemnly undressed Siv and washed away the blood, the filth, and the mud. Roc had explained to Ravna that in the red rock troll belief system, the soul of the recently dead lingered around the empty body until it was finally laid to rest properly. Ravna didn't know if there was any truth to this and though the old red rock troll spoke of worlds circling beyond this one, she didn't know whether there was any truth to that either, but she had pondered it in her heart while she rubbed oil into Siv's clean white hair and along his temples, anointed his eyelids and his mouth with the sweet-smelling oil and tenderly wrapped the strip of woven gold cloth marked with the ancient language of the red rock trolls, that Roc had given her, around his eyes. When he opened his eyes in the life he had gone to beyond this one, Roc explained to Ravna, he would open his eyes to halls of gold and riches beyond compare.

Perhaps Siv had been there while they had done all that. Ravna had imagined she felt his presence there, approving of what was being done for him.

Roc Noc had lifted the body up

while Ravna slid the linen out from beneath him and replaced it with another clean one as per the old troll's instructions. They dressed him in fine robes and Roc Noc had carefully folded up his old clothes, the bolts they had removed from his body, and the cloth he had lain on while they had cleaned him. He would ritually burn them later. Together, they wrapped Siv up in the clean linen and carried him through a nearby doorway and down a flight of stairs into another set of underground caverns.

They had passed sealed doorways carved with intricate runes and hung with amulets; and at the threshold of each door, offerings in bowls and jars sat on the floor, covered with dust. Following a winding corridor, they had finally come to a simple doorway. The whole time, during the washing, the dressing and the walk through the caverns Ravna had remained dry-eyed. She had thought only of how heavy and lifeless Siv's body felt in its shroud. It hadn't even felt like they carried what had once been a living human being and her dearest friend. It had felt like they were carrying pieces of a broken statue. Roc had pushed open the door and Ravna had stepped into a room of dim light and dampness.

She felt famiiar in the round chamber which was small and cool with white limestone walls and a shaft in the ceiling stretching far into darkness above their heads. Several crystals lit the chamber, casting their soft glow across the walls and the earthen floor. They had laid Siv on a dais of stone in the very center of the room, partly surrounded by a thin and constantly trickling canopy of water coming from somewhere overhead. Ravna's eyes had wandered over the walls, carved with intricate runes, many of which had been softened and blurred by other streams of water dripping down the walls. She touched the carvings with her hand. They all spoke of a master craftsman's touch and pride.

"Why would you choose to carve such beautiful images in a stone so soft?" she had murmured to Roc. "See here, the water has worn it away. A few more years and it will be like it was never here to begin with."

"To remind us," Roc Noc had said in a solemn voice while he smoothed a clean linen cloth over the stone table. "To remind us that nothing lasts. The beauty of the carved words and pictures do not matter. The memory of them does. That is what stays."

Ravna had wept then, tears sliding down her cheeks in silence. She wept for the ancient words smoothed away by the passage of time. She wept for Siv, for the words she would never hear him speak again. She wept for everything she had ever wanted to say to him and would never be able to and she wept for her incredible loneliness without him.

She had slung his sword over her back while they had carried Siv down to his final resting place and now she shrugged it off of her shoulders. Clutching it tightly to herself, she walked towards Siv's body while Roc stood over him with his head bowed. He had his eyes closed and his lips moved, but Ravna heard nothing. She bit her lip with tears rolling down the sides of her face and laid Siv's sword across his still chest. Roc lifted his head, his eyes had opened and he had looked straight at her.

"No," he had said firmly and picked the sword back up and placed it back in her arms. "Those of Siv's blood in Whitehall need to be told how their prince fell."

Whitehall... Prince... Those words shouldn't have been alongside Siv's name and yet she had heard the troll stating it matter-of-factly as if it were common knowledge. She wanted to know more, but at that point Roc Noc had turned back to Siv laid to rest on the stone and begun speaking in his deep voice.

The words of an unknown language rolled over her and took her breath like a sharp winter wind. They had in them the power and rhythm of ancient songs and indeed at times it seemed his voice rose and fell and passed from spoken words to chant to full-blown

melody and back again. Ravna had felt it resonate from the ground through her and a bracing coldness flooded her senses suddenly. It felt like plunging into a stream, icy, crisp, and fresh from a spring thaw. Something had brushed against her foot and she glanced down and took a step back with a soft gasp. A green, tender vine had begun to push its way up from the cold floor.

Vines had curled gracefully upwards from around the stone dais where Siv's body lay. They had woven themselves around the carved stone and she recalled the certain tenderness and empathy in the way they had slowly embraced his still body. The vines had spread out from the table and slid up the walls and Ravna had watched them become more and more numerous until the whole room became threaded in green. The leaves unfolded and when Roc Noc's voice had reached the depths of thunder, he suddenly fell silent and Ravna saw in the dim light, stars silently blossoming across the field of green. No, not stars, she had realized when a sweet heady perfume drifted across her senses. Flowers, it had been thousands of beautiful star-shaped flowers that filled the expanse of green foliage.

Ravna had kept her gaze fixed on Siv's pale, serene face until the vines, the leaves, and the star blossoms had finally hid him from her sight.

Roc had turned to a darkened corner and brushed his hand across several crystals in the wall, which lit up in an intricate pattern and the room rang with sweet music. Above, stone ground against stone as further up in the shaft, part of the ceiling spiraled open, letting in a draft of cool but fresh air. The air smelled of snow and winter and a dim grey light came through as though coming from a great distance far above their heads. Ravna had stepped closer and trailed her hand through the shaft of pale light, her fingertips disrupting the thin trickle of the water-canopy at the head of the stone table. The water had changed from a trickle to a steady curtain of clear water surrounding the dais, collecting into specially constructed channels in the floor that whisked the excess water away far beyond her sight

"The vines will seek the light and the fresh air through the shaft once it becomes warmer above ground and spring comes again," Roc Noc had said. "Deep in Darkleaf there are quiet isolated groves where these vines grow and blossom across the forest floor, out of old stone vents stretching far down into the earth. The forest will honor him. Let us leave him now to his final rest. Come."

There hadn't been anything else Ravna could add to that elegant eulogy. Mutely, she had nodded and followed the red rock troll out of the room. He had sealed the door behind him with another gesture and murmured chant and then Ravna had followed him back through the corridors.

Now she lay here in the hammock, holding Siv's sword, watching the artificial lights flicker across vines made of metal. She felt hollow inside and tried not to think about the silent stone door in the dark corridors, a door never to be opened again. "Think of what has always been the key to your survival..." Siv's words seemed to burn in her brain.

"Faith," she whispered, but the word had lost its holiness for her. Perhaps it had saved her, but it had not saved Siv.

"Mistress Ravna," someone said beside her. She turned her head and saw Roc Noc looking down at her. "Come with me, please," he said. She rose and followed him back into his home.

She soon found herself in Roc Noc's study, sitting in a comfortable chair with the sword across her lap. The old red rock troll disappeared for a few minutes and then came back, bringing her a half-hearted smile along with a cup of tea. He sat the tea down on the little table beside the chair and settled himself in a chair directly opposite from her. In his hands, he held Siv's pouch.

Ravna felt numb. She didn't even look at the tea. She sat stiffly in the chair, her head low, her shoulders hunched. When tears started running down her face again, she wiped them morosely away. It seemed she would never know a moment in her life again free of mourning. She felt empty and sick and only dimly aware of Roc Noc talking to her about something; plans and armies. She didn't even care.

"Little mistress," she finally heard the red rock troll say, in a voice that while gentle, nevertheless commanded her full attention. She looked up reluctantly at him.

"Are you listening?" Roc Noc asked solemnly.

Ravna shrugged and a bitter expression darkened her face. "What does it matter? What does anything matter anymore?" she muttered. "Everything I know has been turned on its head. I don't know what's real anymore, who I should listen to, or what I should believe." Her voice rose slightly. "Siv... you said Siv was a prince, of the Whitehall no less. By all rights I should be remembering him as a prince... a prince of royal blood." Her fingers traced the pattern of the rose across the shoulder of the sword. She bit her lip.

"This is not how he would have you remember him, little mistress," Roc said in a grave voice.

184

Ravna's voice sounded dull and tinged with resentment to her own ears when she replied, "How then should I remember him? I don't know if I should be grieving for a barkeep or a prince. He wasn't... he wasn't who I thought he was. I don't know who I am crying for anymore. I don't know who Siv was... and all this time I thought... I really thought I did." Her voice fell to a hurt whisper, the whisper of a child who had been betrayed by someone she loved. "I thought we knew everything about each other. Why couldn't he have told me? Did he truly not trust me? He could have confided in me... He could have..."

Roc Noc sat back in his chair and sighed. He looked down at the papers and a withered flower with soft silver petals that lay in his lap. He stood up, walked over to her, and placed those in her lap. "We are sometimes entitled to our secrets, little mistress," he said gravely. "His was a world he was forced to forget when the Silver Dagger and you, it would seem, became his world. He was a wanted man, child... fleeing the wrath of weavers. One of these weavers had become drunk with the thought of his own power and had attempted to take the life of Siv's brother, the prince of Whitestone Hall. Siv got caught between a maddened weaver and those sent to destroy that weaver, those who carried the insignia of the Order of the Black Arrow. He killed to protect his brother and himself and thereby exposed an Order that none were supposed to know existed. For that there was no forgiveness. He had to flee. He had to be forgotten." Ravna sat in silence a moment. "You are a weaver as well," she remarked, looking up at him and there was a delicate moment then, full of uneasiness.

Roc Noc rubbed his chin. "Once little mistress, weavers were those who wove the mantle of the world. We wove the birthing sheet and the burial shroud of the earth. For that was what was required of us. In exchange was the sacrifice of who we were, the very threads that bound us to this world and this reality. All but a very, very few have forgotten the original reason of why we once wove," he said quietly. He looked steadily at Ravna. "A weaver, however, knows the meaning of sacrifice. Look down at those papers and tell me what you see."

Ravna glanced down, picking up the fragile flower. She laced it thoughtfully between her fingers and studied the papers. "I see plans... Army formations... Names," she said, a thoughtful frown crossed her face as she brushed through them.

"A vast army above us brings Darkleaf to its knees. There is a blizzard overhead, but that has only slowed it, it has not stopped it. This is information vital to those of Whitehall and the Eyes of The Hall, the defenses, and the watchtowers that surround it. It must be taken to young King David as soon as possible, these documents and Siv's sword as well... so that he may know the battle plans of the goblins and that his uncle has left this world for those lofty watchtowers of Darkleaf where none living may go."

Ravna placed her forehead in her hand and felt the weight of everything press like heavy iron upon her shoulders. "I... I can't do this..." she muttered. "I can't... I wouldn't know how... it's too soon... it's too much to ask..."

Roc's face grew grave. Ravna stared down at the flower in her hands. "My dear young mistress... Siv chose to come back to the Silver Dagger rather then take these documents to King David," he said and when Ravna looked back up at him, it seemed his face looked even more lined and old. "The forestwalker knew well the meaning of sacrifice. Yet at the end there was one thing asked of him that he could not sacrifice. He could not give up what had become most precious to him. For that... for you, he died."
"What?"

"For you... he died," repeated the red rock troll softly. "Was it in vain, little mistress?"

Ravna was unable to reply. She didn't know what to say. She only fingered the petal in her hands and stared down at the emblem of the white rose across the shoulder of the sword.

"I will give you time to think..." said Roc Noc in a heavy voice. "It is indeed much to ask of you. There are perhaps some other things we need also..." He paused and a peculiar look crossed his face. He tilted his head and his expression grew still and hard as if something had suddenly pierced his very soul.

"We have company, little mistress," he said solemnly. A faint tired smile crossed his face. "Company in the caverns. We had better go and greet them."

Watcher of the Broken Moon

That first day Thaddeus had brought the boy to the study, he had given the Bean an inquisitive look while the boy had gazed up at the huge ornate walls. "I do hope you know how to read and write, lad? I've no time to teach you your letters," the little dragon had remarked.

"I can read, sir, and write a bit." Bean had smiled with a touch of pride. "The barkeep of the inn where I lived taught me my letters when I would go hunting with him. Gort didn't think a dishwasher needed to know such things, but Siv, he always told me stories, wonderful stories. Sometimes, I'd sneak books in my room at night and stay up reading."

"Splendid! I'm glad of that," the little dragon had said, while he had ushered Bean to a small desk in the corner and motioned the boy to sit down. Around it shelves lined with dusty books, parchments, odd and ends, and rolled-up tapestries had stretched up to the ceiling. Thaddeus had promptly pushed an imposing looking stack of great thick volumes over towards the boy. "You can start with that."

"The top book?"

"Oh no, my good fellow. As good a reader as you say you are, you can take care of the whole stack!" And before Bean could open his mouth, Thaddeus had scuttled up an ironwork staircase to an intricately wrought loft overhead and vanished through a dark red curtain draped over a small doorway. A cheerful "Ta, ta!" floated down to the boy.

That had set the tone for the daily study-times that followed and continued over the next several weeks. For a few hours each day, sometimes longer, Bean had been (in his opinion) rather unfairly coerced to read and re-read the pile of documents and books that sat before him and take notes until his hands ached. He saw no sign of Thaddeus, who would barricade himself in what he called his "office" behind the red curtain for long stretches of time. Many times the tired boy would sneak in a doze after so much mental work, only to wake up to the sound of voices drifting out from within the very walls. Once he jerked awake, at what he could have sworn sounded like Thaddeus and a young woman's voice in an argument. Of course, when he had shaken all the sleep out of his drowsy brain and listened harder, nothing but the silence of the library came to his ears. Yet for all that he heard or thought he heard, he saw nothing. Thaddeus would come down very late into the evening, always alone. When Bean tried to engage him in conversation, the dragon would give him a distant look, his sharp eyes misting over, remembering something apparently important but perhaps only to him. Mostly he rambled on about things of long ago.

So once more this afternoon, Bean found himself in the huge library of Thaddeus's home, sitting at his desk, and reading over old dusty documents. Thaddeus promptly dumped a stack of parchments and old books by him. "Start on those now and don't forget to take notes. I'll be back in a bit, have to check on something. Remember, don't go wandering off out of the library now, there's a good young chap," he told Bean. Bean placed his chin in his hand and pulled down the top parchment and brushed off the thick layer of dust before he set to reading. Odd old-fashioned writing in at least three different hands filled the page he stared at, but thankfully, he found one language he could read. "Observe... Ob-serv-ations Concerning The Wars Of The Helixshires: The Dun-sid-ne Tragedy and Its Re... Reper-cussions," he murmured to himself. Daylight filtering through a stained glass skylight over head cast shadows of red and gold over the boy and over the dark wood floor beneath his feet.

He trailed his index finger along each faded word, moving his lips silently. He got through about three pages, recounting the family tree of the Helixshires and the families that branched off from them, before his attention began to wander back to his own family at the Silver Dagger Inn, to Mama Faerie and Theron who had been so kind to him. He also found himself wondering about the mysterious red curtain and what lay beyond it. After trying to keep his thoughts on the task in front of him, he finally sighed to himself and pushed the papers away. He felt very tired. He also hated feeling constantly alone, not knowing if he'd again sit here late into the night with only a candle against the darkness creeping into the corners of the library. Bean sat back against the wall and stretched his arms, feeling the

strength that had returned to them, and allowed himself a moment of contentment. The boy glanced up again at where the little dragon had vanished and his curiosity irked him to the point he no longer felt he could resist it. "Well... Thaddeus said don't go out of the library... and that doorway must lead to a room still inside the library," he told himself.

Bean slid away from the desk, hopped down from the stool, and stepped up onto the staircase. His boots clanged metallically against each step as he followed it up to the curtained doorway. He paused, listened a moment, then carefully pushed the curtain aside, and found something extraordinary.

A short narrow corridor extended from the doorway and at the end of it, a few steps lead up to a closed round door. However, the most remarkable thing about this corridor was the slender interlacing branches that looked like sun-bleached wood which made up both the doorway and the entire corridor. If any stone construction lay behind this thick latticework of white branches, Bean certainly couldn't see any evidence of it. After all the stone and metalwork he had seen, it felt odd to find this sudden reminder of nature so close at hand.

Bean crossed through the corridor, silently walked up the couple of steps to the door, and stood a moment looking around, unsure of what he ought to do next. Suddenly he heard voices coming from behind the door, one in particular with Thaddeus's distinctive little accent.

"...know, Milady, but there is no other choice. It's utter chaos out there right now, grim as the face of Brutus's granny, just take a look."

"And you will send out a small boy in the middle of it?"

"Who else then? You? Or myself? I imagine the land there is edgy enough from reports coming in and then laying eyes on Brutus come winging in from the skies... I've made arrangements for someone to go with him. It's not like I'm sending the lad out alone on a hobby-horse..."

"Who?"

"Otter will do it."

"The Helixshire elf-woman? Surely not. Thaddeus, think a moment. Why would she...?"

"That's not the issue at hand, my dear girl. That's already been decided. Now away with you..." Thaddeus said in an irritable voice and a long uncomfortable silence followed this comment. Bean heard the little dragon shift around in the room beyond the door and clear his throat.

"I didn't mean...." he began in a rueful voice and then stopped. "Well Thaddeus, a right old curmudgeon you are. She's gone away now." Bean heard the little dragon sigh heavily. After another long pause the boy heard him murmur to himself, "Good heavens...at this rate, there'll be nothing left of the forts to the north... they've taken almost all of the main roads now, filthy little brutes..."

Bean reached out, intending to just lightly examine the door with its inlaid patterns of copper before he turned around and crept back down to the library. He hadn't counted on the door being slightly ajar and the hinges creaking horribly loud in the close stillness of the corridor and the room beyond it...

Thaddeus wore a grave expression on his scaly face. Images of grief and slaughter flickered past his gaze in quick succession; homesteads burned, troops on the march, death, violence, and snow stained crimson. His eyes hooded over in somber thought as he saw the burning ruins of the Silver Dagger Inn. At the loud creak of the door behind him, the little dragon turned hastily, passing his clawed hands over the surface of a large crystal orb embedded in a rickety table nearby. The images instantly faded into a cloudy mist. Thaddeus looked hard at the door and raised a scaled brow.

"Come in Bean," the little dragon said.

The door stood ajar in awkward silence for a moment. Then it creaked again and opened wider. A shame-faced Bean cautiously stepped inside the room and closed the door behind him. He rubbed his arm and his eyes roamed over this new room.

He found himself in a tall and rather narrow chamber with walls made up of what appeared to be more finely laced tree branches. These, however, seemed carved of pure crystal and came together in several huge crystals that formed the ceiling. On one side of the room, beyond the table with the crystal orb, a desk sagged with all manner of parchments, maps, and more books. Some had fallen off and lay scattered across the smooth, black floor, which was spread with a huge tapestry showing a large golden bird divided long ways by a single black arrow. In another corner of the room, a taller desk stood, also stacked with odds and ends. In the center of the room was a low comfortable chair with its back to the boy. Directly in front of Bean and the chair stood several tall mirrors, obviously having a weaver's spell about them from the look of the mists that swirled across their surfaces. The mists cleared a moment and in the silvery reflection of the mirrors, Bean saw Thaddeus sitting in the chair with his small forearms folded. "I'm sorry sir. I wanted to know where you had gone," the boy said in a small voice. He looked around at the empty chamber. "Were you talking to someone?" he asked. "I thought I heard..."

"Bosh! Talking to someone, lad? No one here. I chatter on to myself and this chamber makes odd echoes, is all," Thaddeus said, holding Bean in a careful gaze.

Bean didn't accept this explanation, but picked up on the hint that it would be the only explanation given to him and held his tongue. "I should go back to my studies, then, sir," he said. "It was

rude of me to walk in on you like that." He turned on his heel.

"No, no, bide a while, young lord, if you like. Though I fear there's not much of anything in this room to keep a young chap busy. I've just been tending to some personal business," he heard Thaddeus remark and looked over his shoulder to see the dragon gesture him back. Thaddeus climbed down from his chair and made his way to the desk. He pushed aside a set of papers, picked up a couple of smudged and folded-up letters, and peered at them through his glasses. He put them aside, plucked up an ink quill, and scratched something on a separate piece of parchment, one of many scattered haphazardly across the table.

"You're probably wondering what all this is about, eh lad?" Thaddeus said, without glancing up from his work.

"Yes sir. I have wondered about that for a while now... where it is that you go while I study," said Bean, rubbing his hands together, almost wishing to be back downstairs again. This room by far had to be the coldest he had been in yet. He pulled his hands into his sleeves and tucked them under his arms.

"Well... the truth of the matter is this. Between surveying the damage outside, I've also been writing letters and keeping up correspondences. Up until a few weeks ago, that is," the dragon replied. "The silence from my contacts is not reassuring at all, but it did make your arrival here, along with what the mirrors have shown me, all the more significant."

Bean glanced at the mirrors again. He walked a little closer and held up his hand. The mist followed the movement of his hand and the boy felt intrigued. Cold radiated from the surface of the mirror. He felt a strong urge to touch the mirror, but it being so obviously otherworldly, he was reluctant to indulge that whim. One didn't just go around sticking your hands where they didn't belong, especially if you couldn't be certain they'd come back.

"These mirrors show you the outside world?" he asked.

"Indeed they do, young fellow. Almost everywhere that can be imagined," the little dragon replied and left off his letter writing a moment to turn around and give Bean his full attention. Bean moved his hand and his eyes followed the movement of the mist in the glass.

"Everywhere..." he repeated. The boy gave the dragon an oddly penetrating stare. "Will it show me my father? Where he is right now?" He asked in a quiet voice. Thaddeus cleared his throat.

"I fear it doesn't work that way, lad." He spoke gently, but Bean glimpsed the furtive look in his eyes, as if the little dragon didn't care to elaborate. "Don't ask me why. I'm not exactly sure myself, but it doesn't. It shows me what needs to be seen at the time, whether it be pain or happiness."

Bean turned his back to the mirror and his brow furrowed. The crystals above him shimmered and Bean heard a faint crackling and popping above his head. He glanced up and saw the crystals expanding, growing almost like living plants. He looked back at the mirrors. He thought to himself of all that he wanted... no, he needed to see; things like his old home at the Silver Dagger and Mama Faerie and Theron, safe and unharmed. Most of all, the Bean felt that never was a need so dear to him as a need to see his father, to know where he was, or what had happened to him. He focused all of his thoughts on that, held his hand mere inches from the cold smooth surface of the glass and waited, willing the mirrors to work.

The mist remained. After a few minutes, Bean dropped his hand to his side once more and sighed in disappointment. "Then what's the use of having them if they don't work like they should?" he said. He couldn't keep the bitterness from creeping into his voice. "What's the use of mirrors with such power? There are so many things I need to see. They can't even do that?"

He felt the dragon's hard stare on him again and turned his head to face the dragon. Thaddeus had an expression in his face as cold as the room. "I needn't remind you, lad... that these mirrors belong to me. They work for me. What they choose to show is entirely up to them. Not to me... and certainly not to you, my dear young chap," he said briskly. He let those words sink in for a moment and then his face softened a bit. "Oft times, there's some things that are best left unseen. Just consider what you ask for. It may not be to your liking."

The explanation left the boy more discontented than satisfied, but the dragon's words and his expression made enough of an impression that he held his peace. Thaddeus pulled off his spectacles in the silence. He opened his mouth, stuck out his tongue, and then paused a moment. He coughed, snapped his mouth shut, and hurriedly plucked up a handkerchief from nearby and used that to clean his glasses instead.

"Never mind those mirrors, young fellow," he remarked. He gave Bean a sideways glance. "Was it curiosity alone that brought you upstairs?"

" I..." Bean stopped and thought for a moment. "It was curiosity first, sir, but as long as I am here... I just want to know what I am supposed to do." He drew the sword out of its scabbard and held it in his hands for a moment, studying it. He dropped the point against the floor, resting the heels of his hands on the cross-handle. He drummed his fingers against the metal, bowed his head, and his young face grew grave with deep thought. "The Guardian told me this sword needed to be healed. I've been here a few weeks and you've told me many things that don't make sense and I've read a great many things that make even less sense. I don't think I'm any closer to figuring out how to heal this sword."

"Well, young man, it occurs to me that the answer would be in those parchments on your desk in the other room. They have the entire story of Ganadon and his sword." Thaddeus gave the boy the knowing glance of a disappointed teacher whose student had not read his lessons sufficiently.

"I know his story, sir," said Bean and his drumming fingers took on a tone of impatience.

"From one point of view, princeling. If you're curious as to what you need to do, you have to understand that there are always several angles to any story and Ganadon's story didn't stop when the sword was shattered and he was killed," said Thaddeus climbing down from the chair. "Nor will it stop with you finding it... whether you want it to or not."

Somehow the way the little dragon said that made Bean feel uneasy. He stopped drumming and looked down at the sword.

"So first of all, Bean, before you solve this enigma you'll need to understand the beginning of things. That means more studying." Bean felt frustration darkening his mood. It must have shown on his face for the little dragon continued. "I can tell you what I know, but it would not help you understand, save you read it yourself, and until you know it for yourself. Our time is running dangerously short though. Since you're feeling more like your old self now, I'll need to send you off towards Whitestone Hall to have a talk with our young

king David. I'm trying to educate you all I can, lad. You'll need it."
Thaddeus paused and looked over to the other desk. "Bother, I just
remembered... I have something I've been meaning to give you..."
The little dragon leaped from the desk onto his chair and scrambled
across it to the floor and towards the other desk. In the process,
Thaddeus's claw brushed the orb by his chair and instantly the mirrors came to life.

The mirrors drew Bean's attention at once, almost without
any conscious effort on his part. He felt them demanding his gaze,
felt it through the quickening in the air between him and their shining mist-filled surfaces. The mists vanished.

Through a raging blizzard he saw goblin forces sluggishly
on the move; saw the destruction they left in their path, saw fire,
blood, and anguish in the very heart of the forest that he had called
home. The images moved by him in quicker and quicker succession,
growing more and more intense and heart-wrenching until finally
the boy had to close his eyes and look away. He wanted to cry, but
somewhere inside him he knew all the tears in the world wouldn't be
enough.

The sharp tap of a claw against the crystal orb rang through
the boy's consciousness. "As you can see, it's not only a sword that's
in need of healing... right now this entire realm's bleeding to death,"
he heard Thaddeus say. Bean finally opened his eyes, rubbed at them
with the heels of his palms, and blinked furiously. He lifted his head
and saw one last image in the mirror; that of proud high walls, un-
blemished and white, with nothing more than red sunlight dappled
across them.

"If it's not stopped soon, even the very stones of the Hall will
bleed. I am sorry..." Thaddeus continued, his voice cool and quiet.
The mists swirled back over the surface of the mirrors once more.

Bean turned towards Thaddeus, his expression pleading and
deeply troubled. He swallowed hard.

"What can I do against all of that?" he finally asked in a hollow voice.

"More than you might know, young fellow," said Thaddeus gravely. "But it's not so much a matter of what I tell you to do or what the king will tell you to do or anyone for that matter. It's what you are willing to try, what you're willing to give up, and what you are willing to risk. Not just for your own sake, m'lad, but for others as well. Young prince, I've no doubt you are of a royal line, more than a washer of dishes out in the middle of nowhere. There'll be some hard things asked of you and yet that'll only prove the blue in your blood."

Bean stood a moment in dead silence, rocking the sword back and forth. A distant and sad expression crossed his face. He felt his own fate quickening beyond his control, driving him in a direction he wasn't sure he wanted to go. He didn't feel brave or decisive. He only felt mournful and more than a little uncomfortable with who he was and what he appeared to be becoming.

He sucked his upper lip for a moment. "I'm scared, sir. Very scared," he said quietly. "But whatever is required of me, whatever I need to learn... whatever I can do I will do... I need to do, really." Even as he heard his own words, he felt terribly alone.

Thaddeus gave the boy a comforting pat on the toe of his boot and an expression of pity crossed his reptilian face. Bean had no way of knowing, but Thaddeus's heart weighed heavy in his small chest hearing the boy's words. The dragon felt that the boy had accepted many cruel burdens upon his young shoulders by his honest yet heartbreakingly innocent declaration.

"Then, young fellow... what you can do... or rather what we can do... is get back to that library and get to studying," he said kindly. "Come on, then, there is much you need to learn and time's a-wasting."

"Yes sir," the boy sighed and followed him out of the room.

the Gre-nel

Silence hung frozen in the bitter air and the hunter moved through the woods. It had blood on its mind, blood and a hunger that gnawed at its empty guts and black soul.

Before the snow had started falling, it had been easy for the gren-el to track the boy even with the accursed clumsiness of the goblins. Every step it took now through the ice-crusted mess brought forth vile curses at being hindered and slowed, but curses only voiced within the recesses of its brain. The ice had also bruised and cut the creature's feet and legs but the gren-el welcomed the pain as the whip that lashed it onwards, closer and closer to its goal.

Yet something else had started working on the creature now, the faint mental beckoning of its brothers that drove the thing due north towards the mountains with the accuracy of an ancient compass. Being a creature of the Weave, it could not help but follow this call. However, it knew it would at some point have to answer the summoning directly and thereby make itself and its position vulnerable to its brothers' ruthless mental probing. Through the discomfort and anger and frustration rising up in the back of the gren-el's brain, it consoled itself with the thought that though the way had been rough-going so far, soon it would open up like the belly of helpless prey.

The gren-el turned and found a way through a deep rocky gully. The walls of stone had fended off the worst of the drifts so the gren-el found it could now lope along at a considerably faster pace. Iron-cord tendons rolled beneath the filthy gray skin while its long gangly arms pumped up and down. Its black nails scraped and rasped against the unyielding ice-coated stone. It braced itself against each wall and leaped from rock to rock with all the savage joy of a prowling cat.

The gully opened up on a frozen stream and here precipitation hung in the air, a thick wet mix of fog and bits of drifting snow. It clung to the thing's skin and tattered clothing and lank hair. The gren-el stopped here a moment and lifted its head, its labored breath hanging in white clouds before its filthy un-muzzled mouth. Snow drifted down heavily. The creature stood still, looking through the gray haze and its glare was no less sharp and cold than the daggers of ice hanging from the edges of the gully itself. It stood a long time, oblivious it would seem to the white coating of snow building up on its head, shoulders, and back and the cold creeping into its bones. Then it closed its eyes and reached out reluctantly with the tendrils of its mind, seeking the call that would drive it across the snow-choked woods in the right direction. It came to him and with that direct connection the thing's thoughts were laid open and it knew the deep humiliation of having its innermost thoughts exposed.

An inquiry came concerning the boy, not so much words in the creature's mind for the gren-el had no use for such things anymore. They communicated through a series of mental sensations, cruel demanding stabs coupled with a slow-burning rage and angry bewilderment. The gren-el answered in kind and recounted its experience. It first sent its brothers the satisfying feel of claws rending through the thick curtain of old tangles, then the painful electrical impulse of sudden and unexpected resistance. The gren-el recalled the pungent stink of an ancient weaver's astonishing power in the target's blood and in the blood of the female creature and the roar of the enraged earth commanded by its mistress bursting up beneath its feet, a considerable feat considering how badly she had been wounded. Further demands and the gren-el yielded the sensation of its claws hammering the ground in pursuit of the escaping target. It gave its brothers the salty sweet taste of goblin blood upon the rocks, spilled there by a sword's slash and the ancient cold odor of the claws of a weaver-born beast gouged across the stone. A dragon it surmised and not without a touch of surprise at the evidence of one still living. The gren-el took pains to add feelings of disgust and frustration at the idiocy and incompetence of the goblins it commanded. It received a less than sympathetic reply, a brief agonizing taste of being unmade, reduced again to its weak and original state and a slow-drawn out death. The scornful gren-el exchanged a mental teeth-baring at this answer, knowing full well that such promises were no more than idle

threats from its brothers and equals. However, it could not deny that at the back of those threats lay the silence of the watchful black eyes of the Beast King, waiting with infinite calm like a fat and hungry spider. While its brothers made empty promises, the eyes had sworn an oath upon the gren-el's head that carried far more deadly weight.

The call of the other gren-els scattered in all directions, seeking the weaver's residue left by the passage of the dragon. One last command traveled to the gren-el to continue to follow the frozen stream and inquire back at a set time. The weaver's trail had been cold for several weeks and now the creature found itself left to its own devices and its gnawing hunger for blood. Its claws scraped against the ice while it continued on relentlessly, almost against its will.

It continued along the stream in silence while minutes turned into hours and eventually it lost track of the time. The snow blew on, now faint and grey with a few winding flakes and then thick and ruthless, bearing down on the thing with stinging bits of ice and severely limiting its vision.

Evening drew near and conditions worsened. The gren-el's lope took on an uneven rhythm while it traveled, brought on by occasionally having to lift its front claw in mid-lope to savagely rub at the buildup of ice forming on its muzzle and in the corners of its eyes. Its mind rang with foul and fearsome curses at the storm.

Suddenly through the relentless snow, it smelled the warmth of living flesh quite close by. The gren-el slowed and stopped, panting while it turned its head to the right and then to the left. A painful sensation of warning, planted in its brain possibly by the call earlier to keep it on task made it hesitate, but only for a moment. Then its rage at being ordered about, its hunger, and its unsatisfied lust for death and destruction caused a slow haze of red across its eyes. It knew then that before it could continue on, the dissonance of its own foul instincts had to be silenced first or it would go mad. A grin split its muzzle, the grin of a demented murderer. Saliva collected in the jowls of its mouth in anticipation.

A dog bayed in the distance. After a moment another dog answered, mingling its howl with the howl of a third. The gren-el slunk forward, past an old wooden fence marking the boundary of a small farm standing some distance away. It moved on its belly, with barely a crunch of ice-crusted snow and then settled in the shadow of a broken-down and long-abandoned chicken coop. Under the gren-el's throat, a broken amulet swung slowly back and forth, a memento of a life forgotten. The creature hadn't stopped grinning. The babble of voices and memories in its brain had reached unbearable levels, a pain that set its blood on fire and yet at the same time, a sweet agony it savored. It had to kill before it started remembering again.

The dogs charged through the snow in a fury, their senses alerting them to something horribly wrong in their surroundings and drawing them to the source. They slowed around the chicken coop and paused before moving forward in intent silence towards the shadows in the back. The hairs on their necks stood straight up and their teeth showed yellow against their pinkish gums. Low growls of rage and suppressed fear escaped from their barrel-like chests while they stared into the darkness.

Only silence greeted their growls. Then the darkness leaped at them with a dripping maw full of curving teeth. Red spilled over the blue-shadowed snow, the red light of a lantern when the door to the farmhouse opened a few minutes later. A sharp whistle pierced the air.

"Roc! Packer! Oto! To me, boys!" bellowed the stocky old man who stepped out from the door. He thrust the lantern further out into the cold air, while flakes swirled about him and settled on the scrub-brush of a beard falling down his chest. The old man glanced about, narrowing his eyes in irritation. He pursed his lips and whistled sharply again, then thumped the side of his door with the butt of his cudgel.

In the loneliness of the forest wilderness, the old man was grateful for the protection of those three fiercely, protective hounds. They had served him well over the years, their fierce loyalty keeping him safe against man or beast.

"Hep! Hep! Git in 'ere, boys wit' your foolishness!! 'Ere now!" he bellowed. He stood there a moment longer, then swore softly and snatched up a cloak to drape about his shoulders. He plunged doggedly out into the snow.

"Hep!" he called, casting his eyes around and then stopped when he heard a soft high-pitched whine. He moved forward towards the chicken coop and then stopped in horror at the sight of what remained of two of his dogs. He beheld one dead and one in the last throes of death, savaged in such a precise way that spoke of no forest beast but of something worse, far worse. He hadn't even heard them yelp.

Irrational fear of the darkness pressing upon him and the prospect of an unknown beast turned the man's spine to ice. He backed off rapidly, nearly stumbling on his backside in the snow. He floundered his way towards the warm glow of the open door some feet away. His hand reached up and touched the door and then he stopped, hearing labored breathing somewhere around him, an animal panting.

"Oto?!" he whispered to the darkness. "'Ere boy..."

Something abruptly dropped in the snow beside him. Almost stupid with terror, he turned quickly and saw, half-buried in a drift beneath a window, what remained of his third dog. The breathing sounded closer now. Snow dropped in white chunks in front of his eyes... disturbed from the roof ledge above him.

He slowly looked up into a red-stained grin framed in a fog of white frozen breath. The gren-el allowed him half a scream. Killing was more enjoyable that way.

Sometime later, drunken with blood and the satisfaction of

mindless destruction, the beast tore the inside of the farmhouse apart. No reason or method dictated the slashing of the curtains, the gouging of the walls, or the smashing of the windows. It followed only a desire to befoul and destroy all remnants of any contentment or peace that had once existed under this homely roof. The gren-el ripped through the food supplies, not even caring to devour anything, just to feel the perverse joy of ruining something. It splintered the wooden legs of a chair with a blow and gnawed at the remaining wood as if it had been a bone. It overturned a table and then the bed and sent them both smashing through separate walls. A swipe of its claw sent cold ashes from the fire scattering across the floor and it had set upon the stone of the fireplace, tearing out the stones themselves when suddenly through the pleasant red silence of its mind, it was interrupted with an urgent summoning.

The gren-el tried to ignore it, beating its claws against the stone and dashing a clay pot on the mantelpiece to the floor; then it paused and its head swiveled towards the door almost without conscious thought. The call compelled it. It was not the call of its brothers this time but something else far more powerful. Its target had come within range again. The gren-el could feel it through the frozen air, smell it, taste it as surely as it tasted the stolen life that dripped red now from its jaws. A mixture of feelings shook the creature's mind; disappointment there had been only the old man and his dogs and yearning to continue its gratifying savagery undisturbed. Then through that churning of impressions, something else cut suddenly down to the very core of its being and a trembling shook its frame, not of fear or weakness, but of eagerness that coursed through its body. So close now. So very close. It couldn't turn away now. It had to strike and strike quickly. With no bumbling goblins to hinder its movements, its way lay clear before it.

Its hunger for destruction had not yet been quenched but less than a few miles away lay a promise of something better; revenge and possession of power... and glorious honor from he who now held the oath of the black eyes upon the creature's head. Knowing it would need all of the darkness seething within its soul to achieve its desires, this time it knowingly called up the madness, the screaming, the pain, the babble of voices, and let that lash it into action. It allowed itself one last massive burst of destruction that rendered the farmhouse completely beyond any hopes of salvaging. It burst out of the door and into the snow and cold, moving through the trees back towards the frozen stream once more. It dimly heard the crash of the smoldering farmhouse collapsing in on itself, turning the creatures sight and its surroundings into a crimson-shifting nightmare world.

It would find the boy. It would find the sword. It had to obey. It had to kill... before the blade fell, before the screaming turned to words and before the empty eyes of the Beast King devoured its mind.

212

the DragonSlayer

Day had turned into evening and evening had deepened far into the night before Thaddeus, sitting on his little stool beside Bean, finally said in a brisk voice, "That's done then! We'll call it a night here, young chap." He closed the book he had been skimming through with a satisfactory slam, raising a wisp of dust from the dry pages.

"Ugh..." grumbled Bean. He rubbed his eyes hard and felt very tired. Looking up from the books, he still thought he could see serpentine strands of letters dancing in front of his vision. "That's terribly fascinating," the dragon mused on. "Granted there are still a few gaps that need to be filled. I don't know that we can fill them, though, but it doesn't mean we're beat yet, Bean."

"Fa...fa...fascinating?" Bean stifled a big yawn and rubbed his face drowsily. "There are a lot of names... I don't know that I understand how they're all supposed to fit together, but... I think there were two swords made, right? Mine and another? Both from one sword.

Both filled with 'unspeakable power', so unspeakable I guess, that no one tries to explain it anywhere." He said the last in a lighter tone of voice, trying a half-hearted attempt at humor. Thaddeus looked over at the boy, lowered a quizzical brow, and did not smile in return. After a moment under Thaddeus's blank gaze, Bean's face dropped and he stared down at his hands instead.

"Correct, my dear young prince," Thaddeus said. "And I believe I actually had the acquaintance of the old fellow who forged each of the blades. They refer to him as Portney in the records, of course. Those are his notes you bundled up only a moment ago. In another lifetime, I knew him as the Tinker."

Bean raised his head. "Well... couldn't we find him, then? Surely he'd be able to tell me how to heal the sword?" he said in a hopeful tone of voice.

"Tinker has been cold in his grave for centuries, lad," Thaddeus said. A sad smile crossed his face. "I fear that we can't be asking him."

Bean looked down at the sword where he had laid it across the table. He rested his hand against the white blade and sat silently for a few minutes. Then a light flickered in his soft blue eyes. "Perhaps the key in the healing lies with the other sword. There's something... I don't know how to explain it, rightly... just a feeling of hunger in the blade. Like I feel someone else's hand trying to pull it away from me," he said. "But that may be nothing... the records never say who had it after this Tinker, if anyone."

"Hm. A face and a name would be terribly helpful." Thaddeus held up several pieces of parchment and studied them for a moment. "My guess though is if someone else does hold the other sword, it'd have to be an elf of some sort or elven kindred. Elves are the only race that can weave their essence into objects and most of the time they're the only ones who can stand such objects for long save for the lost trolls and goblins. Very dangerous and nasty habit is the weaving of souls, oh yes," the little dragon said in disgust.

Thaddeus laid the parchments back down again and tapped the table with his tiny claws. His face grew stern with deep thought. "Yet who.... who has the precious thing? It was only recently that your blade chose you. Eh, but who knows? Perhaps it's only some trick of the weave. The other blade could still be hidden for all we know."

"No... No it's not. There is a face..." Bean said suddenly in a grave voice. "I remember now. I saw him, when I was standing in front of the mirror. That picture in my head... the one that made me so ill. An elf, but I don't know his name. I remember though... he had a sword, a sword with a white blade."

Thaddeus looked over at him and raised a scaly brow. "An elf? I was right, then," he said. He looked very pleased with having guessed correctly.

"Yes sir. His hair was white, too, and he was pale... pale like he'd been ill a long time. His eyes were completely black," Bean's voice lowered and softened. He sounded drowsy as if he were talking in his sleep.

"Pity that doesn't narrow it down more. Lots of elves live around these parts." Thaddeus tapped a claw against his teeth in deep thought. "Though I recall now seeing a small pale elven scab that Tinker had apprenticed to himself shortly before he died but... psht!, he'd have to have been a long-lived scab if it was the same fellow."

He paused and shook his head. "No, it couldn't have been. That was a long while gone even by dragon standards. Maybe he could have been a descendant... or if Tinker had hidden the sword away, perhaps it could have been no more than someone who had stumbled onto it." Thaddeus began shuffling eagerly through the papers again. "Maybe a clue in Portney's diary would tell us something. Where'd I put it now? Bean, my dear boy how about you look

216

over..."

Thaddeus glanced over and saw that the poor, tired boy had folded his arms and rested his head on the table. His eyes were closed. The little dragon smiled and nudged the boy. "Here now lad, rouse yourself up a bit and let's get you to bed," the dragon said cheerfully. "I had forgotten you're not like us dragons that can go for days on end without sleep." Bean came slowly awake, blinking awkwardly. He rubbed his face and yawned again.

"Yes sir," the boy mumbled and pushed himself away from the table. The table shifted hard to the right and a tower of books near the edge of the table promptly tipped over, sliding across the floor like a deck of scattered playing cards. They knocked over several dusty leather-bound volumes stacked up untidily on a free-standing column nearby.

"Argh..." Bean gasped, suddenly wide-awake and very embarrassed. "I'm sorry, sir! Here... let me help."

"Oh, careful lad! Some of these fables are older than the fathers of the White Hall!" Thaddeus cried and scuttled anxiously over to the scattered books. He reached down and started to gather them in his arms.

The boy crossed quickly around the table and started picking up as many books as he could. As he picked up one of the volumes that had been stacked up on the column, the pages flapped open to spidery thin writing and a delicate etching that caught Bean's attention. He stopped a minute, laid down the other books, and stared down at the picture.

The dark-haired young lord, horribly wounded and burned, lay dead across a rocky landscape with his eyes closed and his sword shattered at his feet. A huge old dragon, also mortally wounded it seemed, had its head raised and its mouth half-opened in what might have been a snarl if not for the stylized curlicues of steaming black pouring from its mouth and eyes, snaking around the dead man.

Poison perhaps. There appeared to be words following along the symbolic black path, if the intricate dashes and whorls could truly be called words and not decoration. They had an intelligent feel of language about them though, grouped together in even intervals.

As Bean stared at them, they seemed to take on life and writhe serpentine-like across the paper. Off to the side, a smaller dragon crouched defensively, the old one's whelp, Bean guessed. With a start he realized the whelp looked exactly like Brutus. The words flowing in the smoldering black called to his attention again. He stared and at the edge of his hearing, he thought he heard a sibilant hissing and murmur.

The book suddenly snapped shut in front of his eyes of its own accord. Bean's gaze darted up to meet Thaddeus's cool stare. The dragon placed a small clawed hand upon the face of the book and silently pulled it towards him. Bean shifted backwards and tensed.

"The picture... the young dragon... he looked ...," the boy said and his voice sounded strange and awkward in the silence that had fallen around them. A fog of unvoiced questions began to gather, thick and fast, in the space between himself and the small dragon.

"Some things, my young man, are best left for other times," Thaddeus said. "You must trust me in this matter. Do you trust me?" His eyes remained fixed on the Bean.

Bean held his silence while he considered the question. Finally the boy crossed his legs, folded his hands, and looked at the dragon. The grave expression of a relaxed but alert warrior hardened Bean's young features. "Until you give me a reason not to, sir... yes I trust you," he replied in a level voice.

"Spoken like a brave young lord, Bean," said Thaddeus. The little dragon sat back on his haunches and adjusted his spectacles. He let out a long sigh. "Now... perhaps 'tis best we call it a night, shall we? I can see the weariness in your face. Come now... let's get these books up and take you back to your room. Then you can get some sleep. No more doubts and worries about old tales and dusty books." The picture had made the boy intensely curious and suspicious as well, but at the moment he wasn't about to argue and dutifully helped the dragon clean up before walking with him out the door.

Going back to Bean's room, Thaddeus seemed preoccupied and not inclined to chatter. In silence they walked down the shadowey corridors, past the tapestries and the doorway that led to the statue of the young lord. His pale woven face in the tapestries coupled with Thaddeus's thoughtful silence made it even more disquieting. Bean reminded himself that he had said he would trust Thaddeus unless he proved distrustful and did nothing to break the silence between them until they had reached his chamber. Yet the questions nagged at him and would not leave him in peace.

Who was the man? Had the young dragon been Brutus? What had happened so long ago that now dragons ruled this hall? Bean pondered the possibilities, as he watched the little dragon walking ahead of him. None of them set him at ease.

As he expected, his nightclothes had been laid out on the bed with a little mug of warm chamomile tea waiting on the table beside the chair. Bean shrugged the sword off his shoulder, and headed straight for the chair, resting it within hand's reach. With a sigh he climbed up into it, settled back, and sipped at the tea.

"Thaddeus?" he asked. Thaddeus looked up at the boy.

"Yes, my boy?" he asked in a puzzled tone of voice

"Did you kill the lord of this hall?" The boy met the dragon's gaze. His young eyes, clear and unafraid, looked for the soul behind those reptilian eyes and tried to see what sort of creature he had said he would trust.

"You cannot have killed yourself if you're still alive and walking, lad." the dragon answered in a weary voice. Bean saw pain and shame fill those reptilian eyes and for a moment they almost looked human. "You're asking me a hard thing, lad. It's not something I wish to talk about, but yes, I was that young lord and now, through a sore curse, I'm a dragon. There's not much more to it." He sighed.

"You killed dragons then?"

"Bean, did I not ask you to trust me? Then you need to do so. Who I was, that doesn't matter anymore. What matters is who I am now. I don't wish to chatter on about those things, long gone and unable to be changed. Do you understand, lad?" His voice softened, "I need you to understand these things, Bean. I need you to." Bean felt the unspoken ache in the dragon's voice, an ache the boy realized he had unwittingly caused.

"I am sorry sir," the boy said humbly and lowered his eyes. "I was only curious. I did not mean to hurt you."

A sad smile twitched at the corners of Thaddeus's mouth. "And it was many a soul I never meant to hurt either," he said. "We never mean to. However, it cannot be changed and dark days have passed and gone. Now it is present and I have been blessed with a great gift and what is it, you ask? 'Tis life, says I and another chance to help someone else to live right. It's something to cherish, Bean. If all you learn from me is that and not another thing, then you will still live well."

Bean felt an odd chill and held the cup tighter to him. He let the remark pass without further comment and the dragon appeared to be lost in his own thoughts for the moment.

"It's late, young fellow," he finally said. "You'll need to be up early tomorrow morning if we're going to get you where you need to go." The little creature abruptly hopped off the ottoman and made his way towards the door.

"Sir?" Bean asked just as he got to the door. He wanted to ask so many things now: what kind of curse? How had it happened? Yet he thought of Thaddeus's words and the look on the little dragon's face and his own words failed him.

The little dragon waited a moment and then shook his head. "Off to bed now, chap, and get some shut-eye. It will be a grand day tomorrow, you'll need the rest," he said in a kindly voice and with that and a nod, he shut the door.

The high-ceilinged halls echoed thinly with the tapping of Thaddeus's tiny claws against the bare stone floor. The little dragon did not walk with his usual bristling energy, but rather walked as one with a heavy burden on his shoulders. It was in some way a relief to speak to someone else about his past, even if it was no more than a few cryptic words spoken to a boy who couldn't understand the full story anyway. He turned down a corridor and headed into the older part of his home.

The further he walked the more evidence showed a general neglect and damage. Suits of ceremonial armor had been dislodged from their alcoves, sprawled like wounded soldiers on the battlefield. Many of the windows had been shattered and the pieces lay on the floor. Furniture sat quietly in odd corners, collecting dust. A few of the more ornate pieces had suffered damage some ages ago and sat lopsided on the floor, putting the casual observer in mind of wizened old lords trying to keep their dignities even while bodies and minds wasted away.

From the empty windows, a chill breeze blew the ghosts of remaining drapes and small flakes of snow occasionally drifted

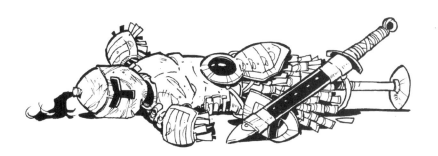

past Thaddeus. He barely noticed the cold for as a dragon he had a unique method of internal warmth. However, he did notice when she silently joined him. Her bare pale feet had made no sound when they touched the floor... but he knew when she came and he knew when she left. It was the way things had been between the two of them for centuries.

"He's a brave young fellow," Thaddeus said to the darkened hall. "He shows promise."

"Yes. He has a sure, strong hand and a clear eye, both good qualities of a young warrior."

She spoke in the voice of a cultured young woman. In the blue moonlight shining from the high windows, she looked the same as her voice; a pale noblewoman in her late teens with dark eyes and long dark brown hair falling softly down her shoulders and her back, touching her feet. In her yellow gown with lace at the high collar and sleeves, she looked like a young woman lately risen from her sickbed and wandering in a feverish dream.

"Provided he has learned what he needs to learn, there will come an hour of direst need that will call to him and none else. He will wield the sword then, with courage and honor, I am sure," she added. When she spoke, a sound chimed in the back of her words, silver afterthoughts that split her voice into strange fragile echoes of itself.

Thaddeus nodded absently. "It was grand for a while to have a warm voice to talk to," he said, with more than a hint of wistfulness. "The lad will move on and it'll be silent again in this old place."

"And myself a mere sighing of the breeze then, Thaddeus?" A tone of impish teasing came into her voice and her face wore a slight smile. "We talk all the time as I recall," she continued.

The corners of the little dragon's mouth quirked up in sudden humor. "You beauty. We do indeed, Madlynn. Ah, but I'm chattering again, words not worth a tinker's curse," he answered and then looked back at her, cocking his head in mild and perhaps morose curiosity. "And what are you, lass... I wonder myself sometimes. Maybe you're someone I knew once in a different life. Maybe you're just me drunken with old dwarven brandy and gabbing on with myself. Am I right, am I wrong?"

The young woman walked between the shafts of shadow and light towards him and another rather unsettling oddness showed itself, for when she stepped in the shadows, she all but vanished completely. She smiled, turned her head in a childish sort of way and bent down to Thaddeus's level to look at him.

"You've always known me, Thaddeus, but now I'm just what's there in the quiet hours. Sometimes we just need someone to talk to, to be there, and to listen. It isn't important exactly how it happens, it just does. So it's all right," she answered.

The little dragon nodded slightly and turned and kept walking. "Still one might question oneself when one chatters on to the emptiness and one day it starts talking back," he said philosophically.

"Only if it was truly empty to begin with," she answered. She walked after him and caught up to him with little effort. The thin echoes of her words broke delicately like spun glass snowflakes and drifted to the floor, leaving shining trails behind that quickly faded. "I never left, Thaddeus. Not really," she said. "You remember when we were small and how you were never rid of me then? I was practically your shadow. I still am. So it doesn't matter."

Thaddeus mused over her words for a while and then sighed. "I still wish I had done something before, my dear. Paid more attention to you and everyone else maybe, rather than indulging in my anger. That's my everlasting shame. But yes, you're right, it doesn't really matter now, it's all over."

She smiled while they walked down the hall, walking through the shafts of light and darkness, now real and a little more than shadow herself. "You made up for that and so many other things a long, long time ago. Look at what you have accomplished. You keep the ideals of the order alive; you still stand watch when there are few left to do so. You remember the reasons the order was founded... it is you that still keeps your family alive.... Thaddeus, you needn't be ashamed. You're the only one who's still holding on to that."

Thaddeus didn't seem very reassured. "Animals have no shame, lass. Humans do. Maybe I hold to that because I've gotten to this state to keep from forgetting what I used to be. Perhaps that's why I hang on to such memories, unpleasant as they might be," the little dragon said in a gloomy voice.

"Oh Thad, don't be such a rube. You're awfully dreary to-night."

"You cannot expect me to always stay cheerful about being a dragon for the rest of my natural born days," Thaddeus muttered and plodded on.

His young companion pondered this a moment and then a tiny sad smile crossed her face again. A hand little more than the weight of a feather brushed across Thaddeus's forehead. Thaddeus stopped.

"It's all right to let go of our old selves, Thaddeus," she said softly. "It's hard. It can be frightening. But when we let go, we can then move on. You told me that once and then I wasn't afraid anymore. Do you remember?"

The dragon's smile mirrored hers. "I'll only remember if you tell me, lass. So help me, if you will?"

"I will. I'll sing the song, too. The one about the butterflies that you love so much," she whispered.

"I'd like that very much, Madlynn," Thaddeus answered. They walked on down the corridor, the dragon and the girl in the quiet night and her little voice echoed around the walls. If her words were nothing more than a whisper of flowing drapes or the patter of snow against the window panes still left, it didn't seem to be worth fretting over. After a while of talking though, she began to sing and while she did, Thaddeus's heart felt lighter and he allowed himself some peace of mind. Perhaps indeed, it really wasn't so important how exactly it happened but only that it brought contentment for a while.

Long after she had fallen quiet and slipped off, long after he had walked in the silence of his own thoughts until he had finally come to his personal chambers, long after all of that had passed, he curled up that night in the old overstuffed chair in the corner of the sparse chamber, closed his eyes, and could still hear her and the other voices of kindred long gone speaking to him and singing softly. The little dragon, after consideration, decided that he could live with such small memories as these. His dreams, though they couldn't be called completely happy, still were able to comfort him for the rest of the night.

Back to the Wood

Bean pulled the beautiful dark traveling cloak tighter around his shoulders and breathed in deeply while he stood waiting on the platform outside of Thaddeus's castle with his gloved hands resting on the pommel of his sword. The air, so thin and bitterly cold, made him slightly light-headed but at the same time it seemed to heighten and sharpen his senses. Beyond the castle, the crisp outlines of the blue-hearted clouds drifted on the edge of the solid world and the silhouetted peaks of mountains leisurely appeared and disappeared. The scene lent itself to the image of a white-capped sea upon which the sails of marvelous ships could be glimpsed. A wind picked up and gusted past the boy, stirring a wildness in his bones, and the boy tapped his pinky finger idly against the grip of the sword. He felt strength running from the blade into his hands and into his blood and felt for a moment, the weight of the sword's heritage upon his shoulders. The presence of the elven king had never seemed closer. Bean let his thoughts lose themselves in the depths of this strange un-worldly sea stretched out before him. In the stillness of his ponderings, he knew himself to be the commander of his own fate and felt himself well near invincible. He felt strong and healthy, his wounds now old scars. Thaddeus's care had been exceptional. He tilted his head back a little and gazed up into a sky painted a rich cobalt blue, a color he had seen nowhere else save for here upon the snow-capped brows of the stern mountains.

"Here we are, lad. All set to take flight?" said a voice behind him.

Bean's head swiveled quickly and he looked down at the small dragon standing there with a pack stuffed to bursting and a water-skin under one arm. A quick exhaled breath whistled past the boy's teeth, the only indication he had been startled and his hands relaxed once more. A faint smile crossed his face.

"I don't know where you get the talent to get right up beside someone without them knowing it, sir, but I wish I could do that," the boy remarked in frank admiration. Thaddeus waved the compliment away and dropped the sack and water-skin to the ground.

"Tsht. Here now, pick up your packet and water. Brutus'll be here any moment," the little dragon said. "There are dried fruits and cured meats in there, plus some cheese wrapped up in brown paper and a few small almond-cakes. That and freshwater streams ought to hold you until you get where you need to go, but if not, your guide knows well enough how to find what you need in the wilderness. She's one of the best, an old friend, and very trustworthy. Here..."

He motioned the boy down and handed him a cloth belt and a rolled-up bit of parchment with a wax seal on it. "Tie that belt around your waist. Got jade bits sewn in the inside lining. It's not much but best to keep it inconspicuous, should you have need of it. You never know. Also..." He pointed to the parchment. "That'll be your proof of good faith to give the young king so tuck it away somewhere where you shan't lose it."

Bean sheathed the sword, took the belt, and tied it around

his waist. He tucked the parchment away in the side of his boot and hefted the sack and the water-skin on his shoulders underneath his cloak. He absently rubbed the fine cloth while he adjusted it over his shoulders again and felt awkward and a bit of guilt for accepting all these beautiful gifts, weighing heavier on him than the items themselves.

"Thank you sir," he said. "I don't know if I could ever repay you for all this... the food, the kindness, the clothes, and everything." "Bah! The food you'll need, the kindness will pay itself when you do what you need to do and send the warning on to those who need to hear it. As for the clothes... well a prince should dress like a prince not a poor bedraggled washer of dishes."

Bean felt very self-conscious. "That's all I've known how to do, sir," he said, fidgeting with the gloves on his hand. "I don't know that I'm anything beyond that, truthfully..."

Thaddeus got a very keen look in his eye and his expression grew stern. "Upon my word! Don't ever say that! There's no dirty dishwater running through your veins, I'm thinking, but blood as blue and royal as the sky over our heads. Do you think a sword with that kind of heritage would have anything less than the hands of a prince to wield it? Pff. Get those daft ideas out of your head, they're not worth a docken."

A quizzical look crossed Bean's face at Thaddeus's pointed remarks. The little dragon drew himself up to his full height and added. "One is born to the crown and trained for it. Act like a prince and the rest comes easy. You're a brave lad with a good heart, it's only natural to be modest and well... your rough upbringing as it was in the wilds of Darkleaf with only brutish old ogres as your models... I suppose taught you humility better than most. I dare say, however, that you have an advantage most royalty do not, my dear young fellow."

"Knowing how to balance a stack of pots taller than me?" asked Bean wryly as he grinned.

The dragon was taken aback for a moment and then chuckled and shook his head.

"Ta, you're one clever, little chap. I was going to say you understand the worth of hard work. That and a song will take you far, as my father used to say. But here now, lift up your chin a bit. If you'd but hold your own self-worth a tad dearer than you have before, I daresay you'd surpass the greatness of even the elven lord who once held that blade. Am I right, am I wrong?"

Bean nodded with some hesitation. "Right about some of it, but the rest I'll need to think over, sir," he remarked. Truth be told, Bean couldn't say he agreed wholeheartedly with anything the dragon had said. Nevertheless, he did admit feeling a growing sense of quiet honor and confidence outside of what he had experienced in the thralls of the sword's power. He finally felt he could find a place in this world for himself, a place and a purpose. Also he had to admit being called a prince gave him a rather nice feeling of pride, regardless of whether or not he agreed with the title, but perhaps as Thaddeus said, one could grow into it.

"Well then..." Thaddeus nodded and continued on in a brisk tone of voice. "Brutus will have to drop you a ways beyond the settlements. Dragons would not be a welcome sight and I'd not like to see my old friend harassed by ignorant farmers. When you land, Otter should be there to meet you and take you on past the forgotten roads. She's one of the Helixshire so mind your manners and be quick to listen and react when she tells you to. Don't worry, Brutus will keep an eye on you if she's not there right away. I wouldn't dare think of dropping you off and leaving you alone. Since no-one but a few traders make their way through that part and in this weather I doubt there'll be anyone out at all. Still mind yourself and mind who you talk to as well, lad."

Bean nodded absently and then heard the rich powerful bell of Brutus's voice echo across the peaks. The figure of the majestic dragon rose then above the clouds, his powerful wings sculling through the mists. He moved purposefully towards Thaddeus and Bean. Bean felt a tug on the side of his trousers and glanced down at the smaller dragon.

"Kneel down here, young fellow. I can't talk to your knees," Thaddeus remarked. Bean did so and the little dragon clasped him about the elbow and gave his arm a hearty shake.

"My last bit of advice for you, Bean," he said in a solemn voice. "Be wary of what you possess for it belongs mostly to itself. It has chosen to bind itself to you and that could be a dangerous combination. I don't fully know what it is capable of doing but beware of its influence over you. It will grow stronger the closer it comes to its other half. Mind also that it seeks wholeness at the price of your free will. Our own light can blind us, Bean, so be careful."

Bean smiled faintly and for a moment he looked years older. "I will, sir, I promise."

"I know you will. You're a good young chap. Remember that."

Bean nodded, stood up again, and adjusted the pack on his shoulder. Brutus circled twice around the castle and swept his wings mightily through the air, causing gales of swirling loose snow to curl and spread across the platform as the magnificent beast alighted on the stone. Bean felt the ground tremble slightly while Brutus lumbered towards them. The dragon lowered his head and gazed at Bean a moment. He turned his head inquisitively as he laid his massive clawed hand on the stone in front of Bean, made a deep friendly

noise in his throat which sounded like "HURRF!" and waited for
the boy to climb into his hand. His warm breath swept Bean's hair
back from his forehead and the boy hesitated a moment. While it
was a relief to be leaving a place of his own free will without goblins
or beasts at his heels, he still felt a great reluctance. For all its myste-
riousness, Bean had felt a bit of peace and relaxation while here with
the dragons. The boy felt terribly sad at the thought of corridors left
unexplored, books left unread, and talks around the fireplace that he
would never hear.

Bean gave a soft sigh, laid his hand on the beast's curved claw,
and stepped up into the broad warm palm, only to sit down hard
when the dragon abruptly lifted him up in the air.

"Good-bye lad, do come back and visit when it's all over and
done. I have always enjoyed visitors!" he heard Thaddeus call below
him.

Brutus closed his other clawed hand over the boy, spread his wings, and crouched before he leaped into the air, arching his massive body with power and surprising grace as he rapidly gained altitude. Bean felt his stomach drop into his toes and turned his head so he could see out of the cracks between the dragon's claws. The sea of clouds and the great unknown lay before him. The boy still felt sadness heavy on his heart, but seeing the peaks of the mountains passing beneath him, he was also aware of a growing thrill of adventure as he wondered where his path might take him next. It comforted him somewhat.

Thaddeus watched the figure of Brutus navigate the mountains and vanish in the mists. The little dragon rubbed his scaly chin thoughtfully and turned his eyes towards his castle once again. Something had gone with the boy, something he had rather enjoyed while it was still here, something he wasn't sure he'd ever have the pleasure of seeing again despite his cheerful admonition for Bean to come back and visit. Having another person to talk to had brought the dragon a few weeks of contentment and happiness. Now the corridors looked emptier and the silence seemed deeper than ever.

"The next thousand years are going to go by a lot slower methinks," Thaddeus said moodily to himself.

"It will be fine Thaddeus," said a little voice near his head. "He will be all right and so will you. Be at peace."

"I know, lass. Some part of me knows. It doesn't make the sadness any less though," he murmured.

A hand rested on his shoulder and he sensed her smiling gently at him. He looked back towards where Brutus and Bean had vanished and a half-smile touched his reptilian face.

"All the fortune in the world go with you lad," he said. It was growing colder now. He turned away to go back inside the castle and the wind whispered around the ramparts and blew across his shoulders.

Otter

With his mind clear of pain and fever, Bean better appreciated the flight this time around, though the area of sight regrettably hadn't improved that much because of the position of the dragon's claws and the dim morning light. At first, the boy dared not move since being in the clutches of a real live dragon had to be unnerving enough, without being miles up in the air as well. Gradually though, the dawn's extraordinary light touched the curved edges of Brutus's claws, a golden light tinted with rose. Garnering a little courage, Bean shuffled around until he found a gap where he could comfortably rest most of his face. He peered out at the frothy sea of thick white mist and felt the bitter air blow past his face. The growing light edged the clouds and made them look like a surreal scene of fiery coals. In the deep silence only the leathery flap of Brutus's wings and the noisy huff of his exhaled breath could be heard. Bean watched the clouds pass and thought of nothing in particular. The peaceful and quiet atmosphere did not lend itself to any sort of deep pondering.

He spent most of the day curled up in the warm dim curve of Brutus's clawed hands, sometimes moving enough to look out at the clouds, sometimes lying on his back and turning things over in his head. He found he missed the interesting books and the little oddities he would find on the nightstand or by the table. Regrettably he'd never know now who had done all that for him. Most of all, he missed the conversations with Thaddeus.

Bean wondered about this mysterious traveling companion that was to meet him. A Helixshire, Thaddeus had said, by the name of Otter. The name of Helixshire was not unfamiliar to Bean. He had once waited on a table of elven merchants passing through on their way to larger cities and he remembered hearing them speak of these others of their race. The way that they had talked of the Helixshires led Bean to believe that elves as a rule half feared them and half worshiped them. Before he could hear more, Ravna had called him over to help her with this and that, then Groggle had needed him in the kitchen, and finally Gort had yelled at him about something or other. By the time he had been able to find a moment's breathing space, the elves had already gone their way, leaving the boy to clean up their leftovers, which had hardly been magical or wondrous for all the first impressions they had left on the boy upon walking through the door. When he had later asked Siv about them, the barkeep had only shrugged and suggested with a wry smile that Bean, with all his eluding of Gort in the ogre's moments of wrath, could put a Helixshire to shame. Bean had felt quite proud of himself until he realized Siv had been teasing him and had then sulked with the barkeep for the rest of the day.

Bean dug into a pocket, pulled out a length of string he had remembered to tuck away before leaving and idly began fiddling with it. At some point between making an elf's-ladder with the string and feeling lonely, Bean dozed off.

He startled into wakefulness when he felt the dragon's claws shift quickly. He clutched at the nearest finger and felt a sudden drop in his stomach while Brutus changed direction and swerved towards the ground. He pulled himself to the gap and rested his chin against the dragon's warm leathery skin. The boy gazed down, seeing the clouds dissolve before his eyes and the dark scrubby tops of the trees rising up to meet him with alarming speed. The air beating against his face took his breath with its coldness. The perspective swung around far too rapidly for his taste at this point so he closed his eyes and clung tighter to Brutus's claws while the dragon, rumbling happily, spiraled in for a landing.

Right at the edge of the treetops, Brutus's claws opened and he took the boy in his mouth as gently as a cat with a kitten. He opened his wings wider and glided into an open area. The dragon landed with a mighty swipe of his huge wings that made a white spray of snow leap up against the black tree trunks and shook snow and icicles from the branches. He lowered his head and dropped Bean unceremoniously into the snow.

The boy scrambled to his feet, which was not an easy task since the snow almost reached his stomach. He brushed himself off and peered through the trees. Not far away lay an open stretch of ground covered in gleaming white snow. A silent figure stood there, concealed in a dark green cloak that rippled in the breeze over the white ground. The stranger pulled the hood back to reveal the dark olive-brown face of a beautiful but stern-looking elven woman. She walked towards them in a calm and easy manner. In height she stood a little taller than Bean and her pale hair floated behind her.

The shadow of Brutus loomed over Bean and the big dragon nudged him in the small of his back, nearly knocking him on his knees again. "What?" he asked, turning to the dragon. Brutus rested his enormous head on the ground, closed his eyes, and rumbled at the boy while he waited and watched the elf approach.

"Well hello Brutus," the elf said when she reached the two of

them. She took off one of her gloves and laid her hand on the dragon's jowl. She patted it and lightly scratched the scaly skin. "Dhaua, dhaua it is so good to see you, cousin. It seems Thaddeus has been feeding you well." The dragon's snort had a tone of amusement in it and he slowly turned his head, enjoying the attention.

Bean stared in wonderment at the beautiful elven lady, wooing the huge beast as it swayed its head and closed its eyes in utter contentment. At first glance, she hadn't looked too dangerous but the boy considered that she had an enormous dragon practically eating out of her hand right in front of him. That made quite an impression.

The elf glanced at the boy. When she smiled, her plum-colored lips stretched thinly over gleaming white teeth. It didn't exactly feel like a friendly smile, more a formality.

"Young man, we haven't much time to stand about and stare. You need to go ahead and say your goodbyes. I wouldn't think you would want to offend him. Dragons are funny like that," she said. An uncertain look crossed the boy's face. He turned to the dragon and hesitated a minute, flexing his hand and tightening it into a nervous ball. Then he reached out and laid his hand on the dragon's snout and patted it. Brutus snorted again and moved his nose against the boy's hand. Bean's eyes brightened and he gave the dragon's nose a good scratching, all the while thinking to himself that this was something he'd be telling them back at the Inn and he knew they'd never believe it. Brutus's pleased rumbling ran through the ground beneath Bean's feet and made more snow fall off the branches around them.

Then the dragon abruptly moved his head, turning it so that Bean could see himself in the curve of the big fellow's enormous eye. He blinked slowly at the boy and moved his head back a little and gave Bean a very wise stare that made the boy momentarily forget that he had been scratching the dragon's nose like he was a friendly old cat just a few moments ago. His blue, bearded throat swelled and a musical noise began deep in the back of his throat. It grew and grew, not so much in loudness but more in depth and richness and Bean stood transfixed to the ground, feeling the strange power of the music running through his blood. The world around him grew blue and hazy and he thought for a moment he saw the white glowing life coursing through the black trunks of the trees. The music stirred up feelings of comfort and courage in the boy. Still singing to himself (singing being the best way Bean could think to describe it) Brutus lifted his head, turned and took a few steps before leaping lightly into the air. The back draft of his wings dropped the rest of the snow off the tree branches and fanned halos of ice across the ground, leaving the boy and the elf alone as he sailed off into the sky. After the magnificent creature had vanished into the gray sky, long after the singing had faded into the distance, Bean still stood there, lost in the memory of that singularly amazing moment. He fancied he still heard that music in his head and his bones

"So... what do we have here?" the elf said, breaking into his daydream. "Turn around here, boy." Bean turned and she folded her arms and studied him closely. Bean stood very still for a good few minutes under her sharp gaze. When the cold and her stare had gone past the point of comfort for him, she finally lowered her eyelids and made a unimpressed noise in her throat. She snapped her fingers in the direction of the open ground beyond the woods. "Start walking and keep up with me," she said and they set off over the snow.

They hadn't gone more than a few footsteps when she broke the silence again.

"Thaddeus said that you were a half-elf," she remarked.

"Yes ma'am." Bean glanced down at his hands. He didn't know he liked the tone of her voice. It felt like an accusation.

"You have an important responsibility, a mission if you will, placed on your shoulders," the elf went on. "You carry a special sword, he said."

"Yes ma'am."

The elf stopped at the edge of the trees and looked closely at him again. "What is your name, half-elf? What is this sword you carry?" she asked.

Bean looked back at the elf. She had the most extraordinary dark blue eyes, the color of the cobalt sky over Thaddeus's castle. He felt that penetrating stare go through his head, demanding the truth from him. "My name is Bean. The sword once belonged to Ganadon, an elven king of long ago," he replied.

Otter said nothing for a long moment. She held him in her relentless gaze, standing completely at ease in the snow. "Prove it," she finally said.

"Ma'am?" A bewildered look crossed the boy's face.

"Prove your claim about this sword. Show it to me," the elf said. "My house clan knows the signets of the old king. A false sword would not have them."

Bean thought a moment, then shrugged off his cloak and pack and pulled the sword from the sheath. He held it out towards her, meaning to give it to her to examine. However the elf made no motion to take it. Her eyes ran sharply over the white blade and the stone, studying it.

"Lhai-dhu ama Ganadon... ama soi, ama?" she murmured suddenly and her eyes narrowed.

"What?" Bean asked. The elf waved his question away.

"Nothing. I asked a question. It seems I received an answer of sorts. That is all, Bean," she said evenly. She took a deep breath, frowned, then turned away and started out across the open ground. Bean stood there for a minute and then hastily sheathed the sword, threw back on his cloak and pack and trudged off after her.

He caught up with her after a few minutes and heard her muttering under her breath, "...dangerous position.... meddlesome dragon, what were you thinking, Thaddeus? A civil war? And knowing the position of the Helixshires, knowing I cannot possibly..."

"Ma'am?" Bean said in a breathless voice and the elf went silent. "I'm sorry.... did I do something wrong? I mean are you..." He cut himself short and a helpless look crossed his face as his courage retreated. "Ma'am... you walk t-too fast for me," he finally said.

She slowed her pace and looked down at the Bean. Her lips thinned in exasperation.

"Listen well, young man. We will set the record straight here," she began. "First of all you will not divulge your mission to anyone. Understand?"

Bean nodded.

"You need to realize that my duty to you is no longer sealed by the word of a dragon but by the honor of my clan and by the oath of an old friend. There is more to that weapon than you realize, if it is indeed the weapon of an elven king," she continued.

"Yes ma'am... I mean... yes, I know. Back in the swamps I... urgh!" A drift suddenly swallowed the boy up to his armpits. He floundered about and tried to push his way through the snow with little success. The elf stopped in her tracks and made her way back towards him. She waded into the snow and grabbed his wrists.

"What I meant... t-to say... I have fought with it b-before... ma'am..." Bean offered hopefully while she dragged him forward

through the deep snow and got him back on his feet. He brushed the snow off and adjusted himself. The elf stood in front of him, her hand on her hip and a bemused expression on her face.

"Sword or not, I can look at you and tell you are no knight," she remarked. "You are entirely too trusting for one thing. You were ready to give that sword to me and here you have yet to ask me my name."

"Well.... Brutus was friendly enough towards you. I didn't suppose you meant me any harm. And I errr... know your name already, ma'am. It's Otter, isn't it?" Bean said.

Otter nodded and waved her hand. "It is." She snorted and shook her head and continued on. "Though the words of a stranger hardly mean anything in a world where truth and loyalties can be bought and sold for little more than a glass bit."

"Thaddeus said you were trustworthy. I trust you, ma'am," Bean said in a humble voice.

"Hm! Did he now?" Otter replied. "I always did think him a bit hasty in his judgments."

Bean, utterly befuddled at this point, stared at the elf while they walked and wondered what kind of traveling companion he had fallen in with. She glanced over at him and smiled her tight smile again and shrugged her shoulders. "If it is any reassurance to you; yes, I will lead you true and yes, I am honest. However, the earlier you learn to be cynical, the better. That way, the world will never surprise you," she said.

Bean did not reply but instead listened while the elf went on, "For whatever reasons, Thaddeus felt it important to send you into the fire so it is my responsibility to protect you and that I will. You will listen only to me and you will act when you are told to do so. I never repeat myself. I do not allow fools and insurgents that luxury. Do you understand?"

"Yes ma'am." Bean tried his best to keep the grudging tone

from his voice. He found himself not liking his new situation very much but it didn't seem he could do anything about it. Otter turned her gaze to the sky and he heard her mutter under her breath, "By the broken moon, that is all we need now... ghosts returning."

Bean didn't know what she meant by that cryptic comment but decided not to inquire further. Instead he held his silence and lagged behind the elf while they trudged across the open ground. The late afternoon light washed the pristine whiteness with overtones of gray but it seemed to the boy that the day had already gone on much longer than it should.

In the far distance, what looked like an old stone column briefly rose above the curve of the hill, marking the crossroads and a clearer road to travel on or so Bean hoped. About that time, fat white flakes landed on the back of the boy's hand. He looked up at the gray sky only to see several more drifting down towards them.

"Are you coming or are you going to stand there gawking?" he heard Otter say impatiently. He turned his attention back to her only to see her standing some feet away. Without another word she turned away and kept walking. The boy gave a noisy sigh while the snowflakes danced around his shoulders and thought to himself that he should have known it wasn't going to be that easy. He set his sights back on the tip of the stone marker in the distance and grimly set off after the elf who was clearing a path north through the snow and had almost disappeared completely from his view.

246

an Unexpected Ride

Several hours later they found themselves at last stepping through more reasonable levels of snow-drifts. Bean puffed and huffed his way up a low hill to stand by the side of the great stone marker and look down at the crossroads below him. He looked sideways at the elf, who had already started making her way down to the roads. She had driven him hard, never stopping and barely glancing back at him. Bean frowned in frustration.

"Ma'am…" he said in a small despairing voice. He leaned against the marker to catch his breath. Otter stopped in her tracks and looked up at the tired boy with his heavy load. She raised an eyebrow, sighed, shook her head, and walked back up to the marker.

"Rest then, but only for a moment," she said.

Bean felt almost stupid with relief to hear those words. He took his gloves off a moment to blow warmth into his numbed fingers and rubbed his hands across his face which was already flushed bright red from the cold and exertion. He brushed himself off and kicked snow off the heels of his boots. Then he dropped his gear at the foot of the stone marker and sat down on it. The temperature felt like it had fallen another couple of degrees and he slipped his gloves back on. The cold did not seem to affect the elf at all. She stood quite still while the snow fell and kept her eyes fixed on the roads with a thoughtful detached expression on her face, looking for all the world as if she were enjoying a breezy summer's day. Bean recalled Siv telling him tales of poor souls trapped on lonely roads by the snow out deep in the woods during the long months of winter where no one would find them until spring thaw. He quickly put those thoughts out of his head.

Bean raised his gloved hand and studied his fingers, thinking back to when he had placed them on the stone hand in Ganadon's tomb deep beneath the mad Collector's lair. He could still feel the cold stone beneath his fingers.

He shivered, then got up, and started pacing again. His mind turned to the Silver Dagger and he wondered if anyone had ever bothered to come looking for him. He tried to calculate in his head how many days or months or years it had been and to his mild surprise, found it to be considerably shorter than he had realized. It seemed unreal that washing dishes at the Silver Dagger felt like it had happened years ago. He rubbed his hands, sat down again, and thought of Groggle and Ravna, Siv and Gort, and the regulars who had come day in and day out of the little Inn. He remembered how bored he had been, how he had longed for the adventure of far away places, and now here he sat out in a lonely gray world with his back to cold stone while the shadows of evening crept into the horizon and snowflakes danced about his head.

He found he missed the Dagger terribly. He longed to be back there again, but now he had made a promise, for all he understood of how to keep it.

At that moment the boy raised his head, hearing off in the distance the sound of a whip crack and a rough hoarse voice barking something loudly amidst the squeaking of rusty wheels and the groan and grumble of some poor over-laden beast. Bean stood up and craned his neck. Otter already had her sword drawn and stood alert with her eyes on the roads.

A great dark shadow appeared on the crest of a hill far beyond the crossroads. It drew closer at a snail's pace and Bean felt a lump of fear and unease settle into his stomach once more, as he moved closer to Otter. When this apparition had almost come into clear view, Bean felt Otter nudge his shoulder. He turned to her, only to be motioned to move behind the marker and out of sight. He had scarcely done so before Otter vanished without a sound over the drifts of snow.

Bean pressed his back against the cold stone and listened to the creak of wheels draw nearer. He heard the grunt of, what he soon realized were mult-oxen and someone coughing and mumbling something. The boy sank further down into the snow and pulled the cloak over his head. Ever so discreetly, he peeked out from behind the stone marker. He saw a four mult-oxen team hitched to two carts lumbering slowly down the frozen road. On the driver's seat sat a weathered old fellow in a dark grubby coat and an old hat like a broken stovepipe.

"Get on there, y'wretched rack-a-ribs! Hup!" he shouted to his team and snapped the reins as the road inclined uphill. The poor beasts groaned in protest. "Ah quit yer belly-aching!" the man shouted at the mult-oxen and stamped at one of them in its hairy rear with the sole of his boots. His hand reached into his coat and pulled out a dented flask and he pushed back the rim of his hat to swig at the flask while he glanced at the surrounding scenery. His disinterested eye rested on the marker, paused, and then a dark smile crossed his bristly face.

"Huooooaaaa!" he bellowed and drew up the reins tight. The old man stood up in his wagon and shook his fist in the direction of the marker and Bean froze.

"I know yer there!" he roared. "Git out here, y'bandits or I'll give ya a taste of the back of ol' Benjamin Rumps' hand! Y'snivelin' yella-eyed devils why I'll..." and the rest of his words dissolved into a string of generous vulgarities that included goats, privies, and the mothers of all thieves in general. The old man stamped his foot so hard the cart bounced on its wheels and Bean ducked farther back behind the marker. "Come out, y'can't fool me!" he bellowed again and cursed something fierce to the wind. "Got eyes in the back of m'head and a nose like a fox! Y'think ya can...." Suddenly his bawling stopped short and ended in a nervous gurgle.

Bean glanced out from behind the marker again and saw the old man standing stiffly in his wagon. Behind him stood Otter, her blade at his throat and a grim smile on her face. The boy's eyes widened. He hadn't even heard her moving through the snow and now there she stood on the cart, in complete control.

"With all that noise you make, human, I could have picked you off with a crossbow long before this," she said calmly.

"Rot-suckin' murderer..." the old man said in a hoarse whisper. "Go on then... cut my throat and steal m'gear and go dancin' for the devil's hangman. I'll spit in yer eye when I meet ya 'twixt the flames."

"If I wanted to kill you, we would not be speaking now," she said dryly. "Now put your hands on your head and get down off the wagon." Her sword whipped down to rest between his shoulder blades and she gave him a light prod.

"Just robbin' me then? Eh, eh I see how it is," the old man whined. With the elf right behind him, he climbed down from the wagon and into the snow. He stole a glance at her out the corner of his eye. "No wonder everyone hates th' elves' guts. A step up from the goblins, you are... oh aye, ol' Ben knows." His voice trailed off in a mumble of obscenities.

Otter's eyes narrowed and her blade did not move. "Bean!" she called.

Bean slipped out of his hiding spot and made his way down the side of the hill. The old codger cast a jaundiced eye towards the lad and he snorted. "A mite fancy in your feathers for a thief's brat, ain't ya?" he sneered.

"Thieves we are not," Otter replied coldly.

"Not thieves? Well that ain't a spoon yer stickin' in my back, elf."

"I commend you, old man. I had not thought you that observant." Otter smirked.

He ignored the comment and growled, "Ain't done nothin' to deserve gettin' stranded in the middle of nowhere. I'm an honest man, I am…"

Otter studied the man for a moment. She relaxed, sheathed her sword, and walked in front of him. She kept her eyes fixed on him and gestured towards the wagon. "Where are you headed, human?" she said in a cold and calculated tone of voice.

He muttered under his breath and then answered, "Culver's Gulch." The old man motioned back towards the direction he had just come from. "Now you gonna let me be about my business or should we just stand here makin' daisy chains and wait for goblins to

come slit all our throats!?"

Otter glanced over at the Bean, who stood uncomfortably in the falling snow. The boy's eyes darted in the direction of the woods, down the road, and then turned back to her, waiting to see what she would do.

"I'll give you a choice then. You will generously grant us passage to Culver's Gulch," the elf said and then smiled sarcastically. "Or if that does not suit you, we will leave you here and take your cart."

"That ain't a choice!" the old man blustered. "Drag you and the brat to Culver Gulch? With naught for my troubles? Look here Mistress' Elf, ol' Ben ain't no fool. If I'm going t'go from a hold-up ta passenger service, I expects compensation."

Otter's free hand flew to her cloak and the man calling himself Ben suddenly got a nervous look on his face and stepped back. Instead the elf pulled out a small bag and tossed it into the old codger's knit-gloved hands. He looked at the bag for a moment, weighed it thoughtfully in his hands before he slipped the string off, and turned it over in his hand. Four uncut jade stones tumbled across his fingerless glove, a fortune that in the skilled hands of the right money exchanger could keep the old man comfortably well off in bits for a good long while. The old man gaped down in amazement and then looked back at the elf and the boy. A greedy smile crossed his face for a moment and then he quickly pocketed the stones somewhere within the confines of his tattered cloak.

"I reckon that's good to start off with," he said slyly. "Off to Culver's Gulch, then milady. Mind now, my good young sir, you're goin' ta have to ride in the back cart there. Not enough room up front. You, mistress elf, can sit up here next to me."

Otter didn't bother trying to hide the obvious disgust on her face. "Come along Bean, it is time to go," she said and delicately climbed up in the front seat with the old man, disdaining his efforts to assist her. Bean tossed his bag into the cart and climbed in, while

Otter went through the heroic effort to arrange herself on the seat as far away from the filthy old man as possible. Bean sat himself down on a large coil of rope and managed a quiet "thank you" to their driver, who only grunted in reply. The old fellow's dark eyes lit up for a moment when he saw the gold glint of a sword hilt before the boy pulled the cloak back over himself. His rough hand pulled at his bristly chin a moment and then he smiled again and patted himself, feeling the jade stones in their secret pocket underneath his coat.

"Only the best for my travelers, eh?" the old man chuckled and climbed back on his wagon. He grabbed the reins, gave them a good snap, and hollered "Let's go, boys, hup-hup now!" to start his animals moving again.

The carts creaked along across the ice-crusted road. Bean rested his chin in his hand, listened to the crackling and crunch of frozen mud under the wheels, and gazed up at the clouds high above, while the snowflakes flitted around him. He felt the weight of the sword resting on his shoulders and thought again of the friendly Brutus and Thaddeus and his mysterious home.

"So who is ya, boy?" the old man barked suddenly, breaking the dismal silence. "And what're you an' your elf friend here doin' out here in the rough, eh-eh?"

A little taken aback, Bean nevertheless straightened himself up and looked over at the old man's back. "I'm Bean... sir and...." He remembered then that Thaddeus had warned about speaking to strangers and bit his tongue. On reflection though, it occurred to him that while this old man most certainly fit the description of strange, he hardly seemed threatening. Coarse definitely and he stunk of ale, but not so much threatening or at least Bean hoped first impressions wouldn't mislead him.

"Bean?" cackled the old man. He pulled the rim of his beat-up old hat back over his bushy white brows and crooked his head to take a closer look at Bean. "Bean, eh. There's a name. What about you, elf? What 're you called?"

"Otter. That is all I care to divulge about myself, human," Otter answered. Bean could feel the chill and the distance in the air created from the elf's tone of voice. He got the feeling that she was no more happy about their situation than Bean was.

"Talkative, eh? Fair enough, mistress." He crooked a thumb back in the direction of the forest. "You're lucky you weren't headin' towards the woods.... Most o' the folks have fled from Darkleaf and them's that's stayed is dead, so I hears. All the towns and the forest itself shot through with goblins. Whole woods prob'ly crawlin' with the liddle maggots as we speak."

He snorted and made a terrible noise for a second before he spit into the snow. "Ashmont was the last place I passed through. They had already caught wind of something brewing and was packing their bags. Says I to myself, I ain't stayin' 'round to let them goblins catch up to me either. If yer smart, you won't dawdle in your travelin' either. Some fool at the tavern even swore he'd heard something of dark creatures stirred up by the goblins trampin' through Darkleaf." He laughed, glancing over his shoulder at Bean. "Pah! Hogwash and tales from drunks. Ain't nothing that scares me."

Bean came out of his thoughts and shifted his attention back to the old man. "I'm sorry, sir? What did you say?"

"'Sir, sir,'" the old man mimicked, very much amused by the term. "I said ' ain't nothin' that scares me' that's all. So anyways, where are ya two goin'?" He all but ignored Otter and posed the question to the boy who seemed to him to be far more inclined to chat than the elf.

Bean swallowed down his irritation at the old man's prodding, thought a moment, and then replied, " We're heading upriver... towards the mountains." It sounded vague enough. He didn't feel entirely comfortable telling this old fellow everything at one go. A shrewd look crossed Ben's face.

"Well... you two are in a right dilly of a pickle, then ain'cha, boy? Where the river forks, getting there alone'll take you a good four weeks, maybe five on foot. For all that fancy dress, I think all y'll get yerself is either frozen to death or snapped up by bandits. Good thing I did come along, though you sure do have a way o' convincing about ya." He glanced at the elf again, spit, and wiped his mouth on the back of his shirt sleeve. His brown eyes gleamed wickedly.

"There's a port down in Culver's Gulch that take you right downriver where y'want to go, no waitin' and no trudgin' through snow and arrows to git to it either. Plus there's wealth beyond your imagination," the old man continued in a cheerful voice. "I'm a zift miner, Benjamin Rumps by name if ya didn't catch it before. I'll be rich-a-plenty once I find me a vein down in the mines."

"A port is agreeable," the elf said. "However, your wealth does not interest us."

The old man raised an eyebrow and allowed himself a brief happy thought that involved pushing the disagreeable elf from the cart. The blade she carried insured that would remain only a thought, though. Bean shifted his weight a bit and an empty bottle turned over and went rolling noisily around the floor of the cart.

"Don't be breakin' anythin' back there, boy!" Ben's irritable roar made the boy jump. Bean hastily caught the bottle and placed it in a crate. The old man gave a sudden nervous grin as the elf shot him a dirty look.

"Gee-up, boys," he called to the mult-oxen, cleared his throat, and in a kinder tone said, "So what're all dressed up fancy like that for, boy? Mighty important-lookin' rags you got... look like a governor's son maybe, eh?" The subtle probe for information wasn't lost on either Bean or Otter. The elf glanced back at the boy for a second and then turned her attention back to the road. Bean caught the warning signal from her and remembered the words from Thaddeus.

Bean rubbed his shoulder. "I'm just a messenger, sir," he answered in a quiet voice. He shifted himself again when they rounded a corner. It was a rough ride but for the most part at least he wasn't walking.

"Hm!" said the old miner, less than impressed. "Y'ever been this far north before, boy?"

"N'sir."

"Fine country it is, fine indeed. Travel it all the time, old Benj'man does. Been working those mountains yonder all m'life... had to come down river a bit late this year t'haggle some supplies off the river-rats... filthy bandits, bad as the goblin-maggots. Ah well. Culver's Gulch is enough up in the hills I don't reckon we'll be bothered by 'em. There's some folks talkin' like it's a war this time. Pft! Them goblins git their danders up every few years or so, I'm sure it'll be gone faster'n a mosquito's fart in a windstorm. Folks'll be back home and planting crops by fall, yep," the old man rambled on with a nod.

He pulled out his flask again, looked back at the boy and grinned while he took a swig. Bean saw dark liquid dribbling out the corners of his mouth and going down his scruffy neck. Old Benjamin swallowed, winced, beat his chest with his other hand a second, and then shook his head in satisfaction. "Hooo-WEE!" he declared

finally. "Earthdweller brandy's got a mule's kick innit. Best brew in Darkleaf." He turned around in his seat and waved the dirty flask at Bean. "Here, boy want me ta toss it to ya and have y'self a swallow? It'll put hairs on your chest."

Bean tried hard not to make a face. He could almost see the fumes spilling out in the cold air and turning the lip of the metal flask black. "No thanks... I don't drink, sir," he said.

"Fah! This'll warm yer soul, I'm tellin' ya. Go on, boy, one sip ain't gonna 'urt ya."

"I'll be fine," Bean replied firmly.

Old Ben smirked. "Ya don't know what you're missin'!"

Bean sighed, remembering the many ale-loving patrons of the Silver Dagger Inn and thought to himself, not a rotten liver, that's for sure. Out loud he said, "You're probably right, sir, but if it's all the same I'd rather not."

"Suit yerself then." The old man shrugged and turned back around. "How about you, mistress elf? This ain't like that eldenberry ditch-water your kind quaffs at high teas, ta-ta... this here's a real drink." He pushed the flask towards her and Otter's lips curled in disgust.

"If you do not remove that filth from my face now, human, you will not get a second chance. I have no qualms about leaving you beside the road with that vile flask forced down your throat and going on alone with the boy," she said in a sharp voice.

The old man harrumphed, but he took back his flask very quickly. "Ta! Your loss, mistress elf." He took another swig. "No wonder...." he began and then got caught by a fit of coughing. He spewed the brandy all over himself, wheezed, and pounded his chest a moment.

"No wonder ya look so unhealthy!" he finished, taking another swallow presumably to help the coughing. Otter rolled her eyes, folded her arms, and stared straight ahead at the snow falling across the road with a sour expression on her face.

The wind started picking up a bit and Bean pulled his cloak tighter around his shoulders. He thought again of how nice it would be to be back at the Inn even if it had been wall-to-wall with drunks like Benjamin Rumps.

"How's about a hard-boiled egg then, boy? Boiled 'em this morning," the old miner said. He did not offer anything else to Otter. He had decided he didn't like her at all. Under his seat, he fished around in a bucket of salty water, pulled out a couple of eggs and turned in his seat to toss them back at the boy.

Bean caught each one and peered at them. His stomach grumbled, reminding him that he hadn't eaten for a good part of the day. He looked at the elf and she, perhaps feeling his questioning eyes on her, gave him a listless wave of approval without turning around.

Bean took off his gloves, cracked one egg on the side of the wagon and peeled it. "Thank you sir," he said and took a big bite. It tasted very, very good.

Fury Unleashed

The snow crunched under the black claws of the gren-el and finally cleared on a well traveled path crusted with ice. In its cavernous chest, the dark heart of the creature beat quicker in anticipation and it passed over the slush and the frozen ground in a swift silence, a hellish hound pressing hard against the elements and its prey, a mere breath ahead of it. Its tongue passed delicately over its reddened teeth several times; its eager breath whitening the air in front of it.

When the air cleared once more it saw its quarry vanish around the corner and it could hear a man's hoarse voice singing. It grinned and veered off into a smaller path, traveling alongside the main road. The beast ran faster to overtake them.

Bean sat with his chin in his hand, half-listening to old Ben belt out the words to his bawdy song in the frozen silence. He watched the dull snow-covered landscape with its drifting flakes of snow pass by them and he lifted his head and gazed at the equally dull gray sky for a moment. The wind swirled mists of dirty ice across the drifts. The cart suddenly lurched forward and Bean caught the side

of the cart to keep himself from being thrown forward. Benjamin cut
his singing short and prodded the mult-oxen in the backsides. The
beasts swiveled their heads around grunting in alarm and backpedaled
in their reins, tugging against each other's yokes.

Otter said nothing as she scanned the ridge. She suddenly felt
very uneasy.

"Get on wi' ya!" Ben bellowed at the mult-oxen and stood up
in the chair to lay about the beasts' thick furry hides with his stick.
Bean winced when the old man began swearing, laying down foul
words on the backs of the mult-oxen as heavily as the blows.
Suddenly the boy stood up straight in the back cart. A sickening
sensation touched the edges of his fingers and made the hairs prickle
on the back of his neck. In the same instant, Otter sat up expectantly.
She drew her sword, muttered something quietly under her breath
in the direction of the old man, and rose to her feet, giving their
surroundings a sharp glance.

"Sir..." Bean said in a hoarse voice and then louder and more
urgent: "SIR!"

"WHAT?" Old Ben yelped, cutting his abuse off short. He
looked back and met the boy's hard stare. Momentarily taken aback
by the intensity in the boy's eyes, his mouth snapped shut.

"Sir," Bean said. "I think we.... tssstt!" A fierce coldness far
beyond the chill in the air assaulted the boy's nerves and made him
noisily suck in air between his clenched teeth. He felt like he had
been immersed without warning into a river of snowmelt. He knew
that feeling and felt the familiar dread deep in the pit of his stomach.
Unfortunately for all of them this warning came a second too late.
On the left side of the road, a snowdrift violently burst apart and a
massive creature leaped at the hindmost wagon, the one Bean sat in.
It slammed into it with its shoulder and all but tore it and the end of
the lead wagon to pieces. Bean found himself flung violently clear of
the wreckage onto the side of the road.

The mult-oxen panicked and jerked the front of the wagon forward. The connectors between the wagons snapped. The poor animals dragged the remains of the lead wagon across the black ice of the road, making a horrible high-pitched braying of alarm while Ben, his leg caught in the reins found himself borne along down the road by his crazed beasts of burden.

Bean had quickly pulled himself out of the drift, beating the snow out of his ears and grew still at the sound of harsh breathing in front of him. He raised his head. His fingers tightened around the hilt of his sword.

Otter having leaped when the wagon took off, landed in the snow-crusted road with a wildcat's grace, poised on her hands and knees. The elf shook her head, leaped to her feet, and spun around. She grew still with horror as she found herself and the boy in the direst of situations. A beast stood before them, grinning at Bean, showing a horror of red-strained pointed teeth. The three of them formed a triangle in the road, and she stood at the furthest end while Bean

was a mere few paces away.

The thing advanced towards the boy at a leisurely pace, confident of a swift and easy kill and a simple recovery of the sword. Otter held her sword at the level. She kept her eyes fixed on the beast and inched forward ever so slowly. Her nerves prickled with restrained energy.

"Bean," Otter hissed. "Bean...fall... back... now."

She risked a glance at the boy. The boy held his sword upright while a death shroud of falling snow began to gather on his shoulders. He stood there, transfixed by the beast moving slowly towards him. He had to be caught in some sort of victim's trance, she reasoned, that mouth-drying fear that paralyzed the helpless rabbit, sitting and watching the wolf coming to devour it. Even if she started running now, she couldn't reach him before the creature did. He might have a slim chance if he stepped back and broke into a run.

"Bean," she spoke louder, still trying to keep her voice calm. Her eyes darted back and forth between beast and boy. She heard the loud deliberate scrape of Bean's foot against the snow-covered ground and allowed herself a small measure of relief. That relief shattered when she glanced over at the boy.

Bean hadn't stepped back. He had positioned himself for a strike. His young face was grim and determined. He pulled off his cloak and dropped it and a bit of snow scattered across the black icy ground. His muscles tensed. His eyes narrowed. The blue light patterned itself across his sword, up his arm and into his eyes and the blue turned fierce and white.

He took off, but not away from the beast. Bean ran hard at the gren-el, covering the remaining ground between them in only a few steps.

Otter ran towards them both, her teeth gritted and her eyes wide with rage and fear, sure the boy would die right before her very gaze. She didn't know she was seconds away from witnessing something far different.

The gren-el had fully expected its quarry to run or at least put up the miserable semblance of a fight. It got instead the unpleasant surprise of a deep slash from palm to elbow when it raised its arm to strike at the boy. Bean danced away narrowly when the vicious creature struck at him, sending loose snow flying and carving a gash of black earth into the white embankment behind the boy. The foe had the advantage of size and strength, but Bean had the advantage of a weapon and instincts that clearly were not his own, which calmly directed his actions and his positions. Hawk-And-Sparrow method first... strike quick, move back quicker... cripple your enemy, wear him down, said the thoughts in his head.

The gren-el spun around and pursued the boy, though a slight limp hindered its speed. It appeared intent on leaping upon the boy, but at the last minute it feinted to the left and lashed out at Bean, hoping to connect. However, Bean proved far too fast as he rapidly reversed his grip on the sword and deflected the blow. He swept the sword around, threw off the beast's claws, and thrust the point of the blade directly into the joint of the leg it rested its weight on. He gave it a quick twist, heard something pop, and pulled the sword free. Bean scrambled back when the enraged beast tried to backhand him. It proved an ill-aimed strike for the boy had thrown off its balance badly. Bean repositioned his grip on his weapon, lunged at the gren-el again while the beast struggled to raise itself up on its hind legs. Within striking range, the gren-el swept out with its deadly claws. Even with both arms injured, it managed to deflect the blade, its claws ringing against the metal.

On the edge of this furious battle, Otter circled, her eyes darting back and forth watching the boy and the gren-el engage each other. She kept her blade balanced calmly in her hand, but beneath her cool exterior, a struggle raged no less fierce than the one she witnessed now. The frustration of the hard-pressed beast and the tenacity of the boy both amazed and sorely vexed her. Never before had she seen one so young fight in such a style that was long forgotten to almost all but her own family. However, Bean's sudden skills, besides leaving her at a considerable disadvantage to get a strike in, had touched off a warning somewhere deep in her warrior mind. She edged towards the action, hoping to take advantage of a careless moment, only to be forced into rapidly deflecting both claw and sword. She jerked back and for a brief second, her eyes rested on Bean. Through a shimmering blur, the elf found herself gazing at a stranger wearing a boy's face. His indifferent blue eyes stared through her and then he turned back to his task. She might as well have been an errant breeze.

The gren-el had grown tired of this child's play. It caught the blade suddenly near the shoulder. Its claws tightened around the blade and red seeped between its fingers while it held the blade nearly immobile. It leaned in closer to Bean and its mouth spread in a horrible smile and then snapped at Bean's face. Bean swung himself to one side and the vicious fangs just barely grazed his temple. The gren-el's foul breath made his stomach turn. He twisted the blade savagely in the thing's claws, freeing it, and jumped backwards. The

gren-el followed suit.

Further down the road in a cul-de-sac, Old Ben freed his leg from the reins and slid off the ruined wagon onto the icy road while the mult-oxen mulled about, their sides heaving with exertion. The old man painfully got to his feet and swore a blue streak. He rubbed his bruised and bleeding back, turned and limped back towards where they had been attacked, and then stopped short, hearing the sounds of vicious combat further up the road. His eyes widened and he picked up his pace.

He climbed up the slope with some difficulty, crouched down, and moved through the deep drifts until the scene of the battle came into his view. "What th..." he whispered hoarsely. Below him, he saw the boy dancing around with his sword, fighting some sort of unnatural beast that chilled the old man's blood to look at. Save for the sounds of the blade glancing off the thing's curved claws, both fought in an eerie silence, each intensely concentrated on the annihilation of the other. The elf woman, sword in hand moved around them poised to attack, but the boy and the creature in the midst of their fray left no room open to do so.

Old Ben gazed in utter disbelief. The more he stared, the more difficult he found it to properly understand what exactly he was witnessing. The boy... his movements didn't seem quite right. They reflected an age and experience far beyond the boy's tender years.

Like, Old Ben thought, someone or something had crawled into the boy's skin and was moving him around like a puppet. The air around the two of them seemed to have a funny quivery quality about it, with the stronger aura concentrated on the boy. The old man felt hair prickling on the back of his neck. He couldn't deny feeling an odd sensation of energy and matter being bent or reshaped while he crouched there and watched.

He told himself it must be a trick of the dim light against the snow or his eyes and brain going funny from being rattled around in his skull because of the recent unpleasant experience of being dragged down the road. Needless to say, he didn't care to get involved, not that he felt any sort of sympathy for the beast, but that the mere sight of it made his blood run cold. If the boy and the elf felt cocky enough to take on that thing whatever it was, they'd be doing it on their own.

He glanced in the direction he had come from and spit into the snow. "Feh, I ain't risking my skin. That moon-shadowed devil can have 'em," he muttered. He turned and fled back to his mult-oxen and wagon.

The gren-el at this point knew nothin but dark frustration. The boy moved too quickly to get a decent strike in. Hardly discouraged, the creature kept trying. Now and then it caught the end of his shirt but more often than not it caught the end of the boy's sword. The blade had a nasty bite and the gren-el strong as it was, had to make a decision quickly before it lost much more blood. It let the rage burn away all pain and thoughts down to one red ember. It fed on that single concentration of darkness and drew strength from it into it's deep dark heart. After one more slash of the sword bloodied its curled lip, the beast tightened the muscles in its body until the tendons stood out on its gray skin. Then in a sudden burst of fury and claws, it descended upon the boy.

The euphoria of battle had taken Bean. It was a wonderful feeling to lose himself in every step and turn, to feel his muscles respond with such control and power, to watch the shine of the reddened blade while it darted and swept through the air. When the beast rushed him, he could have laughed in delight and he gladly met the thing head-on. The gren-el came at him with claws and teeth, snapping and slashing, but instead of trying to overpower him with sheer brute force, the creature cunningly began mirroring the boy's movements in such a way as to draw him back towards the ruins of the wagon. It feigned weaker and weaker strikes, luring the boy into extending his blows further and further. Then it suddenly lashed out, caught the hilt and twisted the boy around so that he had Bean trapped in a space between the wagon and the side of the road and redoubled its efforts. Bean warded off the claws, flipped the sword over, and stabbed the blade through one of the creature's claws to pin it to the ground. He swung over his sword like a catapulting acrobat, landed a blow across the creature's face with the heel of his foot and slammed the thing against the ruins of the wagon. The gren-el tore its claw free and lunged at the boy. It opened its mouth, baring rows of glistening teeth ready to tear the boy's throat out. In the same second, Bean pulled out his sword and leaped at the thing, his eye cold and controlled as the gren-el's eye burned with madness.

The world faded away and Bean's control faded with it. The sword had him completely now. The boy lowered the weapon for the last strike. He looked directly at the beast and their eyes locked.

"I know you... Do you remember your name... Pellanor?" the boy said. The gren-el's face contorted in shock. It did not hear the words of a young human, but rather the voice of a ghost. Memories washed over its brain in a black wave... his mate ... the children ... blood on its hands... his hands... the screaming... the power... the hunger.... the darkness behind the stars...

The beast held back the strike a moment while it touched on the disturbing thoughts. It proved a moment too long. Bean thrust the sword home, hard... right through the thing's throat and into the wood of the wagon behind it with a dull thunk! His feet hit the ground and red spattered across the boy's grim face. His breath escaped from between his teeth in short gasping hisses. Bean held the thing there, pinned to the wagon until its jerking movements grew still.

Something crossed the boy's face then... an expression of anguish, uncertainty, and pity. He slowly stepped back, worked the sword free from the wood and let its weight and the weight of the

beast pinned on it drop slowly to the ground. He stared down at the beast.

It shouldn't have been that easy, he mused. And then came the disquieting thought of it being ... that satisfying...

Otter stepped towards the boy and sheathed her sword. He stood there staring down at what he had done. "Bean..." the elf said. Bean didn't answer. His eyes remained fixed on the twisted remains of the broken creature lying in the snow, his mind lost in some dim and distant time.

"Bean," came a female's voice in the distance, calling him back to the world he left behind. The boy finally blinked, the shimmering in his blue eyes faded and his thoughts gradually returned to that of an ordinary young boy. He turned to Otter with a dazed look on his face and stood quite still gathering his thoughts and what little strength he had left.

Otter picked his cloak up from the ground where he had dropped it and wrapped it around his shoulders. She patted his face. "Come now, young man, bring your mind back down from the stars... it's over," she said. She studied his expression for a moment, and felt pity touch her. He looked completely indifferent to what had just happened. Her eyes went to his blood-streaked hand which still clutched the blade. She made a gesture towards it and suddenly distrust darkened the boy's face. His grip tightened on the hilt and he moved it away.

"Don't touch it," he warned. Weariness touched his voice as well as a peculiar coldness. "You mustn't touch the sword, please." The elf drew her hand back and her face grew grim.

"I have no intention of doing so, but it might be advisable to see if that hand.... and the rest of you... are injured in any way," she said shortly.

"I'm fine ma'am. Really I am," Bean answered and his eyes turned back towards the corpse of the beast. "It didn't hurt me." He felt completely drained.

"I will reserve judgment on that until I see for myself," Otter answered carefully. She looked around at the mess of the broken wagon and then scanned the forest for a moment. "We do not need to linger here at any rate. Come now we must be off." She draped the boy's arm over her shoulder and took a moment to steady him. Bean felt weak and his muscles ached. When he finally took a few steps, he felt a sudden disconcerting sensation like hundreds of years draining from him in seconds. He pressed his hand to his face, closed his eyes and held it there until the sensation passed.

The lowing of a mult-ox sounded in the distance, along with a faint string of swear words. Otter turned her head and listened for a minute, then knelt and held her hand against the ground. Her lip curled with disgust.

"We ought to see if Mr. Rumps is alright," Bean said. Otter shook her head and stood up again. The sounds grew fainter and vanished in the sighing wind.

"I have the feeling that our good wagon master has fled with his tail between his legs. The distance between us grows even as we speak. Good riddance, I say. He had no honor in him," Otter muttered.

Bean opened his eyes and looked over at the elf. "So what do we do now?" He asked in a numb voice.

"We walk. It will take us a little longer than by cart, but I have my bearings now and we will be able to find the town he spoke of," the elf replied. "A few extra days will not hurt us."

Bean frowned. He had enjoyed riding in the cart and the thought of walking only made him feel worse. "Maybe one of his mults is wandering around... maybe we can catch it, rig up something from what's left of the cart and ride on that," he suggested in a hopeful tone of voice. The elf gave him a long, hard stare.

"We cannot spare the time to look for the old man's beasts.

As for the wagon..." She pushed a piece of the wood around with her foot and the answer seemed obvious. The elf glanced over at the massive body of the gren-el. "Besides you must remember that riding caused us to let down our guard," she said. "Better we salvage what we can from the wagon and go on foot. That way we stay alert... and alive. Here..." She threw a reasonably clean rag over to him. "Get some snow and wipe the blood from your face. Then clean off your sword."

Bean mumbled something unintelligible, but caught the rag. While Otter gathered up what she could from the remains of the wagon, Bean did as he was told and when the elf came over after a moment to look him over, he at least had a clean face and a clean sword to show for his troubles. Otter took a moment to check for any major wounds and a faint smile crossed her face while she did so.

"What is it ma'am?" Bean said, mystified at her amusement.

"You are quite the tale, boy. Barely a scratch on you and a knowledge of swordplay that would put many a seasoned warrior to shame," she said. "You have a lot to think about for one so young. Now answer me true. You were not a mere inexperienced boy in that battle. Movements like that takes years, even a lifetime, to learn. Someone else came into your mind and told you what to think and how to move, did they not?"

An odd mix of perplexity and wariness crossed Bean's face. He sighed softly. "What do you mean, ma'am?" he asked innocently.

"The best way I can explain it is to call it borrowed power. Did Thaddeus not go into more detail about the nature of such power?"

Bean stood in deep thought for a moment. "I only know that I had been given a great responsibility... and that I must heal this sword."

"Heal the sword?" Otter asked, cocking an eyebrow.

"Yes. Somehow or other this sword is broken and I must

make it right. I promised I would. I just... I don't know how to do it. Not yet anyway," the boy replied, aware of how awkward his words sounded.

"The sword has some type of control over you, does it not?" Otter asked, looking straight at the boy with a sharp glitter in her eyes. Bean did not meet her gaze but rubbed his arms instead and felt reluctant to respond. Under that cutting gaze, however, he eventually cleared his throat.

"Yes.... yes ma'am. I guess so, but only when I am in danger, when I need it the most. Only then... I swear," he said. He heard the fervent tone in his voice and realized he was trying to defend his actions, as if he had gotten caught stealing cream pasties. It made him feel very ill at ease and he grew quiet.

"Yes, Bean, of course," said Otter in a flat voice. "Only when you are at your weakest and cannot resist. Malnova..." She passed her hand over her face and glanced wearily up at the heavens.

"Ma'am?"

"Bean, you are aware that this blade has an old weave about it, do you not?" the elf asked, looking back down at him. Bean glanced at the sword in his hands and turned it over thoughtfully.

"Sort of," he said in a quiet voice. "Thaddeus spoke a bit of the weave and I read a few things about weaves in books and such. Nothing I really understood though."

"What Thaddeus neglected to explain to you, Bean, is that such power demands high prices of those who wield it. I regret I do not understand it as well as my brother Johann. He is a more scholarly sort. I never had much patience for such things, but I do know that with the use of the weave, one always courts madness along with it."

"Madness?" Bean's face paled a bit.

"Yes, boy. When you let the sword use you like that, your self-control slips away bit by bit and takes your mind with it. That creature that attacked us is also part of a weave. Compulsion, greed, and a lust for power made it what it was. That path could be walked any of us, even you, Bean. Do you want that?"

Bean's eyes glanced over at the body of the gren-el. The moment before the strike had been the only clear moment Bean remembered of the battle. Images had been burned into his mind. He had known the name, had known that thing had been an elf. Bean had known what it had done to itself. The boy silently shook his head no.

Otter nodded with a grim smile on her face. "We need to go, Bean. We have tarried here far too long. Let's see what we can salvage," she said. Bean stirred out of his unpleasant thoughts as the elf tossed him his haversack and a dented canteen.

"What about Mr. Rumps?" Bean asked again as he pulled aside a shattered wheel and found an oilcloth packet of honeycakes, badly squashed but still edible and dropped it in his sack.

"He can fend for himself. Move quickly now and

less chatter. If this beast has brothers or a master, it will be missed before too long," Otter said. They gathered what they could in a few minutes and then started down the road. The elf led the way, keeping a sharp eye on the concealing snowdrifts.

After a couple of hours, Bean noticed Otter had slowed her pace. Though she had not relaxed her grip on her sword, the boy sensed the tension surrounding her had lessened somewhat. She spoke suddenly in a conversational tone of voice: "Young man, I suspect there will be times you will be forced to use the sword to defend yourself. You should understand, however, that you lose more and more of your free will every time you let the sword control your actions."

"But... but ma'am. I can't just not use it," the boy protested. "All I'm good for is cleaning off tables and washing dishes. How else could I protect myself? I mean... I..."

Otter stared down at the boy. "You need it and it needs you, is that how it works?" she asked.

Bean looked perplexed. He dropped his head. "It's not like I can just... throw it away. It comes back," he mumbled uncomfortably. It had not exactly been an answer to her question, but he didn't know what else to say. Her comment had more or less hit home.

"Listen to yourself, young man," Otter remarked in a grave voice. "Do you see how the weave in this weapon is already affecting your mind?" She sighed and stopped for a moment to give the boy a stern stare. "First of all, you must change your mindset. People who go through their lives as you said, thinking they can do no more than clean tables and wash dishes will do exactly that until the end of their days. If... and this is the important part... if they never decide they can do more. Look at me, Bean. Do not drop your head like a child being chastised."

Bean raised his head and met the elf's sharp eyes while she went on. "If you are willing to think more of yourself than that and if you are willing to learn, then I will teach you of the Helixshires, the laws of the dance of blades and the techniques. You need to learn to heed your own voice more than the voice of that sword."

"Yes ma'am?" the boy said, his eyes growing wide. "So you will make me a Helixshire?"

The elf pursed her lips together in amusement. "Knowing how to control a weapon cannot make you a Helixshire," she answered. "My people would say that comes with birth. I have heard though of warriors adopted into the clan through rigorous training. In my lifetime I know of only two that had ever been given that honor."

"Really?" Bean asked incredulously.

"Yes really," Otter replied matter of factly.

"Who?"

Otter snorted. "Do you gather questions like acorns, boy?"

She started walking again and Bean hurried after her. He wondered if he had insulted the elf in some way and just when he thought he would never hear the answer, Otter surprised him by remarking, "Two brothers, as I recall."

"What were..." Bean stopped. "Sorry, ma'am. Please go on."

Otter chuckled quietly. "They had cast off their human names and been given clan names when the Helixshires accepted them as kindred. They were the only names we knew them by, as tradition dictated. You are a khal-zim, one who is outside the family. I cannot tell you their names, I am afraid. However, one had been king of the White Hall, the other captain of the guards. Good men... but the great king, he has gone the way of us all and the stars call him their brother now."

"Is his brother dead also?" Bean asked.

Otter shrugged. "He went into one of the great forests of Darkleaf. No one in the family heard from him again."

Bean pondered this for a while with a somber expression on

his face. When they turned a corner he stopped again and glanced up at the elf.

"Do you really mean to teach me the ways of the Helixshire?" he asked. "It's not just idle talk?"

Otter turned her head and studied the boy. "Why would you think it is idle talk, Bean?" she answered.

"I have to know ma'am," Bean said. "I want to know it is a real and true promise. I... I need to know." The intensity of his voice surprised them both.

Otter studied the boy standing there in the snow. "You have had many broken promises in your life, have you not, young Bean?" she said gently.

"Yes," said Bean in a low voice.

"Then it is a promise that won't be broken," the elf said. "Your first lesson is to learn the value of silence. Think on that and no more talking for now." She turned and without a glance back, continued to walk.

Bean shivered and pulled his cloak tighter around him. He glanced back behind them, anxiously to watch for any more shadows slinking after them, hoping fervently that he'd not have to fight again. He felt vaguely dissatisfied with the elf's indifference but decided to push it aside. He stank of blood and sweat, he felt battered outside and inside and it didn't seem worth brooding about. He wished, however, that he could talk. Being silent allowed him to remember the dead creature they had left behind them in the ruins of the wagon. Thinking about what he had done made the boy feel very dark and uneasy with himself.

At that moment, a small blossom of golden light pierced through the heavy grey clouds settling on the swiftly darkening horizon. Just briefly the light shone, trailing shafts of soft light across the snow, a quiet moment of natural beauty, which then vanished again. Bean realized the skies were clearing up and the threat of snow for now was alleviated. Bean felt a strange sense of peace. Something seemed to reassure him that all would be right. He remembered the warmth and peace he had felt in Mama Faerie's home and the quiet of the off-hours when business was slow at the Dagger and Groggle would send him off into the peaceful cool woods on errands.

Bean lifted his head a little higher and braced his shoulders. He'd go on then, one step at a time. At this point after all the strange twists and turns his life had taken, it was really all that he had left to trust in, his own two feet and where they would end up taking him. That in itself was a small comfort.

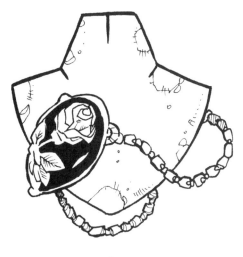

Epilogue

The old underground hall stood silent and dark. Hardly a breath of air stirred the fragile strands of abandoned spider's webs in the corners. Further below in the dead world, flames guttered and died and strewn among blackened bones, the ashes of old ambitions grew cold, but one ember still burned red in the darkness.

An old door creaked and swung open. The smoldering darkness stared out with one maddened yellow eye. It gathered its ragged black robes, staggered out, and leaned for a moment against the door frame. Slowly it collapsed and for a long time it lay still on the stone floor.

Slowly it raised its head. When it smiled, its clenched teeth gleamed faintly in the dark. A horrible rasping command that barely passed as language, escaped its blackened lips. A faint wisp of bluish light flowed from its raw fingers into a stone sconce in the wall and it came to life with a feeble light, just barely enough to see by.

The creature dragged itself across the floor little by little and pulled itself up onto a small table. It dug its claws deep into the dusty wood and then closed its other hand around a decorated brass rod. Using that for support, the hulking figure slowly and painfully made its way down the halls.

Empty suits of tarnished armor and broken statues stood at attention while their lord and master passed by them, trailing threads of smoke and hoarse whispers behind him. His shadow passed over massive paintings that had once hung in a king's chamber but he took no notice in those things he had once prided himself in owning.

Some time later, his burned hand rested against the damaged veneer of his study door which he then painfully pushed open.

Darkness draped the room. He staggered to the center of his study where a chair still sat facing the fireplace. The fire had gone out long ago and a piece of frayed rope lay scattered on the floor, gathering dust.

A sneer crossed the creature's face. In a burst of rage, he swung out at the chair with the brass rod and knocked it into the corner, dislodging a shelf of stoppered bottles. They smashed on the stone floor and the contents of the bottles seeped across the nearby rug. The creature sank to his knees in front of the fireplace and his head lolled back weakly. He stared blankly up at the ceiling with his one good eye. Pain ravaged his ruined body, pain from fire and spear. However, his body shook with amusement and his mouth sagged open and a hideous raw cackle escaped his throat, the laughter of a soul gone completely mad. He had left the traitors though, left them to burn in the tomb of the sword. He sat here, alive, and they lay, bones and ashes, down there in the dark. He had killed them all.

All except one, the gopher.

He fell silent and closed his eye. His lips moved in the cold darkness and bluish light began to grow around him. It intensified, throwing every item in the study in sharp relief against its cobalt glare. Objects sensitive to the weave glowed in response and the light swirled in a maelstrom around the ruined creature. A chant swelled from his chest, throwing the wild blue light around the darkened room.

After a moment, with one final hoarse wail, the light abruptly faded and the after glow of the various weaved objects illuminated the study in a dim light. The creature raised his head and he inhaled the sweet scent of his treasures that surrounded him, a bouquet of moldering books, damp stone, and dust. The familiar scents pulled him back from the oblivion that threatened to consume him.

He scanned his study. Trinkets, cunning devices, and the art of ages long forgotten lined the walls and littered the floor. Everything here he could call his own and yet the only thing he truly desired in the world had been taken away from him by the unworthy hands of a clever brat. A deep anguished groan shook his body and he clenched at his face and closed his eyes, feeling a pain far greater than the burns and wounds on his body. The sword had betrayed him and the silence in his head was more than he could bear.

One eye opened and burned with sudden fierceness. Everything precious to him had broken like glass, but he could not sit here and weep. He knew deep in his bones the gopher had not perished. The betrayal of the sword and the boy's very life stood as the deepest of insults to the red rock troll. He could not let it pass.

He stood up and moved slowly towards a shelf piled high with scrolls, codices, and books. Once he had taken such pride in the knowledge he had carefully gathered over the years and now the memories of long ago, of when he had once been powerful and commanded respect, haunted and tormented him. He had to know though. He had to find the clues that had eluded him while he had been caught up in the rapture of the song.

He pulled them down, flipping through pages of old poems and ancient lore, examining the scrolls one by one and throwing them aside when he had finished. The more he read, the more his thoughts seethed in his mind. Surely, the boy and the sword had conspired against him, planned all this from the beginning. He was a proud red rock troll, one of the eldest race, the first instructors and this was the treatment he had received. His kind had taught the miserable children of Broken Moon every secret and power they knew today.

They had taken that knowledge in their false gratitude and betrayed his kindred with it and now his kindred were all dead and gone. His teeth gritted and his vision clouded in anger. Why couldn't they have left his people to live in peace? Why had the sword betrayed him?!! Why did the gopher still live? WHY?!?

In rage, he tore his hands through the shelves, slinging books and papers everywhere. He flung great leather-wrapped books across the room, smashing many of his delicate valuables, while his thoughts swam with images of death and destruction and the empty cold world above. He pressed his hands against his ruined face and trailed his fingers down the sides in a clumsy half-remembered gesture of mourning. His face was rigid with fury and grief, grief for what he once was and never could be again, grief for the song of the sword he could no longer hear, and fury for the loss of the sword that would never be his.

A piece of paper, rolled up and bound with twine, fell near his feet. His glazed yellow eye glanced down and he knelt down, and picked it up. He sagged against the shelf while he scanned the paper with a dull expression on his face. The weave of his earlier making had been quite powerful and extremely taxing and he felt completely drained by the effects of the abuse of using the power keenly now.

When he pulled off the twine, a pendant in the form of a rose fell into his hand. A dim memory touched his mind, of a solemn-faced woodsman standing in the heart of Darkleaf and holding this in his hand. He had dropped it in the underbrush and walked away and the red rock troll had scooped it up. He now scanned the paper. Spidery-thin handwriting proclaimed the document as an old folk tune called, "The Song of Ganadon."

A song of a dead elven king in one hand and a pendant with the old symbol of the White Hall in the other; the creature's eyes narrowed as the two signs connected in his head. The sword of a king and the throne of White Hall, all were within the eager grasp of one young boy.

"You... are... ambitious, gopher," he croaked. So that was it. The glory the sword had promised the boy had been White Hall, the ancient seat of Broken Moon. Power and the honor of kings... that rightly belonged to him, to HIM! He clenched the document in his hand and the fragile paper crumbled in his grasp.

He shook his head and frowned deeply. He staggered slowly towards the fireplace, held out his hand, and whispered under his breath while he let the pieces of the paper fall upon the charred wood. In mid-air, blue flames burst from the brown paper and scattered across the fireplace. He held out his hand against the fire and continued to mutter. Slowly the wood reignited and warmth spread through the cold room. The red rock troll gazed into the fire while the golden light illuminated the full horror of his ravaged body and face.

The song had died and he was the Collector no longer, but his mind was now clear again and he could think and plan. The pain and the rage was now his song.

"So... the little gopher... knows," he whispered. A black smile crossed his face. "So he seeks... to cut the rose. The rose so white... above the throne. Yes... he thinks to rule alone... his plan to come with... sword in hand. Let the White Hall run red, let him try to command the elven dead." His hoarse whisper grew louder and he began to shake with silent laughter.

"Ring, o Hall with the cries...
There, oh yes, the gopher dies...
Upon an altar of fire... and lies.
Liiiieeeessssss...."

Glossery

Ashmont – A settlement on the edge of Dark Leaf Forest

Badger, The – The savage human general that leads the Beast King's goblin horde army.

Bean (the) – A young orphan and dishwasher who worked for the Silver Dagger Inn until kidnapped by an insane Red Rock Troll and Weaver known as "The Collector". He was taken upon an errand deep within the earth to find a sword of power. He escaped the Collector's design, under the power of the sword, but in attempting to escape was gravely wounded in the swamps of Dark Leaf.

Beast King, The – A malevolent entity of mysterious origins, most likely an Elven prince, driven by an insatiable hunger to subject every known realm to his tyrannical rule.

Benjamin Rumps – A foul-mouthed northern merchant and prospector.

Bindwort – A healing herb, used to heal broken bones.

Borrowed Power – The influence and power of the Weave used to enhance the actions of an individual. Potentially dangerous and highly addictive, the user gains supernatural abilities but surrenders his or her free will, which leads to madness.

Brutus – One of the great dragons that dwells in the craggy heights of a mountain and regularly hunts the southern swamps of Dark Leaf Forest. Like all dragons, he is highly intelligent and possesses an uncanny skill to remain out of sight.

Collector, The – A Red Rock Troll who lives beneath the Dark Leaf Forest among the ruins of one of the many abandoned subterranean cities. He is the kidnapper of the Bean, driven mad by the power of the Weave. He is tormented by past skeletons and the sword of power, once wielded by Ganadon.

Crimson Per – An earthdweller brewer and merchant of Dark Leaf who regularly trades his wares with the Silver Dagger Inn.

Culver's Gulch – A zift miner's settlement in a distant northern mountainous canyon on the border of the stone troll infested mountains.

Dark Arrow – A village in Dark Leaf Forest.

Dark Leaf Forest – A vast forested land, home of the Silver Dagger Inn.

"Dhaua" – An Elvish greeting. Literally translated it is a word meaning the most enjoyable hour of any given time period, so in effect when spoken, the greeter is wishing the one greeted with "the best part of the day."

Docken – A worthless weed.

Dunsidne – A city in the Eastern borders of Dark Leaf and the Mountainous wastelands of the Goblins, that is little more than ruins now. It fell in the days of Ganadon.

Eyes of the Hall, The – A network of vigilant sol-

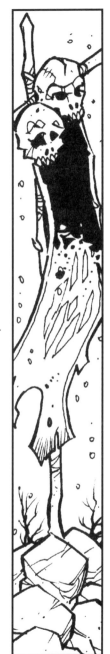

diers stationed in watchtowers surrounding the city of White Hall for the purpose of warning of imminent attack and defending the king.

Faerie Queen, The – Another name for Mama Faerie

Fencer Per – Son of Crimson Per, who completed a tour of service in White Bird's Cove under the employ of the Velumni masters.

Feverfew – A healing herb

Foie-gras – A decadent and greasy meat paste made of the abused livers of force-fed waterfowl; enjoyed only by the richest and most privileged in Velumni high society.

Forestwalker – A discipline of hunter/tracker/scout, capable of thriving in a forest, familiar with flora and fauna of the woodlands, often associated with Elf communities. Forestwalkers become one with the forest, having the ability to understand "the language of nature."

Ganadon – An ancient Elven King who repelled an army of Goblins using the power of the Weave to fuse his soul into his sword. While his accomplishments were heroic, the cost at which victory came was considered by all who survived to be a terrible tragedy.

Gort – The curmudgeonly and greedy proprietor of the Silver Dagger Inn.

Gren-el – Once Elves of considerable rank and prestige, now driven mad in their search for immortality and power through the unchecked use of the weave. Gren-el rejected a life of grace and decency to embrace a life of hideous cruelty and unsatisfied lusts. This monster used its power in the Weave to alter its body for the intent of killing. They were dreaded creatures of pure malice that hated all signs of gentle civilization and beauty. Generally, Gren-el were only heard of in legends and were not found in the places of the living, but through the power of the Beast King, they became evil weapons in his unholy army.

Groggle – The younger of the two ogres, the Silver Dagger's brewer and cook. He set out on a search of Dark Leaf to try to find and retrieve the Bean.

Guardian, The – A creature that guarded the Sword of Ganadon, freed from his mission and curse, once the sword was delivered to the Bean.

Heartleaf – A town in Dark Leaf Forest.

Helixshire – A close-knit clan of elves, steeped in mysterious discipline and tradition. The Helixshires were instrumental in protecting the land of Dark Leaf from marauding armies of goblins in ancient times. They cherished family, freedom, and their privacy.

Honeycakes – A sweet baked pastry.

Johann Helixshire – Otter's brother who is an elf and a scholar.

Khal-zim – The Helixshire name for an outsider.

King David – A human youth, king of Whitestone Hall.

Knotted – All Weavers are considered "knotted." An unknotted weaver would be a person who knew how to work with the Weave, but who has never touched it. A Weaver becomes "knotted" when he or she performs his first Weave. A Weaver's Knot

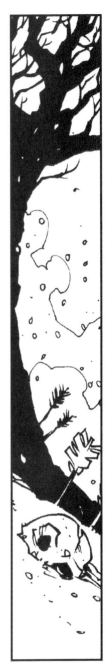

refers to the physical location where the Weaver first touched the Weave, or became "knotted." This physical location can be anywhere in the world; and, for the Weaver, it is the position where the Weaver can draw the most power.

Lampsweet – Sweet smelling incense commonly burned in oil lamps to freshen the air.

"Lhai-dhu ama Ganadon, ama soi, ama?" – Elvish approximately meaning, "And is it your sword, Ganadon... is it you... is it you?"

Lifestone – A stone tied to the life of an individual's soul. The stone enabled a person to sense the general well being of the individual who the stone belonged to. Should the individual die, the stone would turn black.

Mab – The name of Crimson Per's mult-ox

Madlynn - A mysterious woman companion who dwells with Thaddeus.

Maeyve – An earthdweller settler living in Dark Leaf Forest.

"Malnova" – An elvish expression meaning, "Save us" or "Fortune preserve us."

Mama Faerie – A mysterious and kind woman of unknown race and origin who nurtures and protects small and gentle spirits known as pixies. She possesses great power in the Weave to heal and remain unseen from the more malevolent creatures of the Dark Leaf forest. She is also know as the "Queen of the Faeries."

Marathur – An earthdweller settler living in Dark Leaf Forest.

Miri – A pixie

Mult-Ox – A shaggy common domesticated livestock used often to draw carts and plows in Dark Leaf.

Nalia – A pixie

Narva's Seal – A healing herb

Order of the Black Arrow – A group of assassins that detect the use of the Weave and are sworn to slay any Weaver they come in contact with to protect innocent people and creatures.

Otter – An elf woman of the Helixshires and a forestwalker.

Pellanor – An Elf thought to have perished in the wars of ages past.

Pepperbark Tea – An herbal tea

Portney – Another name for Tinker.

Qwen – Another name for Mama Faerie

Ravna – The current "Mistress" of the Silver Dagger Inn, who manages all the tasks that two brutish ogres could never do and keeps the customers coming back. A close friend of the forestwalker/barkeep, Siv.

Roc Noc – A Red Rock Troll hermit sage who lives beneath the Dark Leaf Forest amid the ruins of an ancient subterranean city.

Sallow Bark – A healing spice.

Shepherd's Heart – A healing herb

Silver Dagger Inn, The – An inn nestled in the heart of Dark Leaf Forest, run by Gort, the Ogre, and his brother, Groggle.

Siv – A forestwalker and the barkeep of the Silver Dagger Inn. He entered Dark Leaf to retrieve the Bean and stumbled across an army of Goblins intent

upon destroying the White Stone Hall.

Soul's Tears – A simple silvery-white wildflower native to the Dark Leaf Forest.

Tangle – The power of the Weave tied to a fixed location or object.

Thaddeus – A miniature talking dragon of mysterious origins.

Theron – The kind, gentle, and strong husband of Mama Faerie

Tia-Pho-Phia – A pixie with unusual courage, and the favorite of Papa Theron.

Tinker – One who hid a piece of Ganadon's sword deep in the mountains. His former name is Portney.

Unraveling – The process of dispelling a Tangle.

Vespa – A pixie

Weave, The – A power bound to the World of the Brokenmoon that could be harnessed and used in different supernatural capacities by the various races that dwelled there. One who employs the power of the Weave is known as a Weaver. The Weave is often used for different purposes and in different strengths, depending upon the race, recklessness, and knowledge of the Weaver. Common use of the Weave is highly addictive and leads the Weaver to madness in most races. Teaching or practicing the Weave has been outlawed in all civilized lands and is thus exceptionally rare. All books containing knowledge of how to master the Weave have been destroyed.

Weaver – The title given to any being that has mastered and wields the power of the Weave. Weavers tend to remain close to the land in which they unleashed their first Weave (where they were "knotted"), for it is their place of greatest power. The more they borrow power from the Weave, the quicker a Weaver surrenders his or her free will to its power and succumbs to madness. It is commonly said of Weavers that they do not master the Weave, but that the Weave masters them.

White Bird Cove – the capital city of an empire ruled by humans far to the south of Dark Leaf, known as the Realm of Whitebird, or the Southern Human Realm.

White Stone Hall – (Sometimes called White Stone Hall, White Stone, or the White Hall) Capital city of the Northern Kingdom, ruled by a young human named King David. The city lies on the shores of a vast lake that feeds the Grand River (a major trade route between the Hall and the realms to the south.) The city of White Stone Hall is a place of philosophy, diplomacy, and sophistication and is built upon the dream that all races might learn to dwell in peace.

Widgin-fly – A pesky insect.

Yarrow – A healing herb.

Yellow Gentian Root – A soothing herb distilled in a tea for healing.

Zift – A priceless, "indestructible," and nearly weightless metal found solely in the mountains of the Stone Trolls to the far north.

Ruins of
Dumsidne

Goldleaf

Heartleaf

the Silver Dagger

Dark Leaf Forest

Culver's Gulch

Than Dolell

Linmar

White Stone Jall

the Gate

Velinor's Door

Teroth

Realm of the Elves

Patchwell

Crivell's Port

Cold Leaf Forest

295

Aimee Duncan

Aimee Duncan lives in her own quiet little niche in North Carolina, surrounded by family and a beach or two. There's never been a time when she hasn't been writing, drawing or reading something. This book represents her first venture into published writings. By no means will it be her last. Aimee Duncan also would rather like to be a pirate but has to admit she's better at writing stories than at swashbuckling. Besides which, she can't swim.

Travis Hanson

Travis Hanson has resided in Southern California most of his life except for the 2 years spent in Argentina. He has always had a wonderful imagination and has spent the last 10 years improving his artistic skills to convey the brilliant images within his mind. Currently he is a graphic artist as well as illustrator of several books. His children have provided inspiration for much of his current work and his wife is a constant support to him in his endeavors. Travis, though like Aimee, wishes he was soaring far above the clouds on a giant dragon named Clyde.